IT MUST I

How else could a three-quarters crazy New York bag lady who saw alligators in the street and survived by stealing funeral flowers and re-selling them find the Notebook which contained all the equations for the Destiny Matrices? And what were the odds that this very same Joan the Flower Man and her Notebook would stumble in and out of the lives of the only people who knew that without the Notebook existence was pretty nearly over?

Well, if the truth were told, the odds were impossibly high. But then again, the people searching for the Notebook were far from ordinary. And Joan was more than any of them could have guessed. For not only was she part of the problem, she just might be the solution!

① SIGNET FANTASY (0451)

WORLDS OF IMAGINATION

- ☐ **THE DARKLING HILLS by Lori Martin.** When the beautiful Princess Dalleena and the handsome nobleman Rendall fall in love, defying an ancient law, they invoke a searing prophecy of doom. Betrayed and exiled by their homeland, the couple must struggle to remain together through a brutal siege from a rival empire "An exciting, charming, and irresistable story."—Tom Monteleone, author of LYRICA. (152840—$3.50)

- ☐ **STRANDS OF STARLIGHT by Gael Baudino.** A stunning, mystical fantasy of a young woman's quest for revenge against her inquisitors, and her journey through the complex web of interrelated patterns and events that lead to inner peace. (163710—$4.50)

- ☐ **FANG, THE GNOME by Michael Greatrex Coney.** Here is an enthralling excursion into an age when mythical creatures roamed the lands, men fought for ideals of chivalry, and the majestic dream of Arthur and his Knights of the Round Table first cast its spell on humans and gnomes. "Rich, striking and original!"—*Kirkus Reviews.* (158474—$3.95)

- ☐ **THE MAGIC BOOKS by Andre Norton.** Three magical excursions into spells cast and enchantments broken, by a wizard of science fiction and fantasy: *Steel Magic*, three children's journey to an Avalon whose dark powers they alone can withstand. *Octagon Magic*, a young girl's voyage into times and places long gone, and *Fur Magic*, where a boy must master the magic of the ancient gods to survive. (166388—$4.95)

- ☐ **RITNYM'S DAUGHTER by Sheila Gilluly.** The third novel of Sheila Gilluly's Greenbriar trilogy—a novel of high adventure and dark intrigue. (163419—$3.95)

Prices slightly higher in Canada.

Buy them at your local bookstore or use this convenient coupon for ordering.
NEW AMERICAN LIBRARY
P.O. Box 999, Bergenfield, New Jersey 07621

Please send me the books I have checked above. I am enclosing $_____
(please add $1.00 to this order to cover postage and handling). Send check or money order—no cash or C.O.D.'s. Prices and numbers are subject to change without notice.

Name_____
Address_____
City _____ State _____ Zip Code _____

Allow 4-6 weeks for delivery.
This offer, prices and numbers are subject to change without notice.

THE ABRAXAS MARVEL CIRCUS

Stephen Leigh

A ROC BOOK

ROC
Published by the Penguin Group
Penguin Books USA Inc., 375 Hudson Street, New York, New York 10014, U.S.A.
Penguin Books Ltd, 27 Wrights Lane, London W8 5TZ, England
Penguin Books Australia Ltd, Ringwood, Victoria, Australia
Penguin Books Canada Ltd, 2801 John Street,
Markham, Ontario, Canada L3R 1B4
Penguin Books (N.Z.) Ltd, 182-190 Wairau Road, Auckland 10, New
Zealand

Penguin Books Ltd, Registered Offices: Harmondsworth, Middlesex, England

First Published by Roc, an imprint of Penguin Books USA Inc.

First Printing, May 1990
10 9 8 7 6 5 4 3 2 1

Copyright © Stephen Leigh, 1990
All rights reserved

 Roc is a trademark of Penguin Books USA Inc.

Printed in the United States of America

Without limiting the rights under copyright reserved above, no part of this publication may be reproduced, stored in or introduced into a retrieval system, or transmitted, in any form, or by any means (electronic, mechanical, photocopying, recording, or otherwise), without the prior written permission of both the copyright owner and the above publisher of this book.

BOOKS ARE AVAILABLE AT QUANTITY DISCOUNTS WHEN USED TO PROMOTE PRODUCTS OR SERVICES. FOR INFORMATION PLEASE WRITE TO PREMIUM MARKETING DIVISION, PENGUIN BOOKS INC., 375 HUDSON STREET, NEW YORK, NEW YORK 10014.

This one's for Donna
I know. I still owe you a letter.

The author would like to acknowledge the following people for providing fodder for *Abraxas*:

- The members of **Bluestone Ivory, Stage Door Johnny, Gallery,** and the **Lodge Basement Band.** When's the next gig?

- **John,** for putting down his cardboard box of carnations one night on the Reflections stage and grabbing a microphone. Have you gone to Kansas City yet?

- **Elaine Pagels** *(The Gnostic Gospels)*
  Stephen W. Hawkings *(A Brief History of Time)*
  Paul Davies *(The Edge of Infinity & God and the New Physics)* for writing books that sent sparks flying in my direction.

  along with . . .

- **Denise,** as always, for understanding and supporting all these years, for sometimes being the only sane person in our family and *still* sticking with me. Love has no logic—we prove it.

- **Merrilee Heifetz,** for persistence, pats on the back, and patience.

- **John Silbersack and NAL,** for being willing to take a chance on a book sideways to the genre.

- **Sheila Bading,** for the bowl.

- **Martha Beck,** for telling me why airplanes fly.

  and not to forget . . .

- all of you who used the baseball bats. You know who you are.

Part One

1: Dirk Gets Lucky 13
2: Taken for a Ride 22
3: Joan the Flower Man 31
4: The House on the Hill 41
5: Death with Chowder 49
6: Damp Dreams 54
7: Tarot Incognito 59
8: A Meeting with Relish 66
9: Dirk Gets Lucky . . . Really 77

Part Two

10: The Prophet Harold 85
11: A Bowl with a Mind of Its Own 95
12: Cuisines and Other Relationships 106
13: An Unlucky Moment 116
14: Concerto Coitus 118
15: Popped Questions 126
16: A Tossed Gauntlet on the Side 138
17: At the Old Ball Game 146
18: Kansas City Without the Crazy Little Woman 155

Part Three

19: The Fool, Reversed 165
20: Far Ago and Long Away 178
21: Fate's Accomplice 185
22: Remains to Be Seen 190
23: Dirk Hits the Beach 200
24: Abracadaver 207
25: Weighing the Anchorite 217
26: The Attack on Fort Marvel 224
27: Every Now and Then 241

part one

"All events are related, one way or another."

1: Dirk Gets Lucky

Wednesday had to be the most depressing night of the week in any nightclub.

None of the social energy was there. It was two nights too early for the weekend party crowd, and the regulars had other reasons for being in the place.

The majority of those in the club didn't care if there was live music. Most of them didn't bother to listen to what the band was playing unless it was utterly obnoxious.

Even as he postured and strutted across the stage in front of the sparse crowd, even as misty wisps of dry-ice vapor curled around his ankles and slid like a moldy shower curtain to the dance floor, even as a hundred and fifty decibels of "Animal Love" slammed the back wall after nearly drawing blood from the idiots standing directly in front of the JBL drivers, Dirk Masterson felt like hell.

Part of it was because his real name was James McCarthy—Jimmy, not Dirk. The name change had come because Stan Fedderman, the band's manager, thought "Jimmy McCarthy" inappropriate. Actually, Stan had been a bit more vehement than that, shaking his balding head as he leaned back in his padded leather recliner.

"Your name's too ordinary, babe. Too damn *Catholic* for a band called Savage. Chris'sakes, who's going to be in awe of someone named Jimmy? You can't even be a good president with a name like that. C'mon."

For another, Dirk had forgotten just what town Savage was in and it didn't much seem to matter. He was tired of small college clubs throughout the Midwest. At thirty, he was beginning to look noticeably older than the audience. He was beginning to reconsider the whole idea of being a rock star.

This was "making it"? This was where six years and Stan's promised record contract got you? This was why he'd left Baywood College in the second year of his teaching contract? This was what he was doing with his master's degree in history and the minor in mathematics, with the years of study and a doctoral-thesis-in-progress? It was almost enough to make him long again for the plagiarized term papers, the bored students vegetating in Introduction to Western Civilization, and the brown-nose types who made admiring comments in class and then ignored him in the quad.

Also, he and the lead guitar player were fighting again. Lars wanted to sing the lead vocals on the title cut for their unrecorded second album: *Animal Love (You're a Bitch)*. He wanted it to be a goddamn contest. "Look, *Dirk*, all I'm saying is that we should use the best voice for the song. You sing it, then I'll sing it—let the guys decide which is better." The afternoon's practice session had left Dirk's stomach sour even though he'd "won" the competition.

(Lars's given name was Fred. Stan had turned away from Jimmy and lit his cigar. A fragrant smoke wreath curled about his head. "And 'Fred'! God, what a dork moniker. All a Fred can be is a fat redneck or some geek nerd. Your parents hate you or what?")

Dirk was only going through the motions tonight because of all of it. Depression swaddled him like baggy boxer shorts: he kept pulling at the nagging thoughts. He slid up the G-string of his Rickenbacker bass to an E-sharp as the band segued into "Animal Love's" last bridge, arching his back in feigned musical orgasm as the note throbbed. He grinned at Lars as if they shared some communion of the backbeat. Lars grinned back. Neither one meant it.

Facing each other, they swayed together as Lars laid down a screaming, gliding lead.

The Abraxas Marvel Circus

Dirk wished he could just ram the Rick's tuning heads into Lars's satin-covered crotch.

The final component of his depression was the fact that Dirk had told Alf, the drummer, about a blond groupie who had supposedly propositioned Dirk the night before. "She's fuckin' crazy, man. I mean, no inhibitions whatsoever. I gave her my extra key and told her to come by after the gig. I tell you, she's gonna make Fish look like nothing."

In fact, the blond groupie had been a fantasy Dirk had indulged in the night before. He'd had to do something. In the next room, he could hear the screams and grunts and moans as Alf and the groupie he called Fish ("Because her mouth goes like this, man") tried to push each other through the mattress of the water bed. The only blonde—or anything else—Dirk had had the entire six-month tour of America's backroads had been his own palm. As Alf and Fish thrashed the water bed into tidal-wave frenzy, Dirk found his own release with the mental blonde whose tits defied gravity: a type of voyeuristic mutual orgasm. The only trouble was that afterward it was no fun cuddling with his hand.

Dirk's celibacy wasn't due to the Woman Back Home or even to a lack of offers. Dirk wasn't much of a talker offstage, whether the stage was a nightclub or a lecturer's podium. Actually, he was rather painfully shy and tended toward one-syllable replies when someone tried to strike up a conversation. Dirk needed to be hit over the head with a baseball bat before he realized that he was being flirted with.

And even when, miraculously, things got to that point where he might ask someone to go back to the hotel room with him, he'd start to wonder about how she'd look when the lights came on or whether she'd leave him with some unpleasant and probably permanent reminder of the night, or if he'd be accosted a few months later by a paternity suit.

Dirk's flirtations were haunted by the specters of AIDS, syphilis, herpes, and pregnancy. He half believed every horror story he'd read in the newspapers. If *Time* ran an article—NEW VENEREAL DISEASE SIGNALS

END TO PERMISSIVE SOCIETY—he was certain that all the women he met were already infected. He was surprised that the other guys in the group hadn't died yet.

The one time he'd actually gotten someone in bed with him—an art student named Patti who'd come to see them in the Tiki Club in Terre Haute, Indiana—he'd been so worried that she Had Something that he'd been struck as limp as well-boiled vermicelli. After several vain attempts to impale herself, Patti had given up and gone back to the dorm. Loudly. Everyone in the hotel had no doubt heard her scathing review of Dirk's performance. He'd distinctly heard Lars's giggle down the hall. For the rest of the band's stay in the Tiki Club, Dirk was convinced the coeds in the audience were pointing at him and laughing. He was also convinced that he'd caught Something for Nothing.

> *"Mama always said you can't get something for nothing.*
> *But baby, I got something for nothing from you."*

Dirk thought he'd put that verse in the next song he wrote.

"Animal Love" snarled to an end with a barrage of electronic snare and toms, and a cascade of brass chords from Kyle on the Yamaha DX7 synthesizer. As Alf clicked off the next song ("Hot-Dog Buns") and a few dancers filed out on the floor, Dirk saw her.

She wasn't the blonde of his fantasy. Dark curls swayed around her shoulders. Her face was round instead of angular, her body full rather than fashionably anemic. She wasn't what Dirk would have thought of as beautiful at all, but something about her made him stare as Kyle did a sliding glissando into the intro and Alf battered his ride cymbal into submission.

She had presence.

Her dancing partner had the build of a steroid-puffed lineman. The handsome bunch of muscles was a lumbering dancing bear alongside her.

She moved like a sleek, luxurious cat, as if dancing were some wild celebration of life. She flung herself into the music with a reckless abandon and an unconscious grace, seeming to dance in a trance. As she swayed, she tossed her head back and laughed, her eyes closed. The stale air of the club seemed to spark visibly around her, as if her body was a dynamo throwing off charged ions. Her dance had an intensity and an expressiveness that made everyone else's movements seem contrived. She flowed with the music, became a part of the pulsing beat, so that each movement seemed somehow *right*, as if her interpretation was simply an extension of the song. Her dance was dark and primitive, like some ritual glimpsed through shade; deeply physical, sensual, frankly sexual. Sweat beaded on her neck and darkened the hair at her forehead; her mouth was open, her head thrown back as she whirled with arms wide.

Dirk was not the only one who noticed. Half the dancers had already stopped to watch, alerted by some sixth sense. She was magic, a perfect blend of primal motion. Her dance was a spell; it snared them all. Her skin was glossy with its heat.

Her spinning, ecstatic joy brought her close to the stage as Dirk started to sing the second verse. He stared down at her through the glare of the fresnels. Heavy breasts joggled under her red T-shirt, her jeans were enticingly tight. Dirk's gaze followed the creases of blue cloth to where they triangulated the pubic mound, then slid along the line of the central seam to that place he suddenly and desperately wanted to be.

She must have felt the pressure of his gaze, for she glanced up at him. The unexpected eye contact nearly staggered Dirk. Her eyes were a deep, surprising green that contrasted sharply with the Mediterranean complexion and black hair. Dirk knew that she'd seen his fascination with the hidden, forested landscape between her legs.

Dirk thought she'd respond with a frown, maybe even say something to Mr. Pectorals. *That would be about my luck,* he thought. *Great, a wonderful confrontation after the set for everyone to watch. Lars'll love it.*

But instead, she gave him a laughing grin full of white teeth. Her stare challenged him, and he was caught. Nothing existed for a moment but those eyes, framed in sweat-plastered ringlets. Dirk forgot the fantasy blonde. He also forgot the words to the second verse and stumbled through two lines before he found them again. Kyle shook his head, Alf guffawed good-naturedly, Lars glared.

She'd noticed, too, for she laughed and moved away from the stage as Mr. Pecs frowned up at Dirk with narrowed eyes. Dirk lost her in the stage lights as she stopped dancing and made her way back to the tables. The dance floor remained empty through the rest of the song, as though the others were embarrassed to dance in the afterglow of her energy. Though Dirk watched, he didn't see her again the rest of the set.

"Thought she was *blonde,* man," Alf said as the stage lights dimmed and he slid his way from behind the barricade of drums. "Looks like you'll have to fight off the Hulk first. Not that I blame him. Christ, if she moves like that in bed . . ." Alf shook his head and flexed his own drumming-swelled biceps. "Want me to come with you for protection?"

Alf had kept his own name. ("Drummers can have stupid names," Stan had said. "It's expected.")

"I don't need help," Dirk told Alf sourly.

Alf snorted. "It must be wonderful to be so self-sufficient," he answered.

Dirk gave Alf an automatic finger, leaned the Rickenbacker against his amp, and walked around to the stage door. He nodded to the bouncer stationed there and went out into the club as the house sound system began blaring an old Beatles album in its CD version.

The place looked and sounded like any of the other dozen or more college nightclubs they'd been in lately. This one was multileveled, making it easier for the drunk or stoned students to stumble and cascade plastic cups of beer over the tables—that happened at least once a night in every club Savage had played. Sometimes the fights that ensued received more attention than the band. The lighting was dim and predominantly red. The patrons—almost all students—stood around in clusters shouting into each other's ears over the general din.

Dirk glanced out to where the soundman had set up the board: Jay was already leaning toward some techie type with too many pens in his shirt pocket, pointing to the racks of amplifiers and talking watts and linear frequency responses. Dirk elbowed his way past the students and the attempts at screaming conversation ("Hey man, you gonna do any U2 next set?") to the bar.

He looked around for a glimpse of the red T-shirt, but didn't see her.

"Coke," he said to one of the bartenders, a kid who looked too young to be serving drinks.

"Ooh, the *hard* stuff for the band," the kid retorted. He sniffed significantly and winked. "Need a straw?"

"No. And make it diet," Dirk said wearily. He heard that one at least three or four times a night. Bartender humor. It hadn't been funny the first time.

"Same for me," a voice said behind him—a scratchy, odd alto. Dirk turned. She looked better close up, and the neon beer advertisements behind the bar gave him a good view. She let him stare at her with that tolerant wide smile, her head tilted a little to the right.

"Angela," she said.

Dirk blinked. "Hmmm?"

She brushed her hair back from her eyes; crystal droplets showered the floor. "I saw you watching me. You should at least ask my name now that you're on such intimate terms with my body."

Dirk opened his mouth to speak. Nothing came out. He shut it again. The air between them seemed charged; he could almost hear it buzzing in his ears.

"It would be polite to tell me *your* name now," she said with that strange, dusky hoarseness. One eyebrow arched quizzically.

"Ji—uh, Dirk."

"Your band's got potential, Dirk," she commented, leaning a little closer to him as the Beatles faded into

Genesis. Dirk caught a wisp of fragrant perfume and perspiration, a hint of sexual musk. "The songs are decent, if a little too simple. You made me want to get up and dance. Did you know that it shows that the band's not getting along offstage? If all of you were tighter personally, you'd be tighter musically, too. The keyboard man and the drummer are excellent; the guitar's adequate. Why are you using a Rickenbacker? A Fender's got a fuller bottom end."

Dirk didn't know where to start with that. He picked up the two Cokes the bartender had sat in front of him and handed one to her. He decided to start with something he knew something about. "The Rick's better overall—for sound and fingering."

She seemed to be waiting for him to say something else, then she shrugged. "A matter of taste, I guess." She glanced at him, her lower lip stuck out in a pout. Then that brilliant grin split her face once more. "You're not very good at this, are you?" she asked.

Startled again, Dirk could only manage a weak "Huh? The band's—"

"I'm not talking music," she interrupted. "I'm talking flirting."

"Oh," Dirk said. Somewhere, a faint light was dawning. He could hear the whimpering of his libido. "Look, uh . . ." He stopped.

"Angela," she prompted. "Please try to remember." She softened the blow with another smile.

"Yeah. Angela. I thought you were with—"

"Edgar? He's been trying to get into my pants for three months now. He's barely got enough brains to remember his phone number. He's good camouflage, that's all—even if he can't dance. Don't worry about him, Dirk. He's actually very nice, like a pet Doberman."

The image made Dirk roll his eyes. "Please keep him on his leash, then."

Angela's laugh rang like a crystal wind chime. "There, I knew you could talk like a normal person. So, why were you watching me on the dance floor?"

Dirk blinked, shrugged. "*Every*one was watching. There was something . . . I mean, it wasn't your face or body . . . just—'' Under her smiling stare, Dirk flushed and ground to a embarrassed halt. *Asshole,* he berated himself. *It's magic fingers' time again tonight.*

"You mean that I'm not particularly good-looking and ordinarily you wouldn't have given me a second glance?"

"No . . ." Dirk began. He felt bewildered.

He'd felt the same frustration the one time he'd tried to play a rated chess player. Dirk considered himself a decent amateur at the game, and he'd been the terror of the teachers' lounge chess set. Still, that time he'd challenged someone truly good he'd been thoroughly outclassed. Whenever Dirk thought he'd made a good move, he'd found that it had been anticipated. After the opening gambit, not even that far into the middle game, he was utterly hemmed in, all his strategy blown to hell. There hadn't been a good square open and he'd pushed over his king. Talking with Angela was the same—there was a rook sitting on every conversational file.

Check. "You don't understand," he said.

"I think I do."

The lights on the stage brightened, then dimmed: Jay's signal that the break was over. "Listen, I have to get back."

"If I dance, will you watch me again?" As Angela spoke, a student pushing through the crowd to the bar jostled against Dirk. Off balance, he stumbled up against Angela. Before Dirk could move away, he felt her forefinger trace the bundled pouch under his leather pants. It might have been accidental, but he felt himself jerk in response. His cock howled like a wolf at the full moon. Angela smiled innocently up at him. "Well, will you?"

"Yeah," he breathed. "I will."

"Then you'd better get up there," she said.

Check and mate.

Dirk decided that anything else he might say would only be anticlimatic. He fled back to his bass.

2: Taken for a Ride

"Light cannot exist without darkness. There can be no heaven without hell. Opposites define themselves."

Father Mayer tossed that pablum back at Jimmy McCarthy in the warm, shabby classrooms of Holy Trinity High. This was after Jimmy spewed out the litany of hatred during Ethics and Morals—also known as Religion Class. How can God be both omnipotent and benevolent? Jimmy had raged. Hey, if He's omnipotent, then He has the power to make all things good. If He chooses not to do so, then He's the absolute opposite of benevolent. If He's benevolent, then He can't be omnipotent or He couldn't stomach what we humans do to each other.

Father Mayer had blinked owlish eyes behind his horn-rim glasses, sighed deeply, and uttered platitudes.

Even at seventeen, Jimmy McCarthy (who had no idea at the time that he would one day be a failed rock star and former historian named Dirk) was aware that life was a wallow in the universal midden. He knew this for certain.

After all, Debbie Imhoff had started shrieking when he'd tried to put himself inside her.

Getting that far had been a long, slow process over a period of months—simple kissing, then the touch of fluttering tongues. For two successive nights on her back porch he'd slipped his hand inside her blouse until the lace edging of her bra crackled under his fingertips and he could just feel the hidden softness underneath. It had taken another two weeks before she let him unsnap the awkward hooks and release the budding globes from tricot bondage. A month after that he'd finally gained the plush nest of his obsession and slipped his finger into the moist warmth hidden there. He'd caught the scent of oily arousal.

Two months later on a September evening, he was certain that the Moment had come. They would give each other their virginity in a glorious rapture. The night would be transformed. Skyrockets would pierce the heavens and explode in unsubtle simile.

But when the time came, she'd screamed as if the touch of his probing erection on her thigh had burned her. "Jesus, Debbie!" he'd shouted at her shrill alarm. "Jesus!"

It wouldn't have been so bad it they'd not been in the backseat of his mother's VW Rabbit, if they hadn't been parked in the back lot of Holy Trinity during a school dance, if it hadn't been so warm an Indian-summer night that the Rabbit's windows were down. Debbie's piercing distress carried like the wail of a civil defense siren.

Lights went on in the houses behind the school. Brother Lawrence, vice-principal and chief chaperon at the dance, hurtled from the school building like a burly Archangel Michael, homing in on the Rabbit as Debbie threw the startled Dirk from atop her and fled the car. Dirk had just managed to extract himself from between the seats when Brother Lawrence huffed up, followed by most of the students at the dance.

Brother Lawrence stopped short of the Rabbit and gaped.

Debbie Imhoff sobbed in distress alongside the car, her hands up to her mascara-smeared face, her blouse wide open, and her thin breasts swaying under the unhooked bra. The girl's skirt had mercifully fallen down over her thighs, but her panty hose trailed guiltily from one ankle. Dirk staggered out of the Rabbit, still thinking that he could calm her down and salvage the wreckage of the evening. "It's okay, Debbie. Just be qui—oh, shit."

Dirk saw Brother Lawrence smoldering under the

parking-lot lights and his classmates trying to suppress their glee. "Brother—" he began desperately.

"*Mr.* McCarthy." Brother Lawrence's voice was the low thunder of an approaching storm. "I'd suggest you zip yourself up."

Dirk looked down. His corduroys were around his ankles with his boxer shorts pooled inside. A condom hung like a new foreskin from his drooping manhood. Dirk could feel a flush beginning somewhere down around his knees and spreading rapidly. His face was red enough to give off light. Debbie Imhoff's pink cotton panties were clutched unawares in one hand. Debbie noticed them about the same time and snatched them back with a howl.

That was too much for his classmates. As Dirk turned around and bent over to pull up his pants, the first waves of laughter broke over him. For the rest of his stay in high school, Dirk would be known as Limp Meat.

Rubberman.

Jimmy McCondom.

After that, Dirk decided that there wasn't a God, or if there *was* one, He wasn't anyone Dirk wanted to worship.

A benevolent God would not have humiliated him that way.

An omnipotent one would have at least kept Debbie quiet until it was over.

Dirk felt some of that old frustration again as Savage thrashed their way through the next and final set. Angela *had* danced again, with that same intriguing energy and magnetism—the applause afterward was more for her than the band. Her spirit was more brilliant than the stage lights; some overflow of that brilliance trickled over and set the band on fire as well.

Dirk played mostly to her, with an intensity he hadn't felt in weeks. The newfound enthusiasm sparked the others. Savage played the first half of the set like maniacs. Angela left the floor during the third song. Dirk had lost her in the crowd, but he could feel her watching. The residue of her energy remained. He bounded across the stage with Alf's insistent beat.

When he'd caught a glimpse of her again, it was to see her going out the entrance with the Doberman Edgar on her arm. Dirk's ego came crashing down around him. He was certain that the noise was audible. Lars, of course, had noticed. He heard the guitar player giggle behind him.

Dirk played the rest of the set on automatic. The fire that had ignited Savage fizzled on his dampened ego.

By the end of the set only the usual mix was left. The staff was still there, looking utterly bored and ready to hustle out the last patrons the moment the houselights came on. There was a table near the soundboard, all male and staring too intently at the stage to be anything but local musicians in to scout out the competition. There were a few eternally hopeful students of assorted and indeterminate sex flailing around the dance floor, and demonstrating why, at nearly 2:00 A.M., they were still there to be picked up. At a table to one side of the stage the groupies had gathered, dutifully applauding at the end of every song and making the silence in the rest of the club even more appalling by contrast.

Dirk announced the last song with relief. When it ended, he slammed the Rick into its case and snapped it shut as the aftermath of the band's volume rang in his ears. He stalked from the stage with what he hoped was a dignified pace. Out at his table, Jay was covering the soundboard. Kyle had gone to the bar for a last drink, Lars had been surrounded by the local musicians, and Alf was sitting with the groupies, Fish already draped around his shoulders like a decorative shawl. Alf looked at Dirk. Dirk shrugged back, glad that Alf, at least, seemed to understand. *Friends don't have to talk. Friends know when the other's hurt and won't say anything to make it worse.*

Alf winked at Dirk and settled Fish on his lap. "Stood up, eh Dirk?" Alf crowed. "Guess you'll have to settle for the blonde." The groupies laughed dutifully.

Dirk scowled, hefted the bass's case in his hand, and headed for the mixing board. Jay wouldn't have noticed Angela, Dirk was certain. Savage's soundman and head roadie was a social maladroit who read *Sound Engineering, Science,* and *Byte* the way Dirk read *Penthouse.* Jay didn't make any distinction between genders at all. There were only People Who Knew Tech and People Who Didn't. On the job, Jay didn't notice anything but VU meters and LEDs.

"She run out on you?" Jay asked as Dirk approached. He squinted myopically behind his out-of-date wire-rims and gave a lopsided smile of sympathy.

"You saw her, too?"

"You were kind of obvious, after all. I'm not *that* blind." Jay wiped his hands on his usual white Oxford shirt. He finished putting the cover over the console for the night and patted it with parental affection, as if tucking in his child for the night. "Besides, the band sounded good there for a while."

"Thought we paid *you* to make us sound that way," Dirk said grumpily.

Nothing flustered Jay. He gave a wide, goofy grin; Jay had a mouth that could swallow a softball. "I do what I can with what I have to work with."

"Yeah, that's the way it's been going with me, too," Dirk muttered. He was thinking of going over to the bar to give Kyle his chance to insult him when Angela walked back into the club, peering through the haze of stale cigarette smoke. She'd changed into a peasant blouse that left her shoulders bare. She looked around, waved to Dirk.

Dirk waved back with what he hoped was apparent calmness. He felt the muscles of his face pulling into an idiotic, too-wide smile. Angela nodded and came down the steps toward him. The grimace Lars gave her as she passed pleased Dirk.

"I was talking to her earlier," Jay said behind Dirk. "Programming, mostly; she likes Pascal. She knows sound, too—even noticed that the horn crossover was set a little too high for the room. We tweaked it down a little and the PA sounded better. She's intelligent. You'd better be careful," Jay said.

Dirk had begun to think that maybe his life wasn't destined to be one McCondom catastrophe after another. Now he glanced back at Jay suspiciously. "What's that mean?"

"It means she isn't Fish, that's all. She's special. Different."

Angela's arrival didn't give Dirk a chance to pursue that any further. She gave Jay a hug, leaving Dirk feeling somehow left out. She didn't make any motion to greet him the same way. "How'd the last part of the set go?" she asked Jay.

"Okay," Jay said. "They've been better. The JBLs sounded good, though. Thanks."

"Sorry I didn't get back quicker," Angela said, swinging around to Dirk. "I had Edgar take me back to my apartment so I could get my car. Miss me?"

"He played like shit," Jay supplied.

"Thanks," Dirk said to Jay. "I can handle my own answers from here on out."

"Only telling the truth. I can give you *all* his bad points if you want," he said to Angela. He began ticking them off on his fingers. "For one, he can't dance, and *you* obviously can. He talks to the crowd all night up on stage, but get him one-on-one with a stranger and he doesn't know what to say."

"Jay—"

Jay ignored Dirk. "He's not as serious about music as he should be if he wants to make a career of it. He's afraid to stretch out and really try something serious. He's really better suited for the academic life."

"Jay—"

"He thinks he'd be better off teaching history again. It's safe. With history, nothing ever changes. He likes to think he's strange and different, but he'd be frightened of anything *really* different."

"*Jay,*" Dirk repeated warningly.

"Is that last part true, Dirk?" Angela interjected.

"No," Dirk said stubbornly, glaring at Jay.

"Good. I'd hate for you to be frightened of me."

For just a moment there was an odd harshness in the set of her mouth, in her jade eyes. The seriousness, the hint of sarcasm in her tone, puzzled Dirk. He thought that somehow he'd inadvertently insulted her. Then she shook her head, setting black waves of hair in motion, and the sharp edge was gone from her. She touched his arm, and he found himself holding his breath.

"Let's go," she said, and the tone of her voice was almost resigned, almost sad. The suggestion panicked Dirk. He suddenly felt lost, knowing that he hadn't been able to recall what city they were in; knowing that he didn't know where the club was or what the hotel's address might be. The usual panic threatened to take him—visions of Terre Haute Pattie ran through his head.

"Let's go *where?*" He knew he shouldn't have said it. It sounded dumb, it sounded stupid. He felt as awkward as old Jimmy.

Jay saved him. "I'll take the bass back to the hotel," he said, holding his hand out for the case.

"If you're sure you want to go," Angela added. "I might not be as safe as a dry, dusty history book."

"He likes math, too," Jay added, ignoring the stare Dirk gave him.

Dirk wasn't about to make the same mistake twice. "Okay, let's go." He handed the bass to Jay. He started to put a possessive arm around her shoulder as he might have with, say, Fish. He caught a glimpse of her face as he did so and saw a challenge there, a tilt of the head that was a warning. In that moment, she seemed older and somehow dangerous, as if the vitality that had fueled her dance could suddenly be turned against him. The feeling was only there for an instant, but it was enough.

Dirk's hand came back and brushed his hair instead. It wasn't exactly a smooth recovery, but Angela was the only one who noticed. She regarded Dirk appraisingly, then looked around the room. Kyle and Lars watched from the bar; the attention of Alf and the groupies was directed toward them as well. Angela gave what was almost a sigh.

"Appearances," she breathed, and any sense of peril about her was gone. She circled Dirk's waist with an arm and pulled him to her. Dirk laid his arm gingerly around her back, giving Jay a puzzled, questioning glance. Jay looked back as if he'd seen nothing: he smiled. "I'll take good care of the bass," he said.

"Come on," Angela said. "The car's outside."

The car didn't seem to match her, somehow. In the glow of the club's neon sign (REFLECTIONS, in electric blue), the Chevette sat like a dull gray lump. It was at least a decade old and didn't look as if it had been washed or waxed in that time. Dirk slid into the passenger's seat, his feet crushing an empty Wendy's bag. The vinyl dashboard was heat-cracked, the rugs were torn, the backseat was littered with paper, wrappers, and books.

"You're a student, right?" Dirk said as Angela slid into the driver's seat and tugged at the twisted shoulder harness. She fastened the belt and slid the keys into the ignition. The Chevette grumbled and turned over; Dirk could smell exhaust.

"How old do you think I am?" Angela asked him.

"You're—" Dirk began. Warning bells went off in his mind. Angela still looked at him expectantly. "I don't think I should answer that one," he said. "I have the feeling that I lose no matter what I say."

She put the car in drive and released the parking brake. "I'm not a student," she told him as she pulled away from the curb. The transmission whined like a sick animal. "So your guess is too low."

"Are you insulted or pleased?"

"Neither." Her grin flashed in the darkness. "I expected it of you."

She turned left at the first light. Dirk caught a glimpse of the street sign—Calhoun—but that didn't tell him anything. Further up the street, he saw a larger sign by a drive: University of Cincinnati, Lot 2. Somehow, being able to give the city a name made Dirk feel slightly more at ease. Maybe he'd be able to remember a few street names. . . . Now that they were actually going, he could even ask: "Where's your apartment?"

"We're not going there."

"Ahh," Dirk said. He nodded. "Ummm, where *are* we going?"

"To another place I know," she answered. She stopped for a traffic light with a squeal of worn brake linings, turned on the blinker to turn right, and looked over at him. Her face was neutral and unreadable in the shadowy light of the street lamps. "I'll tell you where if you want, but you don't know this area at all. If you're worried, I'll take you back to your hotel." The tone of her voice told Dirk that the hotel would not include room service. "Up to you," she said.

As her serious gaze searched his face, she put her hand on Dirk's thigh. It seemed to burn near his tightening crotch, perfectly placed—too close to be casual, too far away to be an invitation.

"Surprise me," he said. He tried to laugh. It sounded more like a cackle.

"I'll do *that*," she answered. "I can practically guarantee it."

The light turned green. She took her hand away and turned. The Chevette grated into gear as the heat on Dirk's thigh turned damp and cold.

3: Joan the Flower Man

Angela drove westward. The single working headlamp of the Chevette made a dim yellowed splash on the expressway, through which lane markers fled like startled hares. Dirk sat uncomfortably in the passenger seat staring at the strange night scenery and wondering if this night with Angela would leave him forever changed.

It would, of course (which Dirk would have known if he'd been at all familiar with Angela), but not in the way he was thinking.

It will take them some time to get to Angela's destination. So we'll leave them for a bit, with Dirk growing steadily more uneasy as the city lights fade to suburban sprawl and then disappear entirely. There are other people to meet, for they'll inevitably be snared in this moment. Angela's all too well aware of that. *She* knows that there are other people caught in the web of her life, even if she doesn't yet know their names.

As Angela might have said to Dirk on the way: "Life's that way. It's being shoved blindly out of an airplane along with all your fellows, without instructions and certainly without a parachute. The wind tugs and pulls at you, your fellow sky divers do the same. Maybe you can learn to spin and twist in the wind. Maybe you can slow your descent and seem to drift upward past the tumbling rest of them. Maybe you can even enjoy the ride and the sense that you're almost flying. But in the end, no matter how lucky you've been, there's always the Ground. It might be different if we didn't believe in gravity, but we do. In the final moment, we always go *splat.*"

Joan the Flower Man understood that instinctively. For Joan, without death there would be no life. Without death, there would be no floral funeral arrangements. Without floral funeral arrangements scavenged from grave plots, funeral parlors, and several florists, Joan would have nothing to sell and no way to survive.

In appearance, Joan the Flower Man looked to be an obese, grizzly man bent over with age. The folded cheeks (one of which was always packed with chewing tobacco) looked like tree-covered slopes after a forest fire, stubbled with an eternal week-old growth of beard. The smile was mostly gums, with a few rotting teeth leaning like old tombstones in a graveyard, brown with tobacco juice. A baseball cap was jammed down over the balding head and, no matter the weather, a grimy windbreaker covered a torn plaid shirt. The tips of worn canvas sneakers peeked from underneath baggy trousers held up by a broken pair of suspenders.

It was when you caught Joan's profile that you noticed the distinct breasts, and when she looked at you, you could see that the lines of her ravaged face were softer than you might have thought, that the rheumy brown eyes might have been, decades ago, almost striking.

Joan was a hermaphodite. Her genitalia and secondary sexual characteristics were a mix-and-match set.

"Buy some flowers, mister?" Joan croaked, holding out a newspaper-wrapped bundle of carnations that had lately decorated the casket of a certain Anna Fulsom. Her hand looked oddly delicate to be attached to the grotesque figure slumped in a doorway stoop on Sixth Street. Most people simply ignored her: Joan the Flower Man was a fixture of the neighborhood, part of the local New York City scenery. She shambled down the long blocks, prowled the back doors of area funeral homes and florists, or sat in her usual doorway surrounded by flower stems, wreaths proclaiming "Dearest Departed," and yellowed newspapers.

"Two bucks," she added without looking up.

No one was certain what compelled Joan to accost certain people and ignore the dozen or more others that passed her by in the meantime. No one had ever bothered to ask her, not that Joan herself could have explained it. There was nothing overtly different about this man—another gray-suited clone from the business district two blocks west. It was simply that Joan's brain was as scrambled and confused as the rest of her body.

To Joan, the clamor and bustle of New York was a montage of her life. Past and present mingled in her mind. Fate stirred her synapses with a cruel spoon. She sometimes lived in the here and now, sometimes in a scene from years ago. The traffic noise might be the hooting of owls in the woods, the wail of an infant, or murmuring voices from her past. In the moments between hallucinations, she would sell her flowers.

The clone had stopped. She thrust the bundled flowers toward him. "Two bucks," she repeated. "New cut, too. Take home to wifey, eh? She 'preciate it, betcha." She gave him a knowing leer and wink, then ruined the dubious effect by spewing a thick stream of tobacco juice at her feet. "C'mon," she urged, seeing the man's hesitation.

Her customer shrugged, not without feeling. "Okay, mister," he said. "You got a sale. Give me the flowers."

He reached for his wallet. Joan watched with her gap-toothed smile, the flowers in one hand, the other extended palm up. At that moment, like a leaden soldier tossed into a fire, the man's face seemed to melt and change before Joan's eyes. It solidified into an all-too-familiar face for Joan. "Henderson, you son of a bitch!" she shrieked suddenly.

Joan clubbed at the apparition with her bouquet. Carnation petals showered the gray suit as the businessman raised a hand to ward off the attack.

"Christ!" He backed away quickly as Joan lurched from her seat on the concrete steps. She spat tobacco juice at him; it spattered the woolen trouser cuffs as her customer turned and fled for more familiar territory. "Henderson!" Joan bellowed in a high, androgynous voice. "Come back, bastard!"

Joan took several futile steps in pursuit, then settled back to her stoop, wheezing from the exertion. Around her, midday New York faded into a night lit by glaring, bare bulbs strung from wires. The buildings became patched tents, the pavement a meadow scuffed bare of grass, the whine of traffic a tinny Sousa march played over speakers hung from trees. She could hear Henderson barking at the marks: "Come and see 'em! Glimpse the fantastic mistakes of nature! All live and guaranteed genuine!"

For a time, Joan had been one of the attractions in a carnival freak show, displaying her dubious charms and oddities throughout the rural southeast. The carnie owner—Abel C. Henderson—had purchased Joan from her mother. Joan's stay with Henderson was a haze of pain and neglect. Henderson considered his freaks possessions, much like the motley collection of tents and wagons that was the Henderson Marvel Circus. He paid Joan nothing but her keep, and sold her nights, for a reasonable fee, to anyone whose tastes might run to the bizarre. When, during the winter of '61 (the same year Dirk had been born), Joan caught pneumonia, Henderson had simply dumped her in Tallapoosa County, Alabama.

It seemed reasonable enough to Henderson. The freak shows were losing money. He'd been used to paying bribes to local officials so they would overlook the conditions of his "employees" in the freak tent; it was part of the normal overhead. The freaks had always brought in enough morbidly curious hicks to justify the expenses. Henderson had brought his carnival south eight years ago to escape the creeping liberalism of the north and the oppressive concern for the "rights" of his collection of deformities—"God's factory seconds," as he called them.

Now this humanism dogged his heels in the south as well. The tariff of bribes had escalated out of sight. Local sheriffs and councilmen were quite willing to line their pockets by invoking "decency."

Along with this, Joan was getting old—thirty-nine and looking fifty. He hadn't made any money prostituting her in months. She wasn't holding up her end of the business. A sick freak would be an intolerable drain on the resources.

Sick freaks died, after all. Their life spans were usually short. And a dead freak was a potential bonus for a greedy county coroner. "Hey, babe," Henderson told Joan as he and one of the roustabouts carried her off the wagon and into a small stand of trees. "No hard feelings—it's just economics."

She hadn't died, though there were times in the next few weeks that she wished she had. She'd even managed to make her confused way back north to a dimly remembered New York. There, her memories and the present fused in her mind, she learned to live. Not well, but enough.

There'd been an observer to the latest incident in Joan's confused life. He was a tall and gangly man with a vaguely Asiatic cast to the skin and distinct epicanthic folds around his eyes. He wore a black suit cut in a style out of fashion since the thirties. White kid gloves encased long fingers that spidered down the front of the unbuttoned jacket.

"Excuse me, sir," he said to Joan, who still muttered imprecations in the direction of the imagined Henderson. Joan started. She squinted up at him and pawed at the mucus in the corner of her eyes. New York City snapped back into place around her.

"Who'er you?" she said suspiciously.

A gloved hand proffered a card. "Ecclesiastes Mitsumishi," he said.

Joan cocked her head at him and took the card. Her thumb smeared a brown trail over the white cotton paper. "Hell of a name," she commented. She dropped the card on the sidewalk.

Mitsumishi simply grinned. His teeth were huge. The enamel gleamed like a toothpaste ad. "Missionary mother, Japanese father," he said. "Both with a sense of humor. I saw you today behind my funeral home. You took Anna Fulsom's wreath."

Thoughts chased each other through the warren of Joan's mind. She thought she saw the street turn into a steaming bayou. An alligator slipped from the curb into the slow waters. "You own that flower place?"

"Funeral home. Mortuary. *Remains to Be Seen.* Mom cared for people's souls after death, I look after what's left." He grinned again.

There was too much mirth in the man for a funeral director, Joan's befuddled mind decided. The suit, the gloves; he was more parody than reality. She shifted her large girth on the concrete steps and scowled at him.

"Name like that, you won't be working very long. You new to the business, huh."

"No. Fourth parlor I've owned in five years. Use to run the Corpus Delicti, in St. Paul, then opened The Body Shoppe in Lexington. They went under like all of my customers." Ecclesiastes waited, grinning, but there was no response from Joan. "Just lost my third place last year: The Stiff's Upper Lip in Cincinnati. Had to sell out. Conservative place, Cincinnati."

The bayou shimmered, and for a second, Joan thought the undertaker was a Creole dressed in overalls and a flannel shirt, his bare toes digging into Louisiana mud. She shook her head and the street returned momentarily. "People got no sense of humor 'bout death," Joan observed belatedly. "Strange you get any business at all."

"I'm cheap."

"Huh," Joan snorted. "You better be, or the alligators eat you up." She could hear the muscular tail slashing water. It'd be on this bank in a minute, sure. "We gotta go," she said urgently. Joan spat juice, wiped at the stubble on her chin, and struggled to her feet. Her grimy hand clutched at Ecclesiastes' sleeve.

"What's the matter, mister?" His grin wavered.

"Alligator, man," she whispered ominously. Her eyes focused on something just behind the mortician. "Shit, too late," she cried. With a gap-toothed scream, Joan lifted her just-wrapped bouquet and began flailing. A mongrel unlucky enough to have chosen that moment to be foraging the gutter howled at the unexpected floral whipping and fled with its tail between its legs.

"Damn, that was close," Joan gasped. Petals from the carnations littered the sidewalk, broken stems hung from the newspaper wrappings in her hand. "Big sucker. See those teeth?"

Ecclesiastes had spun around with a curiously graceful pirouette and was standing with his hands extended in what was obviously a martial stance. He glanced from Joan to the hound, who was staring forlornly back at them from the next corner. "Thanks," he said uncertainly. His hands dropped back to his waist.

"You know kung fu, huh? Odd for a Cajun."

Ecclesiastes blinked. He decided to ignore the last comment. "Aikido," he said. "Got that from Dad. Listen, when you picked up that wreath from the trash, you dropped this." He rummaged in his suit pocket and pulled out a wrinkled, tattered sheet of notebook paper. Holes along one side showed where it had been torn from a cheap spiral binder. He handed the paper to Joan.

She sniffed at it. The sheet smelled vaguely of formaldehyde; the scent brought back the noise of the city to her. Louisiana disappeared into the recesses of her mind. When she continued to look at the paper in puzzlement, Ecclesiastes tapped it with a gloved forefinger. "It's what's written on it," he told her. "That's what made me curious."

"Henderson's Marvel Circus?" Joan asked suspiciously. Ecclesiastes shook his head slowly. "Can't read," Joan told him. "Never learned." A sadness spread over her ruined, old-man's face; the eyes became wetter than usual. She sniffed. "Betsa used ta read to me nights. She was the Wild Lady, had to eat raw meat. . . ." The words evoked memory, and the sound of Henderson's carnival began to return. Ecclesiastes saw her awareness drifting and he tapped the paper desperately.

"Carlos Theopelli," he said. "It's signed by Carlos Theopelli."

"—Henderson'd toss her a bloody haunch and old Betsa, she tear at it, growling with the juices just running down—"

"I heard about Carlos Theopelli in Cincinnati," Ecclesiastes interrupted nervously. He was beginning to regret the impulse that had led him to accost this street character. *Everyone in New York is crazy by definition, or they wouldn't live there.* His father had proclaimed that when Ecclesiastes had called him after the sale of his latest fiasco as an undertaker. *So it's only fitting you want to go there, too,* he added.

Joan the Flower Man growled and made tearing motions with her mouth as she gummed the broken carnation stems.

"He was some kind of eccentric genius, they said," Ecclesiastes persisted. "In college, I used read his articles. The professors all said it was nonsense, but . . . This paper of yours is handwritten. I thought—" He watched Joan capering around the sidewalk, making throaty grunting noises.

"Never mind," he said.

Joan stopped, one leg up in the air. She eyed him sidewise. "I got more," she said. "More them papers. Found 'em in the street this morning."

"I'd like to see them."

Joan's eyes narrowed. "Cost ya."

"How much?"

"You give me all the flowers they leave. Give 'em only to me, don't throw none away."

Ecclesiastes' grin made its return. "Deal. You can have anything that the family leaves behind. You drive a hard bargain, mister."

Joan grinned back.

She led him into the building and up a rickety stairwell that smelled of old urine and stale smoke. The second-floor hallway's rug was bare in places, damp in others. Ecclesiastes followed Joan along the hallway to the door that sagged on one hinge. She pushed it open and motioned him in.

The room had the sweetflower smell of a funeral home, overlaid with a stench of rotting greenery. Carnations, roses, lilies, daffodils: everywhere there were flowers in various stages of decomposition, sitting in glass jars with green, scummy water, and scattered over the rickety table, two chairs, and a bed that seemed to be the room's only furniture. The floor was slick with crushed petals. Bugs crawled in the undergrowth.

"Pretty, huh?" Joan said. There was a trace of pride in her deep, cracked voice. "Got more flowers'n *any*body." She moved around Ecclesiastes, who stood motionless at the doorway. He looked down, saw that his shoes were trampling a wreath. "—EST BROTHER," the trailing fabric proclaimed.

"It's quite *unusual,*" Ecclesiastes ventured, stepping delicately over the wreath. He removed his gloves and placed them in the pockets of his suit.

"I get 'em all over," Joan told him, standing in the middle of the room, her arms spread wide. She spat tobacco juice toward the corner. "First check the parlors, then the flower shops, every day. Go out to the cemet'ries Saturday and Sunday, holidays too—them's the big days for flowers. Bring 'em back here. Get paper to wrap 'em wherever. Sell 'em two bucks, cheap. Flowers mean you care," she added, winking.

Ecclesiastes nodded. The odor of decomposing vegetation was nauseating, overpowering. It smelled the way he imagined the floor of a jungle might smell. "What about the Theopelli papers?" he asked, a little too urgently. He could feel his stomach roiling.

Joan nodded, and began rummaging through the jars and stands and piles of flowers on the desk. At last, she gave a small cry and pulled out a thick sheaf of filthy notebook paper. "Here," she said. She held it out to the mortician, then snatched it back when he reached out to take it. "Deal, remember?" she said.

"Deal." Ecclesiastes took the papers. He went over to the open window of the room, both for the light and for relief from the room's thick atmosphere. He began shuffling through the papers, slowly at first, then with increasing excitement. Joan sat on the bed, arranging a half-dead bouquet of posies in a coffee can as she watched.

She saw his eyes go bright, the way Henderson's sometimes did when a new scheme occurred to him. The room shifted before her. The room became her shabby trailer in the Marvel Circus, the sounds outside those of the roustabouts erecting the tents. Ecclesiastes shimmered and became Gil, the cadaverous boy who was the Human Skeleton. Gil had only stayed with the circus a month before he died. Everything he ate, he threw up. His body could tolerate nothing except water.

"My God, I don't believe it," Gil breathed. His protruding rib cage, the skin stretched over it like flesh-colored shrinkwrap, heaved.

And then, at a dead run, he fled the room.

"It's okay, Gil, I understand," Joan yelled after him. She lay back on her bed, still toying with the posies. Outside her window, the roustabouts hammered stakes into the hard-baked southern ground, cursing each other as they worked.

4: The House on the Hill

They were driving westward along I-74. That was all Dirk could determine in the darkness. The Chevette's transmission growled and muttered beneath him, and Angela's attention seemed to be entirely on the road. He'd expected casual, light talk—the "getting-to-know-you" stage of a relationship. He'd gotten nearly nothing. The psychic brilliance of the woman seemed to be shuttered, locked away for the moment. She'd answer his overtures brightly enough, but that was it. Her smile was beginning to seem more of an effort, as if other matters were intruding.

After a few weak tries at initiating a conversation, Dirk lapsed into silence. Despite his intention to watch the road carefully in case he had to find his own way back, he found himself nodding off.

The crunch of gravel under the tires woke him. His head snapped up with an audible crack as the Chevette's worn brakes brought the car to a halt with a screech of metal. Angela shut off the engine, leaving them in sudden, abrupt silence. They seemed to be pulled well off a winding country road that twisted along wooded, black hills. The expressway was evidently long gone.

Dirk was lost. They could be anywhere. He snuck a glance at his wristwatch: 3:15 A.M. An hour since they'd left the club.

"You snore. You know that?" Angela asked him.

Dirk rubbed the back of his neck and pawed at his eyes, squinting through the dirty windshield. What he saw made him shake his head again.

The car had stopped in front of a set of ornate iron

gates, one of which leaned on broken hinges. Iron scrollwork atop the gates spelled out a name: THREE NORNS. Past the padlocked gates and high, spiked fence, the driveway curved up a long hill. Dirk could see the house quite clearly against the starlit spring sky.

It might once have been a gracious antebellum mansion; now the grounds were overgrown with weeds and saplings, and the gabled sides of the house had the gleaming grayness of weathered, bare wood. Shutters hung limp below the windows; most of the glass was missing as well. The spine of the roof was broken. An involuntary chill went through Dirk. *The House on Haunted Hill:* it looked like a movie set designed for Vincent Price.

He glanced hesitantly over at Angela after a moment. If she'd smiled at him and revealed gleaming, pointed, and horribly overgrown incisors, he would not have been at all surprised. The sleep had left cobwebs in his brain. Dire scenarios unfolded in his imagination in garish, comic-book color. At any moment he expected to hear the creepy background music begin. "All we need is a full moon," he ventured nervously.

She didn't turn into Dracula's daughter. Instead, she began laughing, laying her head back against the bucket seat as gales of amusement swept over her in growing waves. She slapped at the dashboard helplessly, tears streaming from her eyes. Dirk watched first in bemusement, then growing irritation.

"What's so damn funny?" he said.

"I'm . . . I'm sorry, Dirk," she gulped, and then succumbed to the laughter again. She wiped at her eyes with the back of her hands. "I'm sorry," she said again, taking a deep breath. "It's just that you looked so *scared*. Your eyes were *this* big." She succumbed again to the laughter.

Dirk stared grumpily at the dark facade of the house.

"Oh, now I've hurt that male ego," Angela said oversympathetically. "Listen, there's nothing wrong with being afraid. I'd be feeling the same way if our roles were reversed. Probably a lot worse."

"That certainly eases my mind."

"You were the one who let himself be dragged out into the country by a total stranger," Angela pointed out, sniffing with the last of the laughter. "I don't remember forcing you into the car at gunpoint. It seems to me that you were pretty eager to come along, in fact. I can't help it if you've an overactive imagination. If you want to go back, we'll go back." With the last sentence, her tone added an unspoken footnote: *And that'll be the last time you see me.*

She sat waiting for his decision, pointedly not looking at him. Her breath spread warm fog on the windshield.

"Okay, okay." Dirk shifted his weight grumpily on the vinyl seat. *Don't get angry, idiot. You'll totally blow your chances. Remember the way she danced. Remember the way she looked at you.* Despite his irritation, Dirk felt expectation stirring. He softened the hurt edge of his voice, lowered the pitch. He let a finger trail along the shoulder of her peasant blouse. "So—now that we're here, what's next?"

Angela's mouth pursed at the question, all amusement gone. She ignored his tentative advance. Her fingers tapped at the steering wheel. From the set of her face, it was obvious that her thoughts weren't in the same place as Dirk's. "That's not quite so easy to explain," she said at last. "We need to get in there, first of all."

"Umm, we could wait until daytime."

The sharpness of her glance surprised him. He glimpsed that unexpected depth and seriousness in her again; the sense of lurking power. She seemed suddenly older, troubled. "Afraid of ghosts?" she snapped, and then the moment was gone.

The flirtatious, charismatic Angela returned. She grinned coquettishly, reached under her seat to grab a pair of flashlights, and opened her door. Running to the gates, she pushed the broken section aside so that she could slip through. Swathed in silver-blue starlight, the peasant blouse down around one shoulder and just revealing the upper swell of her breasts, she turned and tilted her head back to him, smiling.

She was compelling, like some succubus in the night. "Come on if you're coming," she called.

Then she slipped into the shadows beyond. Dirk heard her laughter trailing behind.

He let out an explosive sigh. So far, all the night had done for him was to tie his stomach in knots. It didn't look as if that was about to change. His choices seemed severely limited: he could walk the thirty miles or more back to the city (assuming he got lucky and headed in the right direction in the first place); he could stay in the car until Angela eventually came back (or someone or something else found him).

Or he could follow her.

At least the door made an impressive, echoing crash when he slammed it shut behind him. Hands in pockets, the pebbles of the driveway gritting under the soles of his boots, he headed up the hill toward Three Norns.

The look of the place didn't improve as he approached. Vines snarled the unpainted shingles, shivering in the slight breeze. The veranda sagged as if weary; part of the roof was gone. The steps had dry rot—the lowest one cracked ominously as he put his weight on it. It seemed that Angela had already gone in, for the double doors at the front were open. The interior of the house was utterly dark. Dirk stumped heavily across the veranda and took a step inside.

Achingly bright light stabbed his eyes. "Jesus!" Dirk yelled. Adrenaline surged through him; his heart hammered at his chest.

"Boo!" Angela cooed softly at his ear.

Dirk lowered the hands he'd brought up to protect his face. "Very funny," he said.

"You jumped about two feet straight up." She was giggling again. Her arms came around him and hugged him quickly (the flashlight throwing crazy circles with the motion). He could feel the warmth of her skin, then she was gone again. Her beam swept around the huge entry hall. "It must have been magnificent once," she said. Gilt was flaking from a mural overhead, where mildew had given the cherubic angels terminal dermatitis. Ribbons of wallpaper peeled back from the plaster, paint gathered in piles along the trim. A thick flour of dust coated the ruined tables and lamps.

"Place needs a housekeeper," Dirk commented unnecessarily.

"The locals think it's haunted."

"I don't believe in ghosts," Dirk answered defiantly.

"I'll bet you don't believe in anything out of the ordinary at all," Angela commented. Dirk couldn't tell from the sound of her voice whether she was teasing him or not. "The man who built it was killed on the grounds by southern raiders during the Civil War. His daughter kept the place until the night she was gang-raped and murdered by a band of thieves passing through the area. The next owner's wife hung herself from the staircase here, despondent after a miscarriage." Angela's flashlight played along the banister of the second-floor balcony. "*He* shot himself, though not here."

"Thank God for that," Dirk whispered. "The spirit population's already overcrowded."

Angela laughed once in darkness. "And the last owner was entirely mad, if you believe the neighbors. He died here, too, upstairs."

"In his sleep?" Dirk ventured.

"The police report said it was an accident. The locals aren't so sure."

"Should have known." Their voices had a hollow sound in the entry hall. The silence was oppressive, and Angela's lesson in local history had left a chill in the air. He rubbed at his arms vigorously. Despite his earlier words, it was easy enough to believe in the supernatural at the moment; in this place, after the strange presence of Angela herself. He half thought that if they stopped talking, the silence might bring some manifestation. He didn't want to see an ectoplasmic woman swaying below the railing, or the weeping spirit of the assaulted daughter howling in outrage. He wanted, very desperately, to get the hell out of here. "How do you know so much about this place?" he asked.

"It's all local lore. You can look most of it up in the library's historical references. It's been a rite of passage around here for years for kids to sneak up to this place at night and look in the windows. Usually the boys. Guess they think it proves their manhood."

"Yeah, well, I actually got in. Now that I've passed the test, can we leave? There are better ways to prove manhood."

"Not yet."

He could see the beam of the flashlight at the stairs and heard the steps creaking under her feet. "Where you going?"

"Second floor. His study's up there. Come on." She kept walking. Dirk muttered an obscenity under his breath and followed her. "Here, take this." She pressed a cold cylinder in his hand. The weight and size of it felt like one of the maglights security cops used.

Dirk found the switch. It seemed better to feel the heft of the flash in his hand, and see the warm, bright circle of light that it cast.

The second floor was little different. A few times, Dirk thought he saw a form slink away from the sudden light. He could hear faint scurryings, and there were small tracks through the dust on the floor. Once he felt the brush of a spiderweb against his face, and it was all he could do to stop from crying out. Angela seemed to know where she was going. She went along the balcony and down a short hall to the back of the house. She opened a door festooned with cobwebs. "In here."

The flashlights revealed a large, square room. An overstuffed chair sat by the draped window, its plush covering moth-eaten. Four or five desks of various sizes sat in the room, and the walls were covered with bookcases. There was a strong smell of must and mildew. Dirk sneezed.

His flash showed Angela looking back at him, startled. "Dust," he said.

She shook her head. "Then let's get looking before you have an allergy attack," she said. She set her flashlight on the edge of one of the desks so that it illuminated the bookcase and began pulling the old volumes from the shelves. She looked at them one at a time, flipping through the pages before putting each back in its place. Dirk hadn't moved. "Why don't you check the desks?" Angela suggested.

Dirk found himself moving over to one of the desks, then was irritated that he found himself obeying so meekly. His stomach lurched. *Too much stress. I'm sitting in a haunted house out God-knows-where in the boonies at three o'clock in the damn morning with a bizarre woman in a peasant blouse and tight jeans who's engaged in some kind of larceny.*

He found himself staring at the admittedly enticing rear view as Angela prowled the bookcase. A line from an old Laurel & Hardy sketch popped into his head; he addressed it to his crotch: *And this is another fine mess you've gotten us into.*

"Just what is it we're after?" he inquired.

"You should know better than me," Angela answered cryptically. She shook one of the books upside down, holding the covers open, and then put it back on the shelf. She looked back at him and saw his confusion. "Oh, never mind. It should be a spiral notebook, a red one. Handwritten. Lots of mathematical formulae. You'll know it when you find it."

"Right." Dirk opened the lid of a slant-top desk and peered at the empty pigeonholes inside. "And what are we going to do when we find it?"

In the harsh glare of the flash, her face looked almost sinister. "We're going to *take* it," she said as if addressing a child. "What'd you think?"

"It's not yours. . . ." Dirk began, then shrugged. It wouldn't do any good. He'd seen "The Twilight Zone," playing on motel room TVs after the gigs were over. Dazed, bewildered, you just had to ride it out and pray for commercials. "Red spiral notebook," he said. "Math. Right." He began pawing through drawers.

Two hours later, they hadn't found it. Angela had been through the bookcase twice; Dirk had seen the inside of all the desks. Angela sat on the chair by the window and sighed. False dawn was laying a faint haze over the trees down the hill; faintly, they could hear birds. In the light, the place seemed more rundown than evil and mysterious. "Damn it, it's supposed to *be* here. We were supposed to find it tonight. *You* were supposed to find it."

"Huh? Look, excuse me, but do you know how strange all this is? I thought—"

"*You* thought you were going to get laid." Angela glowered at him from the chair, her chin cupped in her hand. She seemed almost to smolder; her gaze burned. "That's the only reason you're here. You don't care who or what I am beyond that."

Dirk felt unexpected heat on his cheeks at her frankness. "Well, I didn't know for certain, but I sure didn't expect this—looking through some beat-up old mansion for a madman's notebook."

"Not just some madman," Angela said glumly. "Carlos Theopelli." She said the name as if it should have meant something to him. Dirk just shook his head.

"Carlos Theopelli? Who the hell's that?"

Angela looked at him with a sigh. "Historians only believe what they're told," she said inexplicably. Then: "I should've known I'd have to answer that," she said.

5: Death with Chowder

Carlos Theopelli was one of the greatest theoreticians of the branch of mathematics known as the Destiny Matrices.

That is, several decades after his death, he'll come to be known for the matrices. History's funny that way—you wonder how many Shakespeares and Einsteins are lost to us because of some historian's feelings about who was important and who wasn't. At the moment that Angela is trying to decide how to explain Theopelli to Dirk, Carlos is just a fading memory known only as the Madman of Three Norns, now dead the last eight years.

Theopelli was himself rather unappetizing. If his mind was a perfect, polished red delicious, his body was a bowl of year-old fruit. He was a gross man: his face was the color of a rotting peach; his nose was a toadstool sitting on the decaying skin and dripping some noxious ichor. Theopelli was predisposed to bathrobes—he rarely dressed, rarely went out of his home. His bathrobe and he were equally unacquainted with the pleasures of the bath. His flesh was a mass of sores from an allergic skin condition, and an enormous potbelly hung over the cord of his robe, discreetly sheltering the timid, abandoned knob of his manhood.

If his appearance was horrid, he had at least acquired a certain reputation among scholars of his time. Most of his communications with the outside world were by mail; those who had met him on the rare occasions when Theopelli had felt compelled to attend some meeting were inordinately pleased by his reluctance to travel. The mathematics of Theopelli's logic were complicated (and according to many rival theoreticians, utterly in error). Still, we can assure you that in time his teachings would be mouthed by billions. Boiled down to simplistic aphorisms, they resemble the gothic complexity of Theopelli's theorems about as much as a strip of dried beef resembles sirloin.

- *All events are related.*
- *Everything that occurs, no matter how small or insignificant, has its unique role in the ultimate destiny of humanity.*
- *Nothing will ever happen elsewhere that does not also affect you.*

Or, as it is said: "When the poorest fall, the rich bleed."

Theopelli was at work on his unfinished Destiny Theorem, which he claimed would allow accurate prediction of the course of future human events. His colleagues all knew about the work; Theopelli certainly wasn't shy about promoting himself and his work; his peers unanimously declared that the Destiny Theorem was in a league with perpetual motion and crystal power.

As yet, even Theopelli admitted that the theorem was flawed; the only journal that he had been able to interest in the work was the *National Enquirer,* who wanted to call Theopelli as the Scientist Psychic and offered him a column. The angry Theopelli had just fired back a letter rejecting their offer when fate—always smiling—turned her attention to him. It was a superb example of happenstance.

Theopelli's manservant, Alfred Roundbottom, pricked his finger, and therefore Theopelli died.

Oh, it's never quite *that* simple, but the connection can be made. Theopelli was a recluse, living with Alfred in Three Norns. The mansion looked much the same then as it did to Dirk and Angela. Three Norns was an asthmatic's hell. Alfred was not much of a caretaker or butler, but he was unobtrusive—that was the only criterion Theopelli had. As Alfred was fond of telling the locals: "The old shit doesn't give a rat's ass what the place looks like as long as he's fed when he's hungry."

Theopelli had acquired Three Norns (his name; originally it was Sycamore Havens) when the previous tenant had simply handed young Carlos Theopelli the keys. Theopelli had been in Boston at the time. A graduate of Harvard with a doctorate in physics and mathematics, he'd been unable to snag any of the jobs that his classmates had seemed to find waiting, this despite the fact that Theopelli was grudgingly acknowledged as one of the more original minds to come through the school. His appearance and manner were no doubt to blame; even as a relatively young man, Theopelli had the look of an accomplished slob and the social grace of a unhousebroken puppy.

A year out of graduate school, Carlos Theopelli was unemployed and mingling with the other Sad Tales gathered in Boston Commons during the summer nights of 1922. When a gentleman arrayed in full evening dress approached Theopelli one foggy, drizzly evening, Theopelli's only inclination was to ask for a handout. Instead, Theopelli found himself telling the bedewed stranger the entire tale of woe that was his life. Theopelli was never quite sure how that happened, nor why the man was so inclined to listen. They sat on one of the benches in the Commons, ignoring the persistent rain. Theopelli talked as the man nodded encouragingly, occasionally interjecting a question to guide Theopelli along the downhill slide of his life.

"You seem good enough, Carlos," the man said at last. "All any of us ever wanted was a break. The bastards. We'll show them, Carlos—I'll give you the opportunity that was never given to me. Here." He'd pressed keys and a packet of legal documents into the astonished young man's hands. He'd also produced a .45 revolver from under his formal jacket.

Carlos had realized early in the dialogue that his confessor was not entirely sane. With the glimmer of blue steel, Theopelli was certain that his own life was about to end. But the man only smiled strangely, placed the muzzle in his mouth, smiled at Carlos around the barrel, and pulled the trigger.

Theopelli was spattered with brains, blood, and bits of skull. He was also arrested by the first officer on the scene. The next morning, after a night in a precinct cell and an investigation of the circumstances, he was released, a free and newly rich man—the documents put into Theopelli's keeping had been the stranger's will, giving the possessor of the will full and total control of the considerable fortunes of one Willis McAllister.

Carlos Theopelli was permanently changed by that incident in the park. He would never again willingly talk to strangers; he would hate rainy evenings and formal clothing; he would leave Boston and never return. Boston is not known to have mourned.

Over the next several months, Theopelli waited for his good fortune to dissolve like the Boston fog. Surely there was some legal loophole, some clause that had been overlooked. Surely some member of the McAllister family would file suit. Surely there was a mistake.

There were none. Despite some shaky moments during the Depression, Theopelli was able to become a gentleman scholar, a man of leisure. Gifted by fortune himself, he set out on the task of discovering the mathematical formulae that must govern Fate.

However, we weren't talking about his life, but his death. On that day, Alfred entered Theopelli's study to serve the evening meal. Theopelli was engrossed there, surrounded by open books and sheets of notepaper. Alfred unceremoniously shoveled one of the piles aside to make room for his master's tray. Like the rest of the house, the place setting had seen better days.

Setting down the plate, Alfred slashed open his index finger on the chipped porcelain. Alfred's reaction was normal enough for a person suddenly injured, if not exactly proper decorum in a butler: he dropped the plate with a howl, shaking his injured hand. Droplets of blood fell like thick rain. Unfortunately, since the incident in Boston Common, one of Theopelli's minor phobias was the sight of blood. The elderly scholar rose to his feet in haste, backing away from the abhorrence with his face twisted in disgust. He would no doubt have fired Alfred the next day.

It was at that instant that Theopelli's favorite Siamese cat, Cara, startled by the commotion, decided to abandon the room discreetly. Powered by his three-hundred-plus pounds, one of Theopelli's bedroom slippers stomped directly on the cat's tail. Cara reacted as one might expect. She screamed and lashed out with her claws. Theopelli jerked up the offending foot, tottered, and began to fall, flailing desperate arms. Alfred reached for his employer and caught only a frantic hand.

Alone, Theopelli might well have fallen between the desks of his study, bruising himself and perhaps even breaking a rib or two. Nothing more. Now he swung around the pivot of Alfred's grasp and back into the desk.

He struck hard.

The force of his uncushioned (and indeed accelerated) fall drove his nose into the desk at an angle and slammed the cartilage there back into his brain. A letter punch holding his correspondence (Theopelli was a notorious letter writer) slid easily into his right eye, powered by the weight of his body. His hand grasped the dinner tray as he toppled to the floor—Alfred now having let go of Theopelli in horror—pulling the remnants of his meal down on top of him.

In a puddle of steaming chowder, a bun on his chest and a salad over his loins, Theopelli expired in a very few seconds.

The investigators declared the death an unfortunate accident. The will gave the greatest portion of Theopelli's remaining wealth to Alfred, who promptly took the money and disappeared somewhere on the East Coast. The house and land were left to the state, provided that (as the will stated) "I am still dead in ten years."

The state felt that Theopelli was being unreasonably optimistic, but nevertheless decided to wait him out.

As for Theopelli's mathematical treatises on destiny, well, they were never found. In fact, most of his correspondents claimed that they probably never had existed at all.

6: Damp Dreams

Of course, that wasn't at all the story that Angela gave Dirk as they rode back to Cincinnati, their faces toward a tepid dawn. Angela's explanation of Theopelli was truncated by her limited sources of information and by the necessity of keeping her own interests secret. This strange mixture of small details and large omissions was obvious even to Dirk's weary mind—he'd decided that she was some bizarre academic thief or some type of spy (Dirk had read all the Bond novels); she was obviously holding back a good deal of her story. By the time Angela came to the sad events of Theopelli's death, with the sun scrubbing the warm blacktop of I-74, he could only shake his head wearily.

Dirk wished that thieves didn't come in quite so attractive a package.

His stomach hadn't stopped jumping until Three Norns was long out of sight behind them. Dirk was still held in thrall by the iron bonds of Catholicism. Once, as a child, he'd stolen a carrot from a neighbor's garden. His well-sharpened guilt had gnawed at him for days afterward; he was afraid to take Communion lest the host brand his tongue. He was eventually driven to confess his heinous crime—the neighbor had only laughed and absolved him.

Breaking and entering was something far out of the realm of his previous experience. Through the haze of weariness, he could see visions of rusty bars and dank cells. Sadistic guards patted nightsticks into meaty palms; gargantuan convicts leered at him and patted his rear end covetously.

"We could've ended up in jail," Dirk muttered.

"Don't be such a milquetoast. All we had to do was say that we'd heard the house was haunted and we were looking for ghosts. The place is abandoned. They'd've run us out, that's all. Nobody knows how important Theopelli is yet."

"But *you* do."

Dirk's sarcasm bounced off her. Angela simply nodded.

"You also said something about *me* finding those papers," he continued. "You said it was supposed to happen tonight. You're one heck of a fortune-teller."

Her hands clenched the Chevette's steering wheel until her knuckles went white; her mouth tightened as she stared into the smeared wiper glare. It was the first indication Dirk had that she was bothered under that flirtatious, mysterious exterior. "You always get this grumpy when your libido's feeling neglected?" Her voice purred, but there was honed steel underneath that drew blood.

"Look, I'll admit a"—Dirk hesitated, deciding how to phrase it—"a certain sexual attraction was one reason—"

"The *only* reason," Angela interrupted. She gave him a harsh glance.

"*Maybe* the only reason I came along," Dirk conceded. "I think I deserve more. I'd like to know the real reason you dragged me out here."

"You too tired to think with your dick anymore?"

That sent them both into petulant silence for a time. Dirk had been up too long; exhaustion kept diluting his anger with extraneous thoughts. He found himself nodding off and jerked his head up. He rubbed his eyes. They were sweeping around a long curve overlooking the river valley. The city brooded knee-deep in morning fog.

Angela's long fingers were tapping a restless rhythm on the steering wheel. She exhaled explosively. "Okay, that wasn't fair," she said. "You didn't deserve that. I'm sorry."

"Then tell me"—a yawn intruded; he let it have its

way—"why Theopelli's notebook is so important. Tell me why you brought me with you."

"I can't."

"Why not?"

"Mostly because I'm too damn tired to think of a plausible lie."

Even through the sleepy cobwebs in his brain, there seemed a simple enough answer to that. "So try the truth."

"You're a historian. You only think things are true if they follow the correct pattern."

That was all the answer she'd give. The silence had stretched for a few minutes. Dirk abandoned several openings, then fell to arranging a story to tell the band when he returned to the hotel. *Keep it simple. She took me to her place. We fucked our brains out. She knew every position in the Kama Sutra. Her girlfriend joined us. No, two girlfriends joined us.*

They'd never believe it. Kyle would nod sagely, Alf and Lars would laugh, Jay would tell him that the Kama Sutra was for enlightenment, not pleasure. He'd hear Kama Sutra jokes all night on stage.

Yet as they turned off the expressway, Angela suddenly smiled at him. Her hand swept from his knee to midthigh and returned to the wheel. "Listen, thanks for helping, even if we didn't find it," she said. "If it makes any difference at all, I think I do like you. Even if you are scared of the dark."

She pulled the Chevette to the curb a few blocks later, in front of a narrow building on a block of identically grimy houses. The area had the look of cheap student housing. "My place," she said before he could comment. She put the car in park but left the motor running. She turned in her seat to look at him. "Or would you rather I took you back to your hotel?"

In the full light of day, she was still elusive, still darkly compelling. She had an earthiness, a primal energy. Dirk thought that she would smell of ancient loam, of animal musk. Her features were timeless. She could as easily have been twenty or fifty.

Dirk decided that age wasn't an issue. "Here's all right," he said, trying to be nonchalant.

"Don't sound so eager," she answered, but she grinned. She turned off the car, unhooked her seat belt. She went to the front door of the house without waiting for him. Dirk got out of the car with a groan of rusty hinges. His first step was a tired lurch. He blinked, inhaled deeply, and followed her into the house.

He was surprised when her arms came around him as the door thudded shut. Her mouth was warm and open; his own lips widened in response. Her tongue danced along his molars, slid deeper, and then teasingly retreated. He chased it as her arms pulled him closer.

It was a long kiss. When—gently, moistly—it ended, he found her eyes smiling and extremely close. "Very nice," she said, and leaned in to him again.

Dirk found his jeans suddenly very full.

He stroked her hair, her cheek, her neck. His fingers strolled the edge of her shoulder, skied down the slope of her breast. Angela's hand intercepted him, lacing her fingers in his as she took a step away. "My bedroom's in back," she said. "If you're not too tired."

Dirk's hormones were shouting an exultant *YES!* that threatened to drown out his own voice. Adrenaline pumped through him, making him forget the fact that he'd been awake far too long. His manhood did pushups against the roof of its denim cave. "I'm suddenly not particularly sleepy," he said.

Images of Terre Haute Patti shattered. This was going all right. Dirk told himself that he wasn't going to think of anything but those eyes, that mouth, the way her body had moved on the dance floor and would hopefully dance with him. He let himself be led through a hallway to the rear of the house.

Her bedroom was as cluttered as her car. Clothes were strewn over the bedposts. The sheets were rumpled and bunched where she'd thrown them aside. The mirror of her dresser was hung with nylons like Spanish moss on a cypress tree. There were candles everywhere, runneled wax pooled at their feet. Books sat on every available surface. Dirk glanced at some of the titles: *The Gnostic Gospels, Houdini on Magic, Secret Societies, Anthropology and Early Law.* If she weren't a student, then she had truly esoteric tastes.

They sat on the bed. "I'm not much of a housekeeper," she said.

"So I see."

"Do you care?" Her face was very close. Her breath was warm and fragrant. Her eyes laughed under thick eyebrows.

"Not particularly."

"Good," she said. "Give me a few minutes, okay?"

She hugged him and gave him another lingering kiss. Then she rose from the bed and went down the hall to the bathroom. She closed the door.

She came back ten minutes later, clad only in a smile. She stood in the doorway for a moment, waiting for his reaction, but there was none.

Dirk was stretched across the bed, naked himself, but very much asleep.

7: Tarot Incognito

Dirk's dreams were rather more jumbled and confused than usual that morning, a strange mixture of eroticism and fear. Angela was in them, looking perhaps less enticing than the naked reality that—unawares—slept alongside him. They were embracing in the middle of a haunted mansion, with ghosts waltzing around them while Savage played. Theopelli was there, holding his notebook, and his manservant Alfred was trying to bring him his dinner.

In the real world, Alfred Roundbottom was trying to make a buck from the remnants of Theopelli's short life. He wasn't having a great deal of luck. In fact, since that fateful day in Theopelli's study, his life had been an eternal downhill slide. As he knocked on the apartment door in a run-down tenement in the Bowery, it didn't seem as if today would be any different.

When the door to the apartment swung open, Alfred Roundbottom glanced at the interior and gulped noisily. The room beyond was lit with guttering candles; strange shapes hulked in moving shadows. Bluish haze coiled between twitching, spastic pools of candlelight. A battered kitchen table blocking the entrance hall was littered with strange glass beakers and retorts in front of a rack of cork-stoppered jars—a monstrous book was propped up against a Cuisinart filled with a green-gray paste. The place looked vaguely arcane and cabalistic; it smelled of rotten fish and battery acid. It was worse than Theopelli's old place, worse than the dumps Alfred had been sleeping in lately.

"Excuse me," he said, dropping his gaze to a tiny old man in black who'd answered his knock. He had the short arms and legs, the normal-sized head and body of a dwarf. "I think I have the wrong place."

"You Roundbottom?" The apparition's voice was a broken rasp, like sandpaper scraping steel.

Alfred opened his mouth to answer, but a whiff of the foul atmosphere inside drifted into the hall. Alfred coughed, choked, and had to swallow the sour bile that rose in his stomach. The dwarf stared up at him with a rheumy, unsympathetic gaze. His eyes were huge, the pupils narrowed to pinprick dots in the light of the hallway's bare bulb. They were his best feature. His skin was a pasty white liberally peppered with acne, and greasy red hair spilled over his high forehead. His mouth was a twisted slash cut into the flesh stretched between protruding cheekbones.

"I'm Caleb Mundo," the dwarf said. "Inside."

He turned away from the door and disappeared into the murk of the apartment without waiting for Alfred to answer. Alfred stood there for several seconds, regaining control of his stomach and vacillating. "I have your money," the ruined voice said from inside the apartment. Alfred nodded at that, took a deep breath, and stepped inside.

"Close the damn door. Weren't you ever taught manners?" The voice sounded exactly like Theopelli's—tone and inflection. Old synapses flared; reflexively, Alfred slammed the door shut. He stood in the dim hallway waiting for his eyes to adjust to the light. "You people always keep places so *bright,*" Mundo was saying, and his voice didn't sound like Theopelli at all anymore. "You use a searchlight when a match would do. You'd think the night was unnatural, the way you act. I don't see you carrying any papers, Roundbottom."

The abrupt change of topic confused Alfred momentarily. He peered in the direction of the voice and made out the black-clad Mundo sitting in a worn, overstuffed chair pulled up to a coffee table. A deck of cards lay facedown on the table. The dwarf picked them up in a surprisingly long-fingered hand and began shuffling them as Alfred cleared his throat of the remnants of nausea.

"I—umm, well, that is—"

"You lost them." Mundo, his unblinking stare impaling Roundbottom, laid a card down in the exact center of the table. "I already know that."

"No," Alfred half shouted. "I had them. I did. I had the damn things for years now, never got around to throwin' 'em out. I was bringin' them."

Another card drifted to the table to fall crosswise the first, but Mundo's fixed glare never left Roundbottom. "You answered my ad," he growled. "You said you had them, you said you'd sell them to me for the price I named." There was an ominous undertone to the voice, an implicit threat that made Roundbottom back up. He hit the table in the hall, rattling glass. Something spilled and the odor of burning linoleum enveloped him. He coughed again, stumbling away as his eyes teared.

"If you're holding out for a better price, I'll make you regret your greed." Four more cards—they now formed a cross on the table. Alfred barely noticed it. There were only those eyes, dark and shadowed, flickering in the candelight with a life of their own, deep and dangerous.

"I'll call the fuckin' cops, mister. . . ." he blustered, but lost energy halfway through the threat as Mundo started laughing. The little man had a sinister, unamused laugh.

"Look at the vial on the table, Roundbottom," Mundo said, gesturing as he dropped another card to the table. Alfred saw a handful of white powder encased in plastic lying in the detritus of the tabletop.

"That's cocaine, ninety-eight-percent-pure snow. *My* stuff. I supply it to half a dozen dealers in the city. They're not nice people, Roundbottom. They're all paranoid, and they're all strange. Every last one of them carries a gun, and a lot of them prefer automatic weapons that would chop someone in half, very messily. Some of them *enjoy* using them. If I mentioned to them that somebody threatened me with the cops, do you have any idea how long that person would live? I'm also known as the local fortune-teller, but you don't need me to tell you that such a person's life span would be negligible."

His gaze still holding Alfred, Mundo set a last card in place and put the deck back down, his ebon pupils smoldering. "You *did* lose them," Mundo accused. His voice was flint, striking sparks. Mundo continued to stare at Alfred, who was beginning to feel an uncomfortable pressure in his bladder. Theopelli had made him feel that way, too.

"It was just for a second," Alfred said hurriedly, since it was obvious Mundo wanted him to elaborate. "Yesterday. I've been keeping the papers with me all the time since you told me they were valuable. A funeral procession was going by, so I had to wait to cross the street. I bought a dog with kraut. I didn't want to get the papers dirty, so I set 'em down on a bench. When I turned around, the papers were gone." He shrugged, tried on a sheepish smile.

Mundo sighed. "The Princess," he said. "It was her again. Did you see her?"

"I don't exactly get to meet much royalty," Alfred said, allowing a tinge of irritable sarcasm into his voice. He regretted it instantly as Mundo smashed his fist on the table. Cards jumped. Alfred felt the beginnings of a migraine, and he wanted to pee. Very badly.

"*Not* royalty. Especially not her. Just an interfering bitch who doesn't realize the power she's playing with. She'd have dark hair and fair skin. Very attractive. Did you see her?"

"No . . . Maybe . . . I don't know. . . ." Alfred stammered. He crossed his legs slightly. "Listen, you got a bathroom?"

Mundo ignored him, turning over the card in the exact center of the array on the coffee table. Alfred caught a glimpse of bright colors: he could see a dark woman whose crown was a ram's horns. She stood in a grove of trees, carrying a disk, a full body ill concealed in a gauzy, windblown dress.

"Her," Mundo said. "The Princess of Pentacles.

The earth part of earth, a dabbler in things arcane. She's been in every reading since . . ."

He paused. For a moment he seemed confused, passing his hands over his eyes as if weary. He didn't finish the sentence. "She's involved," he said at last. "She's always there."

"I looked for the papers for a long time. Honest. I didn't see 'em, didn't see any woman like that. I know I can find them again. Just give me time."

"You know *nothing*," Mundo told Alfred. "You're an incompetent fool. If *she* has them, she'll . . ." Again, Mundo stopped himself. He grimaced, breathing asthmatically. "It's this place, this damn place," he grated out in an agonized voice. "I can't remember half of what I need to remember."

Alfred glanced around the apartment. "Just needs some cleaning," he began.

"You *ass!*"

Alfred shivered at Mundo's shout, pressing his legs together. For a moment, he was back in Three Norns, which was often as dark and filthy as this room. It was Theopelli's voice again, screaming at him from upstairs and making him feel like some stupid schoolchild. Alfred had hated Theopelli. He'd often wondered if Theopelli's death had *really* been an accident, if perhaps he hadn't subconsciously directed Theopelli's tragic arc into the desk.

"They're gone," Mundo was ranting. "If my magic hasn't been able to find them, what makes you think your bumbling will succeed?"

Alfred had had enough. He could see there was no money to be made without Theopelli's damn papers, and they were gone. There was no sense in standing here taking the dwarf's damn abuse. "Bumbling?" Alfred shouted back. "You're playing with a bunch of goddamn cards, which tells *me* you ain't got a full deck upstairs." The metaphor, so unexpected, rather pleased Alfred; it gave him the impetus to continue. "Magic," he scoffed. "You live in a rat hole. If your magic's so damn effective, how come you ain't got a palace? You're worse than Theopelli, always muttering about his vectors and quantum equations and parallel—"

He stopped, for Caleb Mundo had risen from his chair with a formidable scowl on his ugly, flushed face. One long, knobby finger pointed up at Alfred's nose and sliced off his harangue. "Shut up," Mundo added unnecessarily. He waved his hand as if flicking away an insect.

Alfred cried out, for with Mundo's imperious gesture, the room disappeared. The effect was almost disappointing: there was no spinning dizziness, no puffs of gaily colored smoke as there always was in the movies, no special effects at all. Mundo and his room were simple *gone,* and in their place . . .

The creature was half again Alfred's height, its long, humanlike arms and body covered with shaggy golden fur. By itself, it might have been almost cute, something like a mutated Irish Setter crossed with a baby Tyrannousaurus Rex, but then the thing looked up at Alfred with a snouted, long head and ruined the effect by smiling.

Rows of needled, unmistakably carnivorous teeth lined that mouth, stained with what Alfred knew must be old blood. Gobbets of raw meat were snagged there, draggling over the black lips. Alfred noticed then that it was crouching beside a barely recognizable human body. The creature plunged clawed hands down into the corpse—a storm cloud of black flies lifting noisily with the motion—and pulled a mass of steaming intestinal coils from the abdomen. It stuffed the gory mess into its mouth, chomping noisily.

The thing's breath hit Alfred then, like the inside of a meat locker after a month without refrigeration.

"Shee-it," Alfred whispered fervently.

The creature grinned again. Bloodshot and very expressive eyes looked at Alfred with distinct malice and —Alfred feared—deep hunger. It crooked a finger at Alfred, beckoning.

Alfred shook his head wildly. "Not a chance," he said.

It shrugged. The creature stepped over the mangled

carcass and came toward him. Alfred turned to run and found a very substantial stone wall at his back. He could hear the creature behind him as he pounded at the rock with futile fists, almost weeping with desperation as a hot, foul breath touched him. Alfred screamed, turning to strike blindly at the abomination before it shredded his flesh like the corpse on the floor. . . .

And then it was gone.

Alfred was back in Mundo's room, and the dwarf was watching him with a haughty, superior smile. "You'll find those papers, Roundbottom. Or I'll feed you to the MindBeast one joint at a time. Alive."

Alfred was panting, his heart slamming against his rib cage. He forced himself to calmness. "A cheap hallucination?" he blustered. He'd be damned if he'd show the dwarf how scared he'd really been. "You used some damn drug or something. I ain't scared of your fake magic. . . ." His protest trailed off.

Mundo had looked away, turning over another card on the table as Alfred became aware of a sour odor and a rapidly cooling, disturbing wetness down his legs.

"It's good to know you're so brave, Alfred," Mundo said, and the mockery in his ruined voice shamed Alfred. "But I think you'll find the papers and bring them back here, anyway."

He held up the card for Alfred. On the bright surface, a man in motley danced on the edge of a cliff. *The Fool*, it said underneath. "After you change your pants, of course," Mundo added.

8: A Meeting with Relish

The problem with wearing faded blue jeans on an April morning is that should you piss your pants, you'll quickly discover that winter's mind-set still lingers: wet jeans are very cold and uncomfortable. You'd also notice that faded denim shows dampness far more obviously than you'd like.

Mercifully, Alfred's apartment was only five blocks from Caleb Mundo's. He slunk through several unobtrusive alleyways. Drunks looked at him knowingly from underneath newspaper sheets and nodded. Alfred still had to endure the gauntlet of stares and whispered comments as he crossed the rush-hour streets. He tried to look like a jogger who merely, well, *sweated* excessively.

Joggers, though, rarely run in jeans. When they sweat, they're usually less precise about the location.

To make matters worse, his landlady—Mrs. Seymour—was standing just inside the front door of his building.

"*Really*, Mr. Roundbottom . . ." she began portentously.

"Damn cab splashed water up from the gutter," he told her unconvincingly as he fled up the stairs to his own room, leaving behind a subtle miasma reminiscent of stale diapers. Mrs. Seymour watched, hands on wide hips, as he hit the landing at a dead run, slammed shut the door to his room, and slid the dead bolt over.

"Men," she muttered. "You'd think as anxious as they are to whip the thing out the rest of the time, they'd never have that problem."

About the time Alfred was peeling the fragrant, soaked cloth from his legs, Dirk was beginning to snore beside Angela, and Joan the Flower Man had stopped by at Remains to Be Seen. The twin parlors were empty; Ecclesiastes Mitsumishi was in the basement workroom. He opened the back door at Joan's knock—he'd given up the formal black coat and tails for a lab coat; his gloves were now latex instead of white kid. The silly, unexpected smile was still there; his teeth gleamed. The abrasive baritone of a television evangelist wafted from the interior with him, tinny from the portable Sony's small speaker.

"I'm not religious myself, you understand," he told her. He gestured at the set, which was half turned from Joan; she could only see shifting blue light flickering from the painted concrete walls. "It's just that Mom always had them on. Fire and brimstone makes me feel comfortable and at home even though I disagree with almost everything they say."

" 'Cording to them, then you gonna *feel* the fire later."

Ecclesiastes smiled and shrugged, moving back into the room. "I doubt it. Some people use Musak, I use preachers."

"Huh." Joan stepped inside. There was a strong medicinal smell. Glass jars lined shelves, stainless steel instruments glittered ominously on a counter top. A gurney stood in the center of the room, and the naked body of an overweight, old man lay there.

"The problem is that most people don't have a very good attitude about death," Ecclesiastes said as he fixed a wide, openmouthed grin to the face of the corpse—one Ben Wilson. Ecclesiastes stepped back to admire his work. "You see, that's how we should go out—laughing eternally at fate's last joke."

Ecclesiastes seemed to wait for her reaction, but Joan simply stood there, scratching at the side of her neck, one cheek distended with tobacco. The mortician shrugged and shook his head. "But no, they have to be solemn. Dignified."

He leaned over, shutting the mouth and readjusting

the corpse's lips. Ben frowned as if fate's joke had been on him. Which it had. "I just can't understand that. What's the good of leaving behind a grumpy body?"

"So's they can buy flowers?" Joan asked hopefully. She reached out with a grimy finger and poked Ben's biceps. The clammy skin dimpled under her finger; a small, soiled crater remained behind as she wiped the finger on her windbreaker. "Flowers cheer you up."

"I'm certain the bereaved family followed all the proper customs and there will be plenty of flowers left over for you, Mr. . . ." Ecclesiastes' voice rose with the last word; he looked bemused as he repaired the residue of Joan's prodding. "I'm afraid I don't know your name."

"Joan."

Ecclesiastes thought he'd misheard her past the wad of tobacco and the rythmic chatter of the television. "John?"

"Joan. The Flower Man."

"Strange name for a man, if you don't mind my saying so. Where's you get it?"

"Not a man, y'see. Henderson's wagon said I was a . . . a hermaphodite."

That brought Ecclesiastes' head around. His long fingers, encased in the latex gloves, prowled his chin as he looked again at Joan. He noted the burr haircut under the baseball cap, the stubbled fat cheeks. He shook his head.

" 'See the Bearded Lady,' it said," Joan continued. " 'A freak show guaranteed to be the ninth wonder of the world.' Real gilt lettering, too. Fancy, with pitchers of me and Becky and Gil and the others underneath. Couldn't read it myself, but Becky, she could. . . ."

It might have been the odor of Formaline, but the workroom shimmered around Joan briefly. The corpse of Ben Wilson became that of an old woman, arrayed in a plain brown dress and lying in a pine coffin. Her hands, crossed at her chest, clutched a wooden crucifix. "You're doin' a good job on Gran'ma," Joan told

Ecclesiastes. "She looks natch'ral." Joan spat a brown globule toward a nearby waste can. A rim shot, it dribbled down the side of the stainless steel.

Ecclesiastes shuddered. "Thanks," he said uncertainly. "I think my work's pretty good." With Ben Wilson's face now properly composed, he pulled an instrument stand over to the gurney and prepared the injection to halt the clotting of blood in the body. "I find our attitudes toward death fascinating. Did you know that modern embalming didn't become a standard practice until the Civil War, when it was done so that the bodies of soldiers could be shipped home?"

"You read dem papers?" Joan interrupted, prowling the perimeter of the room.

Ecclesiastes didn't seem fazed by the abrupt switch in topics. He rolled up his shirt sleeves, picked up a scalpel. "The Theopelli material? I scanned it last night." His voice was suddenly animated, his Oriental eyes alight. "Joan, I think they're genuine. The mathematics are either above my head or don't seem to make a lot of sense, but then from what I've heard of Theopelli, they didn't make sense to *anybody*. I suppose I shouldn't be surprised. Neat stuff. I'm playing with it, just to see if I can make it work out."

Ecclesiastes made a small incision in Ben's arm with the scalpel. Joan winced, Ben was stoic. In the relative quiet, the evangelist reached a fevered climax on the Sony's picture tube, his voice lilting with a southern twang that—to Joan—seemed oddly familiar.

". . . and I say to you out there: *shudder and tremble!* The end of our time is roaring in like a twisting black tornado, howling and dancing as it spreads destruction—that tornado is decadence, that black storm is falsehood and immorality and corruption. The lightnings of that horrible storm signal the coming end of our society. Yet if you believe in the *LORD*"—he made the word two syllables—*"you shall not DIE!"* His audience erupted in cataclysmic applause and amens.

"You got no customers if he's right," Joan commented.

Ecclesiastes looked up. "Excuse me? I didn't hear that."

Joan pointed at the Sony. "He said believers ain't gonna die. They don't die, then Gran'ma wouldn't be here and I ain't gonna get her flowers." Reality did a roll in front of Joan: Gran'ma and the pine coffin disappeared again. Joan merely blinked—she was used to such disconcerting shifts. "That preacher guy . . . he know what he talkin' about?"

Ecclesiastes craned his long neck to see the picture on the set. "Him? A hell of a lot of people seem to think so. That's Abel Henderson, after all. Church of Christ the Marvel; in the last five years, it's become the single largest fundamentalist church in the country. Larger than the Episcopals, Methodists, and Lutherans combined. Some people think he's a genuine prophet. Lately he's been on an Armageddon kick, with prayer and checks supposed to fend it off. He sure knows how to get them to empty their pockets. . . ."

If he'd been looking at Joan, Ecclesiastes might have seen the sudden, suspicious lowering of Joan's eyebrows at the invocation of Henderson's name. He might have remembered that she'd bellowed the same name the afternoon before. He might have hesitated, remembering her reaction. Still, it's doubtful that most people would have made the connection.

What Ecclesiastes did next was an honest mistake.

He turned the television set toward her.

He knew immediately that something was wrong. Joan screamed in pure, fierce rage behind him. He turned to see her standing bolt upright, one trembling, accusing finger pointing at the Sony and a righteous hellfire blazing in her eyes. A demonic growling rumbled in her throat. When she opened her gap-toothed mouth, the fury erupted in a piercing, wordless shriek. Ecclesiastes found himself stumbling backward in unconscious flight from the horrible sound, knocking over the instrument stand. His instruments clattered to the floor; he lost his footing and went down himself.

Joan's hands had curled into claws. She jammed the baseball cap down over her half-shaved, half-bald head and leaped at the television. *"It's him! It's that bastard Henderson!"*

Her first vault landed her on the gurney. She planted her foot in Ben's abdomen and pushed off. The gurney flew backward, slamming into the far wall and overturning.

Joan plucked an unbroken jar of Formaline from the floor as she landed and charged. Henderson appeared unperturbed. ". . . the Lord guarantees salvation to those who support his ministries. The vile storm shall not threaten those who listen to His words through me. So I ask you to send a check today. . . ."

Ecclesiastes, half-tangled in the legs of his stand, raised a delicate, beseeching hand. "Joan . . ."

Joan flung the jar with the fluid grace of a big-league pitcher. The picture tube and jar exploded together; sparks snapped angrily as glass fragments showered the room. Ecclesiastes huddled in a fetal ball as shrapnel rattled around him. He heard the Sony topple and hit the floor. When he dared to look up again, Joan—muttering angrily under her breath—was stalking out the door. She slammed it shut behind her.

Ecclesiastes extricated himself, kneeling in the wreckage. Glass was everywhere, his instruments littered the floor, and the stench wrinkled his nose. The remnants of the Sony smoldered nearby. The gurney, wheels still spinning lazily in the air, lay on its side half atop Ben Wilson, whose composed, quiet features contrasted strangely with his ungainly, sprawled body. Ecclesiastes stared at the corpse. Slowly his grin returned.

"My, don't we look natural," he said.

With a bath and dry pants, Alfred headed back out. He muttered threats against "that damn friggin' dwarf Mundo" under his breath, but he made his way quickly to the Roosevelt Park entrance off Forsyth Street. The area looked the same as it had yesterday morning when he'd lost the Theopelli papers. The hot-dog vendor was there, a huge black man with catsup smeared across his expansive apron. Pigeons scavenged lazily under the benches and among the litter in the gutter; the street people who'd been sleeping on the benches earlier had moved on. A street preacher droned monotonously to anyone who glanced his way, ignoring the scowls of the hot-dog vendor. Shadow fingers from the Manhattan towers clawed at the brown grass.

Alfred made a quick tour of the entrance area, looking for the untidy pile of notebook pages he'd stuffed into a paper bag. The only paper bag he saw was wedged deep under a bench. Sighing, he got down on his knees—startling the preacher, who thought momentarily that he'd made a conversion. Grunting, Alfred reached for the bag, then cursed as he slashed his finger on the broken top of a beer bottle. Getting up, he sucked at his finger, then began pawing through the waste can alongside the bench, rooting through apple cores and soiled napkins.

He felt someone tap him on the shoulder. He straightened up guiltily to find the preacher shaking his head sadly at him. "My son," the man said, brandishing his Bible. "Give up your life of alcohol and destitution and come to Jesus. Let the Lord be your bottle."

Alfred snarled at him. The preacher smiled uncertainly and retreated. Alfred looked at the trash and sighed once more.

He sat down on the bench, elbows on knees, head in hands. He moaned. The day had started out so well—seeing the unexpected ad in the paper, anticipating the fortune this Mundo would give him for old crazy Carlos's scribblings . . . and he'd ended with nothing but humiliation. It wasn't fair. He *deserved* the compensation for the years he'd spent catering to that gross fool in his rickety mansion. The money from the will hadn't been enough; it had gone quickly. Too quickly. The papers were all that he'd had left.

The sound of an argument brought him out of his reverie. Alfred glanced up to see a short, rotund man in a baseball cap and windbreaker screaming at the preacher. The guy looked familiar—Alfred seemed to remember him selling flowers at the park this morning. He didn't have flowers now.

Instead, Joan—who had just stormed victorious from the battle of the funeral parlor—was prodding the cowering street preacher in the chest with a forceful forefinger. Tobacco juice sprayed over the poor man's suit; the fellow was vainly trying to back up, but Joan had pinned him against the wrought-iron fence of the park, leaning forward as the preacher bent backward away from her. He held his Bible in front of him like a shield.

"You bastard! You're one of Henderson's men."

"The Lord can ease your suffering—"

"You get rid of us freaks and start talking about how *good* you are."

"I only speak the truth of Jesus—"

"I won't let you do it, hear? You stop people from *dying*, I don't get no flowers."

"Sir—"

"And I get all the flowers I want from the funeral guy 'cause of the papers I give him yesterday. He gotta have *bodies!*"

With the last word, Joan shoved a forefinger deep into the wrinkled front of the preacher's suit. Pushed past the point of equilibrium, he tumbled over the fence, his Bible flying loose. He scrambled to his feet, grass-stained, with a wild panic on his face. "You're the devil," he intoned, wagging a shaking finger at Joan. "You're in league with Satan."

Joan picked up the Bible. She threw it, hitting the man square in the head. The preacher retrieved his Bible, gave her one last look, and fled across the park. "You let those people die!" she shouted after him. "You hear? Let 'em die!"

The vendor applauded.

Alfred had watched the confrontation desultorily. But at the words "papers" and "yesterday" a vague suspicion had begun to glimmer. He remembered the carnations, wrapped in scraps of newspaper. . . .

Alfred rose from his bench and went over to the panting Joan. "Excuse me, mister."

Joan wheeled around like a clumsy dancing bear. Her grizzled face frowned up at Alfred. "What?" she barked, one eye narrowed, her head canted to the side. She shifted the wad of tobacco from one cheek to the other.

Alfred backed away a step. "Umm, you were here yesterday, selling flowers," he began.

"You wanna buy?" Joan's voice softened a little, hopeful. "Two dollars, cheap." She looked around suddenly, and shrugged. "Ain't got 'em with me, though."

Alfred shook his head. "No . . . you see, I lost something here yesterday."

The suspicion had returned to her face. A tiny rivulet of brown juice trickled from a corner of her mouth and down the stubbled, rolling landscape of her cheek. She looked as if she were about to spit. "Some sheets of notebook paper," Alfred added hopefully. "With writing on them. Mathematical stuff—you know, numbers and things?"

Joan blinked, as if Alfred had simply disappeared for a moment. In fact, to Joan, he had.

For Joan, there was only one apparition that she disliked more than that of Henderson. Abel C. Henderson, former carnie owner and now evangelist, simply threw her into a rage. But her mother—*she* invoked sheer terror. Joan's mother had hated the abomination that had come from her body. She'd despised the child, as if it were a visible condemnation for the adultery that had spawned it.

Her husband had been in the service, stationed overseas. Joan's father had been the owner of a used-car lot, for whom her mother was the secretary. He'd always been a good salesman; he'd sold Joan's mother on the fact that there was no danger. "The doctors, they told me I could never have a kid. Some kind of blockage or something. So don't worry, honey. Just enjoy it."

Two weeks later, her usual monthly visitor declined to arrive. Eight and a half months after that, Joan was born.

She'd moved away from town by that time. She kept moving, dragging the hated albatross that was Joan with her. She abused the child shamefully, fleeing more than one apartment just ahead of the authorities. Yet she'd kept Joan, attached by the last shred of her guilt. In Tulsa, utterly destitute, almost suicidal, she'd finally made up her mind. When Henderson offered her a hundred dollars for the then nine-year-old Joan, she'd taken it gladly and disappeared.

But Joan still remembered. Joan still saw her. Mother was the most evil and feared of the monsters in her head.

"Numbers and things?" The words caused Alfred to shimmer in front of Joan and take on another form. Mother stood there, seemingly twelve feet high, leaning down and shaking a ruler at her. Joan cowered. Numbers and things meant pain. Always. "You're so damn *stupid*," Mother would say next, and then the beating would begin. "You're ugly and deformed and you're stupid! You're just what I deserve."

"No, Mother!" Joan screeched. "I'm sorry, I'm sorry, I'm sorry." Her arms clamped over her head to ward off the ruler, Joan ran, sobbing. She turned left past the hot-dog stand, zigzagging across the traffic on Forsyth and then turning north.

Alfred stood dumbfounded for several seconds. Then he waved his arms and followed in pursuit. "Wait! I have to ask you about the papers!"

But the hot-dog vendor had moved to block his way. He shoved Alfred back with one meaty, dark hand. "Hey," he said ominously, "you don't bother Joan. Got that? Let her go. Have a dog instead, huh?"

Alfred glanced at the muscular shoulders and arms of the vendor and decided discretion was called for. "Sure," he said. "Hey, I just wanted to buy some flowers, that's all. You called her Joan?"

"Yeah," the vendor grunted. "Joan the Flower Man. Everyone around here knows her. She sells flowers, all the time. Daytimes, she's walking around; nights she hits the clubs. Sometimes she sings; ain't got a bad voice, actually. You want flowers, she'll be around. You just wait. Don't bother her; she's a little confused.'' The vendor tapped his forehead. "Y'know what I mean."

"So I noticed," Alfred said. Joan had disappeared across Forsyth. There wasn't any sense in going after her—she looked as if she could outrun him with any kind of head start. But she couldn't be that hard to find again, not such a visible street character.

He'd go to Mundo. He'd tell the frigging dwarf with the cheap illusions.

"Gimme a dog with everything, then," he said.

9: Dirk Gets Lucky . . . Really

Mornings weren't Dirk's forte. It was generally a struggle to climb from the pool of subconscious fantasy and back onto the dry land of reality.

Foggy dreams of Angela still coiled around his libido; his morning erection was warm against his belly. Dirk groaned and levered his eyelids open. Light slammed hard against his retinas and set alarms ringing in his head. He hurriedly shut them again.

After a moment, he cautiously opened one eye a slit. He frowned, disoriented, before he remembered that this brightness wasn't the hotel, that this was Angela's bedroom. He lifted his head from the pillow, squinting with the sunlight streaming across the covers from the window. He saw her then, wearing a terrycloth robe and sitting cross-legged on the floor. Her head was back slightly, her eyes closed, her hands clasped lightly on her lap. An array of cards was spread in front of her. She must have felt Dirk's gaze, for her head swiveled down, she opened her eyes, and she smiled at him. "Hi, sleepyhead," she called softly.

"Good afternoon."

"Is—" The word came out as a croak. He frowned at her quick laughter. "Is it that late?"

"Uh-huh. I've been up a couple of hours."

"Meditating?"

"Kind of."

Angela began gathering the cards. Dirk watched, rubbing his mouth with the back of his hand and swallowing to get the sour stickiness from his throat. "That a tarot deck? Looks different from the others I've seen."

"It's a little different. Not much."

"Are they what told you we'd find those papers you were looking for last night?" He couldn't quite keep all the skepticism from his voice.

Angela shrugged. The corners of her eyes were crinkled with some inner amusement. The pupils had the green of a deep, clear pond. "Partially," she answered. "And even though you're not going to actually *say* it, inside you're thinking, 'Gee, real *effective*, weren't they.'"

"Shot myself in the foot with my mouth, did I?"

The crinkles deepened, the corners of her mouth tugged upward. "Almost. I'd just be careful about mocking something I didn't understand. The tarot doesn't tell the future, after all; it gives an indication of possibilities. And they indicate that there are forces actively interfering with us from a distance."

Dirk let gravity take his head back to the pillow. He closed his eyes again. "You know," he said sleepily, "I have you pegged now. You're a time traveler."

She laughed at that, too, with a strange heartiness. "Just how do you figure that?"

"You're a refugee from the sixties or maybe the early seventies, one of the flower children who never let go. Meditation, the tarot, your books, the candles and incense, the way you talk—it all fits. In your mind it's still the summer of love. The dawning of the age of Aquarius." He rolled to one side, put his head on his hand, and looked at her. She was still grinning. "Am I right?" Dirk insisted.

"Maybe half-right. Which isn't bad for a musician who was once a history teacher."

"Let me keep going, then. You've been in the university system ever since high school. You've never been out in the real world at all—got your bachelor's, liberal arts, of course; went right to your master's after choosing a specialty which assured you that you couldn't find a job. You're probably working on your doctoral thesis now, which has something to do with esoteric mathematics or science, which is why you're after this old Theopelli's papers. Am I still close?"

"Not even a little bit. There's no university, no doctoral thesis. I *have* studied quite a bit under someone, but I doubt that you'd exactly call it science, not with your orientation."

"It was occult stuff, then. Weird shit. Astrological junk."

"You'd think so, probably." Angela shrugged. From her lotus position, she gazed at him blandly.

"That's all you're going to volunteer?" Dirk asked at last.

"What else do you want to know?"

"I'm not sure—anything, I guess. What you like, what you don't like, your background, where you came from . . ."

She seemed to turn pensive with that. Her voice was dark, almost sad. "I've been *here* so long that the past has gotten a little fuzzy. It doesn't seem real to me anymore. Sometimes I think my memories must be someone else's, a fantasy I've borrowed from a book."

"Too many drugs does that."

Dirk regretted the words instantly—his jocular tone shattered the mood. He could almost hear the ice forming in the air between them. Angela glanced at him sharply, her mouth snapped shut in a thin, taut line, and her eyes narrowed.

"Sorry," he said. "I'm not awake yet. I didn't mean that."

"It's okay," she said quickly, but Dirk knew that the moment had gone. She'd locked the intimacy away. Angela straightened the deck of cards, reaching to one side for a large square of colorful silk. She wrapped the tarot gently, then placed the deck in a wooden box beside her.

"What did the cards say this morning?"

Her glare was a challenge. "You don't have to pretend an interest, Dirk. Honesty might be a refreshing change, you know."

He winced, holding his hand over his heart. "Ouch," he said.

Angela shook her head, but one corner of her mouth lifted and the frost in her eyes thawed slowly. "Guess

I'm not quite awake either," she said. "Hey, I'm sorry, too. It's just that I thought I knew you better, and then you say something that tells me you're not exactly the same."

"We just met last night. How well can you know someone after breaking into a haunted house? Or are we talking about the cards again?"

"Your mind's closing up, Dirk. I can hear all the doors slamming shut inside. Why should I tell you the truth when you won't believe it?"

"Uh-huh. All I'm saying is that neither one of us knows the other person very well."

Angela shook her head. "Not true. I think I might have known you for a long time. Years. That's why I made sure it was *you* that came with me last night. I wanted someone I could trust. I wanted a friend."

"Sure. You know a *lot* about me. And what's my name again?" He said it lightly, not wanting to admit confusion. He found himself hoping that Angela wouldn't answer "Jimmy McCarthy"—that would simply be too strange. He wasn't quite sure what she was talking about; he couldn't find her face (or her body) in his memory at all. He was certain he'd be able to recall a definite presence like her—she was too distinctive to forget.

What she *did* say was almost as bad. "The Dirk I know isn't named Dirk at all. . . ." He couldn't read her face or the odd, sudden intensity to her stare. She uncrossed her legs with the limber grace of a cat.

"He's quiet, usually, probably too withdrawn for his own good. Moody . . ." She rose to her feet. The mattress bounced as she knelt at the foot of the bed.

"He usually wakes up with a terrific hard-on in the morning. . . ." Angela snatched down the covers. "And he loves it when I do this." She lowered her head and licked what she found there.

Dirk groaned.

After far too short a time, she looked up again. "And when he comes, he makes this cute little squeak, like a mouse."

"I do *not*," Dirk protested breathily.

She didn't answer directly. She loosened her bathrobe and straddled him. As she knelt there, poised, visions of Terre Haute Patti and the others lumbered through Dirk's mind. His drift in attention was noticeable. Angela leaned down to him, brushed his lips softly.

"Hey, come back," she said quietly. "It's just me. No one else. There's no pressure. Just relax and enjoy what's going to happen to us." She kissed him again, her mouth opening to his. She took his hand, brought it to her breast. Her breath was hot and sweet and slow.

"Yes," she said. "That's better." Her hand guided him into warm, clinging softness.

A long while later, she rolled off and snuggled against him. "Squeak," she said with delight in her voice.

Dirk was shaking his head, his eyes still closed. "How'd you know? I never noticed that before."

"You've never listened to yourself, have you?"

"Neither have you. Believe me, I'd've remembered *you*."

He'd thought she would smile at that. He turned his head to look at her. Sweat beaded her forehead, small black ringlets of hair clinging over her eyes. She was smiling, but there was an inner tension to the gesture. "So how'd you know?" he persisted. "No, don't tell me—I can guess. It's that seeress stuff again."

She rolled away from him, leaving his side cold. On her back, Angela stared up at leaf shadows on the ceiling. "Another lover," she breathed. Dirk thought that was all she was going to say, then she licked her lips and spoke again. "A very special person. You . . . he was a lot like you. So I thought. . . ." She closed her eyes as if pained, and when she opened them again, moisture shimmered in the pupils. She seemed very far away. "He's been gone a long time."

"He died?"

"That's probably the best way for me to think of it."

"Then he . . . then you two fell out of love. The

relationship didn't work." Dirk was surprised at the relief that flooded through him at the thought.

But she shook her head. "Not at all. Everything was working well. Perfectly. It's just . . . we live in different worlds now."

Angela shivered and crossed her arms under her breasts, hugging herself. "Listen, I don't think I want to talk about it, okay? Just . . ." She sighed and rose from the bed. Standing beside it, she looked down at Dirk. "Hey, I'm sorry. Really. I shouldn't have dragged you into this. It's probably too dangerous."

"Drag me into *what?* So far it feels more delightful than dangerous."

"That just shows how little you know. The Mage is here; the cards say so. Everything's mixed up, including me." She padded to the door of the bedroom. Dirk watched her—a runner's legs, gently rounded buttocks, a deep inward bend to the spine just above them, a muscular back, her skin touched with Arabian olive. She turned at the doorway.

"The keys to the Chevette are on the dresser. Take it. I'll meet you tonight at the club, okay?"

"Angela . . ."

"Please, Dirk." There was no pleading in her voice despite the words, no asking. "I need to be alone for a while." She tried to smile at him, patted the doorframe with a hand, and disappeared down the hallway. Dirk heard the bathroom door click shut.

Great. Dirk searched around the room for his clothes, saw them piled untidily alongside the bed. *I meet someone I like, we go to bed and it all works, we get along, and she tells me it's because I remind her of her real lover. Great.*

He pulled on his shorts, tugged his shirt over his head, struggled into his jeans. The car keys were buried under a scarf, two belts, and a bra. He put them in his pocket. At the bathroom door, Dirk raised his hand to knock and call good-bye. The fist swayed, hesitated, and then he lowered it again. He headed for the front door.

"Squeak," he muttered.

part two

"Everything that occurs has its own unique role."

10: The Prophet Harold

The coves and bays of the Gulf of Mexico down from Tampa were laid out by a drunken coral snake. They wriggle in and out of the chain of half-attached islands between the Gulf and the mainland, touching little beach communities with overcute names like Treasure Island or Clearwater or Pass-A-Grille Beach.

Most tourists never find themselves more than a few feet from the neon of the main strips. Which is fine—that's how the residents prefer it. The houses of the rich are those back from the open water, preferably on a little dead-end tongue of land tasting the salty brine.

Abel C. Henderson owned such a house, on one of the inlets where Route 699 runs out of land and Boca Ciega Bay and Tampa Bay meet the Gulf. Actually, the deed was in the name of the trustees of the Church of Christ the Marvel, and this was where Henderson kept his pet prophet.

Henderson took the hand of a waiting guard and stepped from his launch to the wharf. " 'Afternoon, Reverend,'' the man said. "And nice to have you back here. How was Washington?"

"Our little meeting with the president went as expected, Jim. I think we'll all be pleased by the support for our program." Henderson grinned his good-old-boy grin. His voice was deep and resonant, striding confidently from somewhere deep in his ample stomach. A practiced southern twang smoothed and lengthened the vowels. His tanned skin was the chestnut brown of old leather; his gray hair was poufed and carefully brushed back. A gold tie tack in the shape of a cross threw slivers of sunlight from the diamond embedded in its center. "How's Harold today? You boys takin' care of him?"

"We've been trying, sir. Had a little trouble this morning—he found a jellyfish on the beach and started to eat it. Had a temper tantrum when we took it away from him even though it stung his hands pretty good." Jim shrugged. "Cook made up some clear gelatin for lunch. We told him it was jellyfish sushi and he was happy again."

"Good, good. Have to keep our prophet happy."

Henderson clapped Jim on the back with a meaty hand, straightened his sunglasses, and took a deep breath of salt air. It was a tourist postcard day. Wavelets patted the shore, gulls wheeled overhead and dove into bouncing swells, the sky was a drenched dark blue with a few bleached clouds parked on the horizon for contrast. "Good," Henderson said again, as if he were somehow personally responsible for the scene. He headed for the main house as the crew moored the launch to the pilings.

The air-conditioning held the Florida heat at bay except in Harold's room on the second floor, where the windows were wide open to catch the breeze off the Gulf. Henderson felt sweat beading on his brow as soon as he swung the door open. "Whoo-*ey*, boy," he said, tugging down his tie. "You should take advantage of modern technology. No one has to be hot in their own home anymore."

"Air conditioners dry the air and put out the wrong type of ions. Bacteria breed in the filters; the motors are noisy. You close all the windows and doors and isolate yourself from your environment. Air conditioners are a symbol of our civilization's demise."

It was vintage Harold gabble; Henderson grinned. "*You*," he pointed out, "would eat a jellyfish."

"Jellyfish are part of the great cycle," Harold retorted sullenly. "The ebb and flow of the universal tide, the warp and woof of fate's canvas, the dots on God's dice. Jellyfish and humankind are all connected."

Harold was seated on a Naugahyde recliner facing

the balcony overlooking the grounds, his bare feet half out of the room. In fact, his scrawny body was entirely naked except for a soiled loincloth of ragged denim. He turned to scowl at Henderson, showing rotted, pitted teeth with discolored crowns. The thin mouth was camouflaged behind a scraggly beard; the hair was long, matted, and unwashed, hanging in strings and dreadlocks down his chest. His eyes were dark, large and wild, constantly in motion like a pair of startled blackbirds.

"Besides, jellyfish taste just like Jell-O," Harold added.

Henderson ignored that. "My boy, you don't *have* to look like a filthy John the Baptist. Now, that's not the proper image of a prophet anymore—you need to look respectable before people will believe you, not like some wino sleeping in the gutter. Take a bath, have a dentist come out and look at those teeth. . . ."

"Just so long as I don't leave my little prison here, isn't that right, *Reverend* Henderson? My own little padded cell for the crazy man. The padding's the softest velvet, the bars are gilded, but it's still a cell." He giggled in a high manic voice. "Of course, this beats the old Marvel Circus. I can act the way I want to here and no one bothers me or stares at me or stops me. I ask you, what's *wrong* with dirt and decay? That's the beginning and the end of the wheel."

Harold's diatribe gained speed and volume, rising to a near shriek as he levered his body slightly up from the chair with his hands. "From the rot comes the flower, which dies and turns back into compost. The rotting bark of a dead tree is teeming underneath with life—beetles and sowbugs and termites. Deny rot and you deny yourself. Deny the shit inside you and you turn into shit."

"Now, Harry . . ." Henderson began, backing away.

The crescendo came—Harold passed gas. The flatulence was world-class. Henderson was surprised that the loincloth didn't flap with the violence of it. "Intake and elimination," Harold intoned, letting himself fall back into the chair. "Jellyfish farts. There's nothing horrible about the smell of life once you understand it. It's a celebration."

Henderson shivered and breathed through his mouth. It didn't help much. "Whoopee," he said.

Harold turned back to the window. "Sarcasm doesn't become you. And you didn't come down here just to talk diet," he said from the Naugahyde depths. "You want satori but you still haven't realized that you already have the knowledge you need."

"I wanted to talk to you, Harry."

"You wanted to *use* me, Abel."

Henderson looked pained at that. "Son, you're talking to someone who has been given God's work to perform." With a movement that had become habit, he raised his gaze momentarily to the ceiling. "I wondered if the Lord had blessed you with more visions."

Harry belched. He scratched at his armpits. "Yep," he said. "It's the crux, Abel. The year of decision. The ones you call the sorcerer and the whore are here. They'll change everything if you don't stop them. It's time for you to decide what you're after. If you want power, you have to grab it now."

Henderson had acquired Harold for the Marvel Circus in the last year of that institution's operation, long after he'd dumped Joan for dead by the side of the road. Harold had looked neither worse nor better then than he looked now. He professed to be college-educated, a Mensa-qualified genius. He'd been banned from university life after he'd stalked through the campus stark naked, climbed to the roof of the Center building, and urinated on anyone unlucky enough to be passing below, all the while bellowing nonsense verses from Lewis Carroll at the top of his lungs.

"I am the Gyre and the Gimble," he told the first officer to clamber up after him. "I am the Mome's Rath, the Jabberwocky at the end of the world." The university seemed to think it some strange fraternity hazing, enhanced by drugs—Harold was smart enough not to dissuade them of that opinion. In return for his promise to leave and never return, the university agreed to drop charges.

Eventually, he'd wandered into a field outside Estill, South Carolina, where the Marvel Circus had set up its tents. Henderson, always quick to see potential profit in the bizarre, immediately latched on to the filthy outcast with the bizarre proclamations.

Harold had been "Idiot Savant—Touched by God." He'd spouted an odd mixture of dire foretellings of the apocalypse, grotesqueries, and prognostications at those who paid money to enter the tent. In short, he'd merely talked to them the way he talked to everyone. As it was, Henderson would have been satisfied with Harold, his screaming sermons and penchant for exposing himself and his various bodily functions: his entertainment and shock value was high. But the prophecies . . .

In Garnett, a little down the road, he told a recently widowed and destitute old woman that her husband had hidden a small fortune under a loose baseboard in the dining room—she came back the next night to thank him; there'd been fifty thousand stashed under the floorboards. Henderson had cocked his head quizzically at Harry; he'd also managed to extract five thousand from the woman as a "finder's fee."

In Eden, Georgia, on the banks of the Ogeechee River, Harold went into a froth-mouthed trance and told the audience that a murder had been committed the night before; if they would drag the river at a spot just upstream, they would recover the body. A county sheriff was in the audience, and had nothing better to do the next afternoon. He found Ellen Bonestell's bullet-riddled body, weighted down with stones. Her husband had reported her missing the day before; the slugs matched those of his hunting rifle.

Under intense questioning by the sheriff as to how he knew, Harold insisted that he'd seen it in his fiery vision. It took a five-hundred-dollar bribe from Henderson before the sheriff would agree to let Harold leave the county—but Henderson wasn't about to let Harold slip away from him now. Word was spreading.

In Pembroke, near Fort Stewart, the strange, filthy man suddenly began screaming and backing away from some scene visible only to him. "The mountain—the mountain has felt God's wrath! Ash and fire are the portents! The time is upon us!" Harold sprayed spittle, he shoveled handfuls of red dirt into his mouth, he writhed on the ground as if screwing the very earth. The audience had pretended to be appalled, but they stayed. They'd seen people afflicted with holy insanity before, but this divine madness was more dangerous and primitive than any tame speaking in tongues and faintings in church. Harold, if nothing else, had a true gift for invention—a fake or not, he was inspired.

And the next afternoon, Mount St. Helens had blown its summit into dust.

Henderson had quickly realized that there were gems buried in the garbage spewing from Harold's mouth. Too many times, Henderson heard truth in the nonsense. For some time, he'd been considering a convenient conversion. Henderson could sense the swing of the country's mood—he'd renounce his sinful life and become a preacher.

The Marvel Circus was an old scam, more trouble than it was worth. A carnie had to *work* to bilk the marks. With religion . . . ahh, well, *religion* was simply a Marvel Circus of the mind. A preacher was a barker dangling hellfire and brimstone in front of the crowds in place of freaks and oddities. A preacher sold salvation, but you had to die to get it, which meant that no one was ever going to come back and complain about being gypped. A preacher didn't have to deal with dissatisfied customers; if things weren't going well, it was always *their* fault, to be fixed by prayer and tithing.

Henderson even owned a genuine prophet, not one he dared show to his flock, of course, but there was nothing to stop him from claiming Harold's predictions for his own. . . .

It had worked as he'd known it would work. In five years' time, he'd built a religious empire unparalleled in recent history. He was Abel C. Henderson, Prophet of the Airwaves. The Church of Christ the Marvel had a larger GNP than many developing countries. It had a worldwide membership even the Roman Catholic Church envied. *Time, Newsweek, U.S. News,* and *People* had all featured Henderson's round, genial face on the cover. He was invited to White House dinners to discuss policy.

And the Supreme Reverend Henderson was becoming increasingly worried.

Either his oracle was going totally bonkers, or there was something very strange afoot.

"Harry," he said wearily, "are you going to give me the sorcerer-and-whore horseshit again?"

Harold tsked reproachfully. "Such language," he said. "Abel, are you going to tell me I'm crazy? Didn't the visions tell you to back the Republicans? Didn't they warn you about the IRS audit? Didn't they tell you that Bakker, Swaggart, and Falwell would self-destruct? Didn't they—"

"All right." Henderson waved away the arguments, frowning as Harry grinned. "It's just that this one sounds so . . . so *weird.* I mean, you're telling me these people aren't even from this *world.* I ask you, how am I supposed to sound rational talking about people from *outer space,* by God?"

"They aren't from outer space, Abel. They're from another reality entirely."

It was the calmness with which Harry said the words that bothered Henderson. He smiled as if he'd said they were from New Jersey. "Oh, good, that *does* sound better."

"Sarcasm again?" Harry lifted up his loincloth and scratched viciously at his pubic hair. He waggled his penis between thumb and forefinger and glanced thoughtfully at Henderson. His pupils skittered about. "Did you ever realize that a really flexible person could give himself a blowjob?"

Henderson looked away, his mouth a tight line. "Harry . . ."

Harry let the loincloth flop down over his thighs. "I suppose you want to hear about the vision?"

"That *is* why I came."

Harry sighed. He put his hands behind his head and closed his eyes. "It's vague, Abel. The universe speaks in icons and symbols; like every other, its language is a cipher that means something different to each person. Just by talking about it, I change it."

"Tell me anyway."

"Icons and symbols and codes—oh, my. More frightening than lions and tigers and bears, don't you think? Did you know they bound Judy Garland's breasts so they wouldn't show? I wonder at the significance of such a denial of reality in a fantasy medium. Her tits like squashed jellyfish—"

"Harry, please . . ."

"Damming the stream of consciousness again, Abel? A pity—" Harold was quiet for a moment. When he spoke again, his voice had changed; deeper, huskier, it trembled. Henderson pulled a chair close to the recliner and leaned forward to listen.

"I was sitting here just watching the gulls flock around the trawlers coming in from the Gulf. It was evening; the sun was a bright, huge, and blood red eye on the horizon. The clouds were gathered there like golden Hostess Twinkies. Just as the sun touched the water, it flared. And the water was gone—*zap*, Abel, just like that. The fish were flopping around in the mud, gills heaving; the boats were wallowing on their sides like beached whales.

"I could see trails in the hidden landscape that had just been revealed. The path led outward from me, and then it came to a place where other ways led from it. There was a city along one path, with delicate and beautiful crystalline towers and gossamer, winking threads spidering between, though the land around it was barren and stark. Another trail led into mountains, and there I saw both harsh stone and soft grass, and there were caves in the mountainside with night lying inside. And yet another way led to the dark and forbidding forest, the trees casting a shade through which shades moved and eyes watched.

"They were both at the junction, the ones you call

the whore and sorcerer. I'll admit I watched the woman more. I could feel her pull at me; I wanted to part those luscious thighs and dive in. All I would have needed was for her to look at me and smile, and I knew the sorcerer felt the same. He kept glancing away from her as if her gaze burned him, and he never let her get close enough to touch, staying bitter and hidden behind his spells.

"They were arguing, each pointing one way and the other. And there were others who came up to them. One of those was a corpse, dead white like the belly of a fish, and he had a book. It was the book I've seen before, Abel, the one in which a hand wrote the future. The sorcerer and the whore read the book and nodded. The woman licked her lovely lips and said in that husky voice of hers: 'Well, we can't allow *that*.' They motioned to the others and started to turn toward one of the roads. . . .

"But I heard a roar like music as the waters returned, cascading and foaming, furious at being held back. There were jellyfish in the tidal surge; huge ones, flanking the dangling tendrils of a huge man-of-war whose back bristled like an island covered with skyscrapers. I thought the man-of-war was going to sweep over me as well, and I covered my head with my hands, screaming. When I looked again, the sun was just below the horizon and the Gulf was calm. The trawlers had moved on into the bay, taking the gulls with them."

After Harold had remained silent for several seconds, Henderson cleared his throat. "So," he said. "What's it mean?"

"It means that you should watch out for jellyfish in the surf." When Henderson only stared at him, Harry stuck out his lower lip petulantly. "No sense of humor at all. You take all the fun out of being a translator. Whore and sorcerer: the flesh and the devil all wrapped up together—such a great carnie hyperbole. You should be able to mold that into a wonderful, furious sermon complete with jellyfish. You've done a great job with the storm—even if you don't believe I'm telling you the truth about how important it is. But this last vision . . . ?'' Harold shrugged. "How many islands do you know that are covered with skyscrapers, Abel?"

Henderson didn't answer. In the tropical quiet, Harold stared out at the green gulf waters.

"Go to New York," he said at last. "That's what the man-of-war means. They're waiting for you there. Oh, and Abel—take me with you. It's the woman—I have to meet her; it's destined. We're to be lovers."

11: A Bowl with a Mind of Its Own

The jellyfish of Harold's desire had spent the last four nights in the warm, pounding surf of sex with Dirk, who (to strain the metaphor unduly) was not about to rock the boat of this new relationship. Actually, he hadn't expected her to show up at the club after the emotional ending of their first time together. Yet she had, all smiles and affection. If their conversation since that time adroitly sidestepped the tender subjects of old lovers, strange houses, and fortune-telling, Dirk was satisfied.

More than satisfied.

"Dirk, you're smitten," Jay the soundman observed on the break between the first and second sets Sunday night. Jay leaned over toward Dirk, half shouting against the din from the crowd and the club's stereo system. Angela had gone with Fish to the women's room.

"C'mon, Jay. 'Smitten'? You've been reading too many romance novels."

"Infatuated, then. Snared. They're all perfectly good descriptions. You're in love. It happens fast sometimes." Jay tilted his chair back; his wide, toothy mouth grinned. "You don't even realize it yet, do you? Everyone else can see it, though. I'll bet you haven't told her the news, either." He tapped the mixing console and shook his head. "On the road, you should only get close to your own equipment. It's bad luck to get attached to someone you meet traveling, Dirk. It never works out."

"I'm supposed to take advice on my love life from a guy with twelve pens in his pocket protector?"

"Ignore me, then. You still know it's true."

It had been a very good weekend. The club had been jammed. With Angela watching every night, Dirk played with a new enthusiasm, driving himself and the other band members. And Angela's presence had its effect on the others.

Alf the drummer flirted relentlessly and hopelessly despite the groupie Fish's obvious jealousy, giving Dirk covetous looks when his attempts at seduction had absolutely no impact on Angela. Kyle brought her up on stage before the job and demonstrated all the myriad voices his keyboard midi controller had stored in its digital sampler—he smiled like a fool when Angela seemed genuinely impressed. Even Lars grudgingly flashed his improvisational genius, sitting on the edge of the stage with his Stratocaster and running short flaring licks up and down the fretboard while pretending to ignore the others.

Once a set or so, Angela would glide onto the dance floor. She was like a catalyst dropped into a waiting soup of chemicals; slowly, a free space would open up around her as she whirled, as if her intense energy pushed the others back. By the end of the song, she would be ringed by onlookers, clapping in time and charged with the overflow of her wild, free dance. She'd find Dirk with her green, startling eyes and she'd smile.

The radiance was nearly as blinding as the spotlights.

"Jesus, Dirk, is she like that in bed?" Alf asked after one set. Dirk shrugged, but he grinned helplessly. "Never mind," Alf said. "I can tell." He looked at Dirk with grudging envy.

The band played like a mean, nasty machine. "Animal Love" cranked like a monster; "Hot-Dog Buns" swayed and teased. The songs had an edge and drive that ignited the audience, and their reactions fed the fire in the band, which in turn screamed back from through the speakers: an endless feedback loop of energy that had the club jumping all night. The place was standing room only every evening from the middle of the first set on.

Stan Fedderman, Savage's agent and manager, caught rumors of Savage's rebirth and flew in to see the group on Friday night. In Angela's presence, he was mellow and expansive, buying drinks and joking. The band's brilliance wasn't lost on him. He sat alongside Angela at the table by the mixing console, an untouched drink in front of him, chomping on his unlit cigar and nodding.

"You boys didn't sound bad at all," he said afterward. On the Fedderman scale, this was highest praise. "Let me see what I can do."

Which led to The News.

Stan called the hotel Sunday afternoon. The band was scheduled to stay in the Cincinnati club for another week. Stan had changed those plans. "Listen, I stole a break for you guys. There's a new club opening in New York, and I've managed to get the booking. Pack up after the gig Sunday and head east. Be there Tuesday night. This could be important—I have some people coming in from Warner. They heard the tape a while back but I've been telling 'em that you guys have matured and you have to be seen live. Now they want to see you. We could be talking contract, boys."

New York. Contract. The hotel room had exploded with gleeful shouts. A celebratory pipe had begun making the rounds. Dirk had joined in with the rest for a few bowls. In the euphoric fog of the grass there didn't seem to be any problem about what he might say to Angela. He'd stayed at her place every night— she'd only just dropped him off while she went grocery shopping. She'd go with them, of course. She didn't seem to have a job (in fact, he didn't recall her ever saying what she did for a living), had no family, no commitments. At least she hadn't mentioned any. . . .

Of course, she'd go with them. He'd tell her tonight.

"She's got her own life," Jay said, breaking in on Dirk's thoughts. Dirk could see Angela and Fish making their way back to the table. "You're asking to get your ego stepped on."

"You just watch."

Jay shook his head dolefully. "Not a chance. It's going to be too ugly for my sensitive nature."

"You guys look awful serious. What have you been discussing?" Angela slid into her chair with a smile.

"Volatile chemical reactions," Jay said. "Like sulfuric acid and water." He put a friendly arm around Fish before she could sit down, pulling her away from the table and ignoring Angela's curious look. "I think Alf was looking for you," he told Fish. "Let's go see if we can find him before the explosion." With a wave and his usual lopsided grin, he threaded his way into the crowd, taking Fish with him.

"What was that about?" Angela asked.

"Nothing. Just Jay being Jay. Listen, I have good news. Fedderman called this afternoon. We're going to New York tomorrow."

Dirk watched Angela's face carefully as he told her about Stan's phone call. Her smile went wooden after the first sentence, a slash carved into her face with a dull penknife. Dirk faltered, limping through the rest of it. Her gaze never left him. There was a chill in the dark eyes; he could feel himself sweating in response. He touched her hands, folded on the table. She didn't move then away, neither did she complete the gesture.

"You're leaving tomorrow morning." She still smiled. Her unblinking gaze stared at his discomfiture. "That's fine. I suppose it could be a break for you. I can understand how you feel you have to go."

"Yeah." Dirk fidgeted in his chair. The tape in the club stereo switched tracks. If this wasn't going the way he'd expected, at least it wasn't the fireworks Jay had promised. He told himself that there was hope. "So," he began, and stopped.

She'd cocked her head with the word, and he could see something dangerous simmering just below the surface of her eyes.

"Let me ask *you* something before you ask me the same thing," she said. "Why don't you quit the band and stay here with *me?*"

"*What!*" Surprise slammed Dirk back in his chair, eyes wide. "You've got to be kidding—"

He stopped himself, closing his eyes. "Umm, I walked into that one, didn't I?" he said in a voice barely audible over the racket of the club. "You lay nasty traps. That's hardly fair."

"Fish told me you were expecting I'd go with you. Why's it fair for you to ask me to walk away from my life, and not fair for me to ask the same of you?"

Dirk could see the conversational pit yawning before him. There were probably pointed rejoinders at the bottom. He licked his lips, considering his answer. Angela watched him expectantly, her smile mocking. "You're twisting my words," he answered. *That's clever—nothing like a cliché when you're debating the future.* Dirk scowled at himself and plunged on. "There's nothing wrong with your asking me."

"Except that *I* knew what your answer would be. *I* wouldn't have asked."

"I have to go. It's important."

"And I have to stay. That's just as important. I have to find something."

"Are we talking about this Theopelli character again? I thought you'd given that up. We looked; those papers weren't there. You can't tear the mansion down to look behind all the walls."

"There are other ways to look."

Dirk spread his hands wide, exasperated. "Now we're talking tarot cards and fortune-telling again." He knew it was a mistake even as the words came out. His hands dropped back to the table.

Angela's chair scraped against the floor as she pushed away from the table and stood up. Glasses clashed and tottered. She glared down at Dirk, two bright spots of color flaring high on her cheekbones. Her mouth tightened as if she were about to say something, but she gave only a disgusted exhalation like an overheated engine venting steam.

She kicked the chair over, turned, and pushed her way into the crowd. The closest patrons muttered and stared at Dirk. He could have pursued her. For a moment, the wake of her passage left a clear space through the mob of patrons.

Dirk started to get up, hesitated. In that space, the trail closed behind Angela.

He sat back down again.

The second set was a fiasco. The third was a disaster. By the time the break came after the third, most of the patrons were gone, so the last set was merely boring.

Dirk slid the Rickenbacker into its case with more care than was needed. Kyle was disconnecting cords with silent vehemence; Alf heaved his sticks backstage and headed for the dressing room; Lars muttered under his breath, the Strat across his knees—he leaned into the polishing cloth as if he were trying to take the finish down to bare wood. Nobody looked at Dirk. The houselights glimmered through smoke blue murk, the house speakers died in midsong. The local roadies they'd hired rolled out the crates and covers.

The stage was thick with unspoken irritation. Dirk headed for the soundboard where Jay was coiling speaker lines.

"Wasn't the best last few sets, huh?"

Jay glanced up. He pushed his glasses back. "Wasn't even particularly mediocre the last few sets. Good thing Angela wasn't here to hear 'em."

"I guess."

Jay laid down the wrapped cable. "So what happened?"

"She didn't really even give me a chance to ask. And she wasn't interested."

"Did you tell her *why* you wanted her to go with you? Did you tell her how you feel about her?"

"What do you mean?"

Behind the wire-rims, Jay's eyes rolled heavenward. "Never mind. That tells me you didn't. Listen, Dirk, if I handed you a bottle and said, 'Drink this,' would you do it? Not a chance, right? What if I handed you the same bottle and said, 'Hey, this tastes fantastic; I'd like you to share it.' You'd at least think about drinking it then, right?" Jay picked up the cable, slipped it into its case. "On the other hand, you can just call it a convenient affair. You had a good time for a few days. Another groupie to notch on your bedpost. No commitments, no big deal. Who knows who you might meet in New York?"

Dirk stared at the stage. He grimaced. "Umm, look. Tell the others I'll be back later, okay?" Dirk didn't wait for an answer. He headed for the door, breaking into a trot.

"You're welcome," Jay called after him. He began packing away the console.

Dirk was surprised at the relief he felt when he saw the Chevette parked in front of Angela's house. Behind the blinds, yellow light splashed between the houses. Dirk paid the cabbie and stood in front of the house, listening to the early-morning quiet reasserting itself as the taxi drove off.

He knocked on the door, half expecting that she wouldn't answer. From the corner of his eye, he saw the curtain lift at the front window, then drop back. The knob rattled, turned.

"I'm an asshole," he said.

She was dressed in a silk robe, ornately brocaded at the waist and shoulders and loosely tied. He could see the inner swell of her breasts, the curve of her thigh. Her hair was free and wild, stray curls falling over her cheeks. Her eyes were rimmed with puffiness. Dirk could smell incense burning in the room behind her, strong and pungent. Angela rubbed her eyes as if she were tired, then stared at him over steepled hands.

"I noticed," she said.

"It's 'Be Kind to Assholes' Week. Can I come in?"

A faint smile ghosted over her lips and faded. She stepped away from the door, leaving it open. Dirk followed the rustle of her robe into the living room. All the furniture had been moved back against the walls. In the center of the room a wooden table held one of the candles from her bedroom, an incense stand in which a jasmine stick was burning, and a delicate pottery bowl.

The bowl diverted Dirk's attention from the words

he was intending to say. The glaze was dark, a rich ultramarine background. Golden figures danced on the rim, swirling into geometric patterns. Dirk squinted. "I've never seen that here before, Angela. Egyptian? Not exactly my field, but . . . What is it? A copy of something?"

"It's original. Twenty-sixth dynasty, just before the Ptolemies took over."

Dirk scoffed, but he didn't take his gaze from the bowl. Delicate shimmerings moved in the azure glaze; the inlay seemed alive. He wanted to touch them, caress the smooth sides, cradle the flaring bowl in his hands and examine the hieroglyphics. "I don't believe that," he said. "You don't keep twenty-five-century-old museum pieces in your house, and you certainly don't keep them out in the open."

He'd shuffled forward slowly. He could feel Angela watching him, but he stared at the bowl.

Dirk had almost forgotten why he'd come. The beauty of the thing snared him. The bowl asked to be touched, asked to be admired, compelling. He reached out, waiting for Angela to stop him. She said nothing, watching.

The contact was disturbing. The glaze was slick and incredibly cold, as if the bowl had been refrigerated. He pulled his fingers back, shivered involuntarily, and touched it again. This time he picked it up.

Dirk gasped. Holding the bowl, his hands were moving of their own accord: up, down, a looping, intricate series of arcs to the left, then to the right. For an instant, only an instant, he seemed somewhere else. He could feel heavy vestments on his back, some heavy wrapping on his head. His fingers were knobby, ancient, and he peered into a humid darkness swirling with sweet vapors. From the smoky void in front of him came a chanting of several voices, in a language that seemed mockingly familiar, though the sense of it eluded him.

And then it was gone.

In the apartment Dirk heard the shuffling of feet and the clearing of a throat. An extremely masculine throat.

The image faded from his mind; he set the bowl down, his hands trembling from the weird shift in reality.

Doberman Edgar was standing barefoot in the hall archway, wearing a bathrobe that matched Angela's and a scowl. His massive fist patted the molding significantly. "Angela?" he growled.

Behind Dirk, she sighed. "Edgar, why don't you go back in the bedroom? I'll be along in a few minutes."

Edgar grimaced. He gave Dirk a long, appraising stare, seemed to smile mockingly, and then turned. Dirk, still shaking from the intensity of the vision, hardly noticed: he stared at the bowl. Any desire to touch it again had fled. When he looked back at Angela, her face was carefully blank. All the words had gone out of him. He took a breath, then another.

"That was strange," he said. "For a second there . . ."

"It's a very old piece," Angela said. "A lot of rites have gone through it and the bowl remembers. You know—that occult junk."

"You don't expect me to believe that."

"No," Angela said. "I don't."

She said it without mockery and with a sadness that made Dirk scowl. And then Dirk remembered Edgar. Combined with the lingering disorientation from when he'd touched the bowl, he felt like someone had just jabbed him in the kidneys.

"Guess my timing's not very good," he said at last.

"It depends on what you expected, Dirk."

"I didn't expect this."

"What is it you think you're seeing?" Angela shifted her weight, a muscular leg slipping out from the folds of her robe. Her question was intense, insistent; her almond eyes relentless. "Tell me—what do you think is going on? Or has that skepticism of yours kicked in already?"

Dirk floundered halfway between shrug and grimace, feeling clumsy and embarrassed. "You and Edgar . . . well . . ." He clamped his jaw shut. "Look, I'm sorry I interrupted," he grated out. "Whatever you're doing, it's none of my business."

"You're right about that, at least. I don't have to give you explanations, Dirk. I don't recall either of us making permanent commitments to each other. You made that clear enough earlier. I needed someone tonight. I would have preferred it was you, but . . ."

Then her face softened, and the weariness he'd seen before returned. For the first time, he noticed the darkness under her eyes, the lacework of veins in her eyes—whatever she'd been doing, it had taken a physical toll on her. "Damn it, Dirk, you're standing there bleeding emotions all over the rug and I didn't want to hurt you. I like you. And I think that maybe, if we had the chance sometime, we'd find that it was something a lot more intense than that. Maybe you'd even have opened your mind a little."

Angela laughed softly, and Dirk could hear the exhaustion in her voice. She lifted her hair in her hands, stretching, and let the strands fall. She stood behind the bowl and looked down into the lapis glaze. "God, don't we let those little confessions loose when we're tired? Dirk, it's been a wonderful week. I've enjoyed being with you more than you know. I wish we could have had more time to explore this and I'm damn sorry it's over, but it is and I've got things to do that I've been putting off."

"With Edgar," Dirk said.

Her head came up. Her eyes shimmered with moisture. "Please, Dirk. Why don't you just go and make this as easy as it's going to be?" She swiped at her eyes with the back of her sleeve, angrily. "You don't believe in anything that I believe in. Fine. I don't need mockery and I don't need jealousy."

"Angela . . ." he began. *Tell her why,* Jay had said. Dirk shook his head and dove in. "Angela, no one else I've known has hit me so hard and so fast. I wanted you to come with me because I wanted to see where we could go with that. Same as you. I like you; given time, I think it could be more. I wish you'd change your mind, but I'll understand if you can't."

Angela was crying openly now.

"Damn it," she said. Her voice was throaty, torn

velvet. "Why do you say the right things so *late*, Dirk?"

Optimism swelled like a balloon. Jay had been right; he'd been so stupid not telling her in the first place. Now she'd change her mind. Now Edgar in the bedroom would be the one dismissed. He'd managed to avert catastrophe. "So you'll go with me." The relief almost made Dirk laugh.

Her fingers closed around the bowl. She looked down into its glossy depths and not at him.

"No," she said. "I won't."

Her words ripped a long rent in the balloon. All the air went out in a great mocking raspberry. She wouldn't look up. Dirk stared at her, at the bowl she held. He thought of all the words he could say, all the arguments that might, finally, convince her.

He swallowed them. He turned and left.

12: Cuisines and Other Relationships

The lights were out on Mundo's landing. Alfred pulled a Bic lighter from his pocket and rolled his thumb over the wheel, finding the door by the shuddering flame. He knocked.

The MindBeast answered the door.

On top of its furry, snouted head was a policeman's cap, and in its right hand was a severed human forearm, held like a gory scepter.

The Bic-revealed details, backlit against the light from Mundo's apartment, registered in the instant it took Alfred to catapult himself across the too-narrow hall, his back pressed against the wall as if he could sink through the cheap plasterboard by sheer force of fright. The lighter clattered on the floor and away.

"Mundo," Alfred called shakily, watching the creature warily. "Goddamn it, Mundo—"

The MindBeast scratched its massive back with the forearm, grinning blissfully like a hairy, stunted dinosaur nightmare. " 'Evening," the thing croaked. "Alfred, right?" It took a bite from the arm afterward, destroying any illusions Alfred may have had that the arm was a prop. There was pink muscle and white bone under the waxy skin. It chewed noisily, staring at the cowering Alfred.

"Out of the doorway, please!" Someone struck the MindBeast from behind, and it grunted, backing into the apartment and leaving Caleb Mundo to grimace at Alfred. "What are you standing there for? Come in."

"I thought that thing was a trick, not real. Somethin' in my mind."

"In *my* mind, not yours. You haven't room for anything extra, believe me. And I needed her here for the time being. Get in—I don't like having the door open."

The dwarf half pulled Alfred into the apartment and slammed the door shut behind him. He slammed the bolt shut. In the next room, Alfred could hear the shuffling of the MindBeast. "It talks," he stuttered.

Mundo just nodded, arms akimbo.

"It had an arm. . . ."

"She's carnivorous," Mundo grumbled, but he, too, seemed uneasy. His anger was too pat, too convenient. "She has to eat just like you. You think I'm going to feed her dog food?"

Synapses clicked dully in Alfred's mind. Headlines of the last few days skittered through his head, making uncomfortable connections in thirty-six-point Helvetica Bold. "Jesus H. Christ," he muttered. "The cop that's missin', the 'Bowery Butcher' murders . . ."

"They weren't murders," Mundo said uneasily. "Alice doesn't kill indiscriminately."

"Alice? You got a pet man-eating monster named *Alice?*"

"It's her name; that's what she wants to be called. How a thing is named determines how we view it—haven't you learned that yet? Would you feel more comfortable with her if she were called SharpFang or FleshRender? She has morals, too, Roundbottom. I happen to know that all three of the Butcher victims were already dead; a robbery, a fight, whatever—it happens every night. Alice can sense violence about to happen. She'll watch, and when it's over, that's when she'll eat. The officer was self-defense," Mundo added. "He shot at Alice. Because she looks dangerous doesn't mean she is."

"Absolutely not." Alfred's hands were still shaking. "She just tears bodies to pieces and eats them. Keeps the streets from gettin' cluttered. Almost a public service. Alice is a very nice MindBeast with a very nice name."

Mundo glared into Alfred's jittery sarcasm. "What she does makes more sense to me than pickling bodies and sticking them in boxes. And I expect her to be more efficient than you at finding Theopelli's papers." Mundo's short arm shot out and jabbed Alfred in the stomach; the breath went out of him with a grunt. "Or have you managed that simple little task already? No problem, right?"

Alfred grimaced, rubbing his stomach. "No problem" was what he'd said to Caleb Mundo after he'd found Joan the Flower Man and realized that it was she who had taken the papers. How much trouble could it be to find her?

Yet it had been. Those who knew her seemed decidedly reluctant to tell him where she lived, and though he found out where her usual selling spots were, he never seemed to be there at the same time. He made the rounds of the nightclubs since the hot-dog vendor had told him that she sometimes made the rounds to sell her flowers and would even sing with the bands, if they'd let her. After spending a small fortune in cover charges, that finally paid off. He followed her to her apartment. The next night, at Mundo's threatening insistence, he'd broken into the flower-strewn apartment.

There'd been paper enough in the place, but not Theopelli's manuscript. That was simply gone.

He had the sinking feeling that the notebook's pages were scattered through the city, having been used to wrap her miserable bouquets of carnations.

No problem. Sure.

"I checked everywhere," he told Mundo. "I waded through rotting flowers and moldy newspapers full of roaches and fleas. Nothing. She probably gave it away sheet by frigging sheet with her damn flowers."

"That's not what my sources say."

"*Your* sources? What: drug dealers? Monsters? A pack of cards?" Alfred watched Mundo's face go florid; a slow chill ran up his spine and he waited for the dwarf to do something. But Mundo simply stepped back and gestured him in. Alfred breathed a slow sigh and followed Mundo into the living room.

The place looked totally different. The decor was a bizarre mixture of upscale tech and medieval arcana, a scene from some Gritty Future After the Fall motion picture. *Mad Max Meets Dr. Faustus:* Alfred figured Theopelli would have loved it.

The throw rug covering the splintery pine floor of the main room had been moved aside. A tiny flat-screen TV sat on a VCR in the center of the room, the unset time winking blue white numbers at Alfred through wires netting the setup like brambles. Chalked around the tangle was a rough pentagram, at the points of which guttering candles were embedded in dribbling wax. There was a Christmas scene on the candle nearest Alfred: Santa Claus rode his sleigh up the taper into the descending flame. Rudolph was already obliterated.

A Macintosh computer lay on its side in the far corner, the monitor flickering with random fractal patterns. Mundo's tarot deck was arrayed before the computer on a black silk scarf, the cards carefully fanned wide. A cheap map of the city was thumbtacked to the wall opposite the window. Thin wires did a cat's cradle across the room at about head height, and a quartz crystal the size of Alfred's fist was suspended on the wire nearest the window.

And in the midst of it, the wires almost touching the leathery neck and her thick reptilian legs splayed over the VCR, stood Alice the MindBeast. Her short arms were wide spread as she faced the moon-struck window and the crystal, her improbably long, clawed fingers extended. The policeman's arm, looking chewed, was at her feet.

Furry Tyrannosaurus Rex in Moon Salute. It was not a pretty picture.

"You came at the right time," Mundo said behind Alfred. "We were just beginning the incantations."

"Incantations," Alfred repeated dully. "Oh."

"You couldn't bring this Joan the Flower Man to me. Despite the waste of my energies, I decided I must do it myself."

"With a spell."

"Theopelli's manuscript is important. You must realize that."

"Incantations. Spells. Witchcraft. Utter nonsen—" Alfred glanced at Alice and the razored incisors peeking from underneath her long jaw and decided against finishing the word. "You're talkin' 'bout weird stuff," he added lamely.

"*Your* people abandoned this path. That's your folly, not mine." The dwarf fixed Alfred with a black glare. "It's just as real as anything you call science."

"Sure. You even use computers."

Mundo scoffed. "You watch too many bad movies. Just because you don't understand something doesn't mean it isn't real. To produce results, certain things have to be done in certain fixed patterns. I could do it the old way if I needed to, but why bother?"

"Blood," Alice interjected. She was still staring at the moonlit window, arms wide spread. The patterns on the Macintosh screen were changing rapidly now, and Alfred could smell a definite ozone tinge to the air. The hairs on his arms tingled with static electricity. He brushed at them and discharge crackled.

The lights in the apartment flared and went out. Alfred nearly screamed at the suddenness. The Macintosh and the VCR arrangement stayed powered, glimmering. There was a sense that something was about to happen and Alfred decided he didn't care to be here when it did.

"Blood would help," Alice said again.

"Umm, I'm sure it would," Alfred said. Mundo had slipped behind him again as if he'd anticipated Alfred's impending retreat. Alfred heard the door slam and the lock turn. "Mundo, goddamn you—" Alfred turned and the protest died in his throat with a whimper.

Mundo was holding a butcher's knife and a large stainless steel bowl. He leered, an evil gnome in the shadows.

"No," Alfred moaned. The hypercharged air of the apartment seemed ready to explode.

"You piss your pants again and I'll make you lick up the mess," Mundo rumbled. "All I need is a few drops. I was going to do it myself, but since you screwed up and made all this necessary, it's your job. Hold out your arm."

Alfred didn't move.

"Hold out your fucking arm or I'll have Alice chew it off."

Reluctantly, Alfred complied. Mundo grinned. He brandished the knife. "You can look away if you want. It won't hurt much."

Alfred closed his eyes. He felt Mundo's hand close around his wrist, the dwarf's fingers surprisingly strong. He doubted that he could have pulled away. The knife's keen edge slithered along his forearm. Alfred gasped: a hot and sluggish warmth trickled down his arm.

"Here." Cloth patted the small wound. Alfred opened his eyes as Mundo wrapped sterile tape around the cloth and his arm. There was a small red pool in the bottom of the bowl. "It's all over," Mundo said. He swirled the thick liquid under Alfred's nose. "Squeamish?"

"*Now*, Caleb," Alice grunted from the center of the room and Mundo took the bowl away as Alfred's stomach did a quick handstand. Despite his skepticism, *something* was happening, something Alfred couldn't explain.

Theopelli would have claimed to understand. "There's nothing you can't understand," he'd always scoffed. "You just have to figure out whose fault it is and ask." But then Alfred wouldn't have been in this situation without Theopelli. It was all Theopelli's fault and *he* was well beyond asking.

The ozone smell was much stronger; in the darkness, the computer's monitor was a blur of motion and the wires were thrumming to some unfelt vibration. Mundo scuttled around the chalked pentagram, spilling Alfred's blood in each corner. As he splashed the last chalk mark, the wires sang a clear, high note and the crystal tilted up. The radiance of the full moon flared at the crystal's tip and a searingly bright beam lanced from the crystal to the map on the far wall. A brilliant dot of moonlight crawled the inked streets of New York and then stopped.

"There," Mundo cried triumphantly. "We've got her. Now, let's open the portal."

In the center of the room, Alice moaned. A thin fog had begun to wreathe around the map, swirling about the vortex of the crystal's focused light. Alfred blinked—the fog was rapidly becoming denser, the bands of cloud thickening, and then map, wall, fog, all of them, were gone.

"I'll be damned," Alfred breathed, staring.

Where the wall had been, a shimmering opening had appeared, which looked into another room. It seemed to be a small lab of some sort: tile walls; cement floors; racks of chemicals; equipment lined along a shelf with a sink. Two empty gurneys were double-parked along one wall, the black leather partially covered by white sheets.

And Joan was there, the baseball cap screwed tightly down over that ugly, bristly face. She gazed back at them, her mouth moving as if she were chewing something. Her lips pursed and she spat a globule of tobacco juice. It arced through the portal and landed in Mundo's apartment with a wet *schlopp*. Joan seemed totally unsurprised by the fact that she could have stepped through a rift in reality into Mundo's apartment.

"A dwarf, dragon lady, and roustabout." She frowned. "Okay, where's the bastard Henderson, huh? He send you? You tell Henderson old Joan'll punch his face in, betcha." Her hands cocked and fisted as she went into an unsteady boxer's crouch, bobbing and weaving like a pudgy puppet.

Mundo gave her a smile that held all the warmth of a shark. He extended his hand, moving close to the portal but not touching the glowing, sparking edges. "Joan," he said coaxingly. "No one here wants to hurt you. Please, step through."

"Nope."

Mundo grimaced. The smile vanished. "I command it. You must come." He made an imperious gesture but Joan only straightened, her hands dropping and her rheumy eyes narrowing.

"Caleb?" Alice asked. She was peering back at him, her body still facing the window.

"I don't know," Mundo muttered irritably. "She's resisting somehow."

Mundo beckoned to Joan again. For a moment, the tableau held, Alice with her head craned over her shoulder and Alfred lost in a gaping stare. Then Joan's eyes widened as she looked at something beyond Mundo and the others. "Gosh," she said in wonder.

Kwump!

The sound was a shattering blend of thunderclap and gong. A blinding white flash washed over the room from behind Alfred. His eyelids slammed shut reflexively; Joan covered her face with her arm. After a moment, Alfred cautiously slitted one eye. Through the dancing purple afterimages, the room seemed unchanged. Joan, Mundo, and Alice were all staring at something behind him. He turned to look.

The wires laced around Alice were taut and glowing a soft red. Beyond them, the moonlit window had vanished and been replaced by a far more enticing landscape.

Another shimmering hole had opened. In the room beyond this portal and hanging what should have been ten feet above the street outside, stood a woman with dark brown hair and strange emerald eyes. She was utterly and deliciously naked. Her body was full and sensual, lush rather than model-skinny. Behind her was a well-muscled (and well-hung, Alfred thought with unconscious jealousy) young man who was also unclothed but for a bandage much like Alfred's around his right arm. The woman put her hands on her hips, her stance wide and defiant.

"The Mage!" she exclaimed, looking at Mundo.

"Princess of Pentacles," Mundo said to no one in particular. His large, light-sensitive eyes were watering.

"A peep show, too," Joan said loudly. "Henderson, you bastard, you're here, sure."

In the room where Joan stood, a door opened and a cadaverous Oriental man dressed in an out-of-date black suit came through. He stopped, gazing in shock at the scene before him. Alfred shook his head, his gaze swiveling from Joan back to the more erotic scene behind. "Getting too damned crowded here," he said under his breath.

Mundo seemed confused and angry. He still gestured to Joan, who wouldn't move. Alice shivered between the wires, the glow of which was growing stronger. Alfred could almost feel the heat from them. "Caleb," the MindBeast croaked. *"Hurry."*

"She won't come," he snapped back.

There was laughter from the naked woman, bright and easy. "God, I've been so stupid. You're in New York, aren't you? I should have gone with Dirk."

She gave a complicated wave of her hand—the opening into her room vanished as suddenly as it had come but without the pyrotechnics. "Shit!" Mundo howled.

"Caleb . . ." Alice was shivering. Sweat made her golden fur dark.

"Shut up." Mundo gestured again to Joan. The man in black behind her was still frozen in shock. Joan gave Mundo the finger and then, haltingly, imitated the gesture the woman had given. Alice screamed in pain.

Alfred hit the floor.

The wires around Alice went white-hot and then parted with an audible *thwang*. Droplets of molten metal sprayed, the crystal streaked across the room like a glittering cannonball and ricocheted at head height.

When Alfred dared to look back up, the portal was gone. Smoking black pinpricks dotted the walls and floor, the VCR groaned and expired, the Macintosh screen displayed an icon of a grimacing computer. Alice the MindBeast sat heavily in the middle of the floor, her reptilian tail wrapped around her, exhausted.

"The ugly one had power," she said accusingly to Mundo. "You didn't tell me."

"I didn't know. I doubt *she* knows. And we opened

ourselves up to the damn Princess, too, whoever she is.'' Mundo paced the room. He brushed cooling metallic shrapnel from his cloak. His black, twisted regard came to rest on Alfred, who was still huddled in a fetal crouch, wondering if it was safe to move.

"It's *your* fault," Mundo grumbled. "You'll pay, too."

Alfred had no trouble believing that.

13: An Unlucky Moment

Ecclesiastes gaped at Joan. His hand was still gripping the door handle, and he realized he'd been holding his breath for what seemed like minutes. Joan was stalking back and forth in front of the wall, mumbling. There was just the faintest trace of smoke hazing the air at the back of the lab. At least he thought there was; it seemed to be fading even as he squinted to be certain.

"The wall was just . . . *gone*," he uttered shakily. "There was a monster, a dwarf, some naked people. . . ." He gave Joan a bewildered look. "You were talking with them. . . ."

Joan nodded, glancing back at him without stopping her agitated pacing.

Ecclesiastes took a deep breath and calmed himself. He let go of the doorknob. "You saw them, too?" he asked. "The very same ones? Through the wall?"

" 'Course." Joan regarded Ecclesiastes like a parent puzzled by a slow child, her forehead furrowed under the grimy baseball cap. She rubbed at the stubble on her jaw and moved the wad of tobacco from one cheek to the other. "Ain't you always seeing the same things's me?"

Ecclesiastes thought he'd better dodge that question. "Hallucinations aren't contagious," he said, more to himself than Joan. He walked past Joan to the wall and deliberately kicked the porcelain tiles. There was a solid *tchunk;* his toes tingled with the impact.

"Shit!" Ecclesiastes grimaced, decided he'd only look foolish hopping around on one foot, and closed his eyes until the pain subsided. Then he pushed against the wall—it remained solid and unmoving.

He wasn't sure if that made him feel better or not.

"You can't catch a hallucination like a cold," he told himself again. "I'm sure you can't. I mean, I *like* the idea of life being unpredictable, but this . . ."

Behind him, he heard a soft, gasping cry. Ecclesiastes turned to see two great tears track slowly down the furrows of Joan's face. The look on her face was both disconsolate and frightened.

"Joan?"

"Henderson's coming. The bastard—" Her rounded shoulders heaved under the tattered windbreaker and she put her hands over her face. Her body shook with the sobs.

Ecclesiastes watched the grieving Joan for a moment, then shook his head again. He walked over to her and placed his thin arms around her. Trying to ignore the smell of tobacco juice and her strong, distinctive body odor, he patted her.

"There, there." He stroked her shoulders gingerly. "It'll be all right."

He kept his gaze on the wall, though. Just in case.

14: Concerto Coitus

The stage was very tight. There wasn't as much room as they were used to. Dirk frowned at a wood-block set about three feet behind his mike stand. The block held a metal clip filled with a gray powder flecked with black, and two wires trailed away behind it into the twisted spaghetti of the remote cables.

"Isn't this thing too close?" Dirk asked nervously. "It's not that I don't trust you. . . ."

From the balcony where Jay was setting up his console, Mikhail D peered down. "No sweat, man," Mikhail said. "I changed the mixture."

Stan Fedderman had hired Mikhail to run lights and special effects for Savage during their New York stay. "He's an expert—a little eccentric, sure, but he'll make you guys look great."

Mikhail was a thin, nervous, and twitchy little guy in his forties with a penchant for black powder. He looked and sounded like he'd escaped from the late sixties. What was left of his receding hair was long, straight, and tied in a ponytail that went halfway down his back. His denim jeans were frayed and festooned with mismatched patches, and the T-shirt he wore was tie-dyed. Mikhail's last name was something Slavic and unpronounceable. He'd demonstrated his skills in the back alley behind the club, leaving an inch-deep divot in the asphalt after the explosion.

Mikhail grinned, wreathed in flashpowder smoke.

Dirk would have been willing to bet he was the type of kid who'd put cherry bombs in his Revell B-29 plastic airplane models. He had a hard time imagining the 1968 Mikhail waving a peace sign in front of National

Guard troops and handing them flowers. He looked more the SDS type, gleefully and righteously blowing up campus labs.

"It won't be a problem, babe," Mikhail added. He smiled. The man had just about the darkest smile Dirk had ever seen. There was no enamel on Mikhail's teeth at all, and his gums had receded down to the roots. His front teeth looked like someone had shaded them in with a number-two pencil.

"You're sure?"

"Trust me, Dirk. Really."

"Right. I can't even produce your last name."

Mikhail rattled off a burst of guttural syllables ending in "ski." "You gotta have the explosions," he added. "Without smoke and fire, there's no magic. Great rolling clouds of pure white smoke, a gout of yellow flame, the concussion hammering at the audience's chest: man, that's an entrance. That's magic."

The talk of magic reminded Dirk of Angela. Thinking about Angela hurt. There was a sore place in his head that he kept stumbling over, like a broken tooth your tongue won't leave alone. "Give it a rest, Mikhail."

"You don't understand, man. Explosions are primal. They shout 'Pay attention!' with the roar like a Tyrannosaurus might have made in the swamps, chasing the cavemen."

"There weren't any cavemen with the dinosaurs—"

"*Boom!*" Mikhail flung his arms wide, his head back in near-religious ecstasy. "The universe snapping its fingers. God flinging Mother Nature down the steps."

"Mikhail . . ."

"Jailed and enslaved energy shouting 'Freedom!' Entropy doing a breakdance."

"*Mikhail!*"

The shout brought the litany to a ragged halt. Mikhail shook his head at Dirk. "It's magic, man," he said again. "You just gotta have it."

From behind his console, Jay shrugged to Dirk, who nudged the flashpot with a sneaker-clad toe and hopped down from the stage. Mikhail went back to rigging the fresnels.

It was a mistake to turn on the houselights in a rock club, Dirk decided. This place—whatever it might be called—was no exception. The red-and-black plaid carpet was sticky and discolored with spilled drinks, worn down to the nap between the tables, the parquet dance floor was gouged; tiles were missing around the edges. The tables were canted and shabby; the ceiling was a landscape of peeling black paint splashed with islands of duct tape where previous bands had laid wiring and lights.

Maybe Mikhail was right. To bring magic here, you might need heavy demolition.

Dirk went to the bar, where the rest of the band had liberated one of the beer taps.

"This place smells of desperation," Dirk said.

Kyle looked at Lars, who rolled his eyes. Alf snorted. "A little Lysol and you'd never know it," the drummer said.

"No, man, I mean it. All these clubs we've been playing in are the same. People come here hoping to find something: someone to be with, a great time, oblivion, escape. Sometimes they get lucky; mostly, they don't. They leave their scent behind. The pheremones seep into the carpet with the beer."

"When's the last time you heard one moan?"

"Huh?"

"A fairy."

"That's not funny, Alf. Not funny at all. You have to make everything into a fucking joke."

"You're just horny 'cause that Angela didn't come with you," Alf observed. "You can fuck someone new tonight, if you get lucky. Have a beer."

"Just don't spill it on the carpet with the moaning fairies." Lars guffawed. "Fairy moans. Shit, that's pretty damn good, Alf."

"You guys don't know what I'm talking about."

"I know fucking bullshit when I hear it," Lars grumbled.

"You've been pretty moody since we left Cincinnati," Kyle said soothingly, shaking his head at Lars. "Forget the chick and think about playing. Stan says Phil Collins is in town and might drop in, there's the people from Warner coming in Friday, and who knows who else Stan'll be bringing by. This is important, Dirk. Angela made her decision."

Kyle's advice sounded friendly, fatherly, and reasonable. Dirk started to nod.

"Yeah, she's probably humping that other guy right now," Lars added. He leaned back on the stool and spread his legs obscenely. "Ooh, stick it in me, baby. . . ."

The vision jabbed an ice pick into that mental sore spot. "You son of a—" Dirk began.

SSSSSSSSSSSSSSSSSSS.

A million snakes waggled tongues at once; a thousand ghetto blasters between stations clicked on at the same time; the grandfather of all sunspots garbled every available transmission with high-decibel static; the entire world hissed at the joke humankind had played on it.

Dirk's retort was cut off by a stunning wash of pink noise from the stage speakers: Jay testing the sound system. The amplified roar thudded in the subsonic and rattled the walls, shrieked like a lost banshee from the tweeters. Anything Dirk could have said was lost in derisive speaker roar. Lars grinned at Dirk through the aural fog.

When it suddenly, achingly, went away all at once, Jay's voice, like that of a high-tech deity, rumbled over the PA. "Get your butts off the bar stools and on stage. I need a sound check."

Lars sniffed and headed for the stage without looking at Dirk, Alf downed his beer and slammed the mug back on the bar, Kyle patted Dirk affectionately on the shoulder and headed for the bank of keyboards.

Dirk stood there and thought of fifty or so things he should say or do.

"Dirk," Jay pleaded. "Now. Or I'll have Mikhail make magic under your rear."

"Boom," Lars said into his mike. "Is that a stick of dynamite or are you just happy to see me?"

"The universe beating off. Mother Nature cutting a fart." Alf did a roll from the snare to the floor tom, crashed the cymbals. "It's magic, man."

For Dirk, it was a very long sound check.

He was feeling marginally better by evening.

The club was fairly well packed from what he could see from the dressing-room door. Stan had two of the Warner executives at his table in front, already well lubricated with the contents of the several empty glasses adorning the table. The other tables were full, and a crowd milled around the bar in the back. A group of dancers was just leaving the floor as the last chords of the latest Winwood album faded.

The stage lights dimmed. "Let's hit it," Alf said, and bounded up the steps to the stage. Dirk and the others followed. From the balcony where the light and soundboards were set, Mikhail D's dim smile leered down at them, and Jay's voice whispered over the stage monitors. "Make it good, guys."

Dirk strapped on the Rickenbacker. Alf's sticks clicked softly. *One, two, three, and—*

Lars flailed a power chord from his Strat, Kyle's DX7 wailed, Lars punched at the kick drum and pounded the cymbals, Dirk hit a wide-open double-octave G on the Rick.

At the same instant, the lights flared and the flashpot behind Dirk exploded with light and a resounding *KRUMP!* that illuminated the place like a hundred strobes. Quick heat spread over Dirk's back.

The crowd screamed; Dirk heard Mikhail D's exultant laughter even above the sound system. They launched into a hard-edged, upbeat version of Dylan's "Watchtower" as the audience applauded; as Stan Fedderman nodded; as choking wreaths of flashpowder smoke continued to drift past Dirk's head.

Yeah, it *was* magic, Dirk had to admit, as the band charged through the first measures, as the crowd continued to yell and point.

The glorious concussion still echoed in his ears, and the excitement in the crowd was infectious. Dirk kicked a leg up on the next beat, dancing toward his microphone.

"Dirk!" Kyle shouted. Dirk turned to him and grinned, though he couldn't see much through the lights and the cloud left by the explosion.

The crowd cheered with him. Yeah, this was wonderful! As the smoke slowly began to clear and the band roared toward the first verse, Dirk's eyes narrowed. His breath caught.

In that moment, he was inclined to believe in Mikhail's magic.

Angela was out there.

Her walk, her electric presence were unmistakable. She came from the crowd by the bar, heading down the steps to Fedderman's table and sitting alongside him. The Warner execs made hurried room for her.

Dirk made a mental note to thank Mikhail after the set. Dirk laughed, he swayed, he danced in the magical flashpowder haze. He felt *good*.

But the smoke was still flowing past him without abating, and the stench had turned nasty. The crowd continued to yell and those who had come out to dance were standing still, looking up at him with awe.

"Dirk!" Kyle yelled again. "Your *hair!*"

Dirk suddenly frowned and patted the back of his head.

He heard a dry, crackling sound. Hair dissolved into ash under his hand. The crowd applauded.

Dirk looked up to the balcony. Mikhail had buried his head in his arms.

Mikhail D would have attributed it to the magic of pyrotechnics, if he'd been there.

But he wasn't. Immediately after setting Dirk afire, he'd hurriedly left his seat alongside the mixing console and departed the club. "Gotta go, man," he told Jay. "I'll be right back, huh?"

Jay ran the lights as well as sound for the rest of the night.

Stan had arranged for the band to do two one-and-a-half-hour sets a night for the week. Despite the initial accident, the band stalked through the sets like a snarling beast and the audience was howling for more at the end. "Not bad," Jay said through the monitors after the last song. "Not bad at all."

The Warner execs were nodding and flirting heavily with Angela, Stan Fedderman was smiling and coiling his pudgy arms around each of them affectionately. The club manager was smiling. It was magic, Dirk decided. Angela made it magic.

"My boys," Fedderman said to the Warner people. "Ya gotta love 'em. Now, let's talk about this idea of having them open for Van Halen. . . ."

Afterward, Angela and Dirk went out into the early-morning blaze of city light, arms around each other. Dirk's face ached from smiling. "God, I'm glad to see you."

"How's the hair?"

"It'll grow back."

"The new fashion's short anyway."

"The damn flashpowder scorched the hell out of my pants. I'd like to have a long talk with Mikhail."

"It's okay as long as you didn't burn anything crucial. I'll cut your hair when we get back to our hotel room."

"*Our* . . ." Dirk began.

Stopped.

Manhattan lights shimmered from her smile. "I could get a room of my own," Angela said. She snuggled against him. The night was suddenly very warm and very fragrant.

"No. It's okay, I guess. I mean . . ." She stopped his words with her lips. Her tongue did a quick inventory of his mouth and then lingeringly withdrew.

"You *are* glad I'm here?" she asked.

"Yes. Absolutely. Our room. Right. Angela—" He stopped again.

"What?"

"I'm very glad you're here. Thanks." He could feel

something burning in the corners of his eyes, and he sniffed. "I feel . . . well, *incredible*. I missed you."

"But you're still not asking the question you should ask." Her eyes were bright and serious, though her mouth still had a trace of the smile.

"What question?"

"It'll come to you." Her lightheartedness of the moment before was entirely gone now. She touched his cheek in a manner that was almost sad or wistful. "Just ask when it does. I won't lie to you."

"Your moods change quicker than anyone I know."

"It's a Pisces trait. We're moody."

"Astrology too. I should have known."

"You don't like anything that's out of the ordinary, do you?"

"I'm rather fond of you."

That brought back the smile. She kissed him again, harder this time, and then bounded away, holding out her hand for him. They began walking again.

"And just what is it about me you like best?" she asked.

15: Popped Questions

The room smelled of sex.

Like a wave of foaming tidal brine.

Like the insides of Fanny Hill's underpants.

Pheremones swung giggling from the chandeliers. Vapors rose from the rumpled bedsheets like satiated ghosts. The bedsprings complained softly of abuse to the carpet.

The aroma would have made a musk deer proud. It would have sent Dirk's eighth-grade nun, Sister Rose Julie, fumbling for her rosary beads.

"What is that *odor?*" she would have said, as cold as the skeletal penguin she resembled in her robes. "That's the stench of lust. Don't you dare smile at me when I'm talking to you, child. I tell you the devil will *burn* that horrid thing right off you for your dirty thoughts, burn it black and charred and dead until you never, ever think of lust again."

Sister Rose Julie (called Sister de Sade behind her back by the parish priest) thought puberty an invention of the Horned One.

The spirit of old Pan, who had wafted in on the familiar scent and stayed to watch the proceedings (though he'd fallen asleep at some point—it was tiring, being an old god), lifted his hoary head and smiled. He had an erection as thick and veined as his forearm and as long. He waggled its ruddy, knobbed head at Sister Rose Julie.

"Your priests modeled Satan after *me*." He grinned. "And I'd never burn anything as nice as this. Why don't you let me pump some juice into that desert between your legs?"

Sister Rose Julie fled, shrieking. Pan sniffed delightedly: the room was armpits and moistness and secret places; it was primal urges well satisfied. Pan fell back to sleep and dreams of horny nymphs, chuckling.

There was life in the old boy yet.

Unaware of the supernatural traffic jam in the room, Dirk and Angela snuggled together in a tangle of bedsheets. Angela's hand slid up Dirk's thigh and stroked what it found in the nest of stickily moist pubic hair.

Dirk had fallen asleep. Angela's ministrations made him groan and wake once more. "My God, woman. Have some mercy. I'm sore down there."

Angela gave him an evil, lip-licking grin and hooked a leg over his thigh, pulling him into the humid curve of her body. "Obviously you're not as young as you used to be." Her hands pulled his newly cropped head to her, a few stray burnt ends crunching under her fingers. She kissed him, openmouthed and wet, then fell back on the bed with a gasp. She brushed sweaty ringlets back from her forehead and closed her eyes as she touched herself.

"It's just as well," she said. "I think you've scrubbed me raw inside. It felt delicious, but everything's puffy. I have to pee and it's going to hurt. I'll be right back."

She bounded from the bed, which complained screechily once more. Pan whistled from his corner. Early-morning sunlight threw dusty beams past the curtains and folded appreciatively around the curves of her body. Dirk surveyed the landscape as Angela padded to the bathroom.

"I think the modern infatuation with skinniness is crazy," Dirk said. "You know that?"

"Ouch." Through the open door, Dirk heard the bright splash of water in the toilet. "You saying I'm a little chubby, Dirk?"

"I didn't say that. Not at all."

"Sure. And you've got a nice body—for a man your age."

Dirk scratched his head. "Won't you let me give you a compliment?"

"I'd love it. I just haven't heard one yet."

"I mean it. You don't have the standard beauty. You don't look half-starved, your arms and legs aren't stick-thin, you're not tall and statuesque and hard, you've got a bit of a stomach—"

"Watch it," Angela said warningly, but there was laughter in her voice. The toilet flushed; Dirk heard water running in the sink.

"You have some presence. You make people look at you and pay attention to you just by being in the same room. You make them turn their heads. You're . . . I don't know . . . confident, maybe. Sure of yourself . . ."

The brain engineer fell asleep at the controls of his train of thought. It derailed loudly as Dirk lost track of where he was heading with all this.

It didn't particularly seem important. He shut up and yawned.

Angela came from the bathroom holding a towel and a washcloth. "Lay back," she commanded. "Me and my big stomach are coming on the bed."

She knelt beside him. The washcloth was deliciously hot on his genitals. Dirk closed his eyes as she softly cleaned and dried him. "God, that's nice."

"Good. It's another little rite," she said quietly as she touched him. "I like doing it, and I like having it done. It makes me feel close."

"I'll remember it. Next time it's my turn."

She smiled, and for long seconds neither one of them said anything. They grinned at each other like idiots. Then Angela, chuckling, tossed the towel and washcloth on the floor and cuddled against Dirk again.

Sunlight crawled patiently down the wall. Pan snored in his corner. Angela's breath was loud in Dirk's ear. They lay in that state of oblivious contentment lovers sometimes find, wandering in the imagination over breasty mountains and fleshy pillars, tiptoeing around pools of reflection with the shirttails of ego comfortably untucked from the pants of caution.

Something splashed in the pool. A tentacle reached over and tugged at his trailing ego.

"Why *did* you follow me to New York?" Dirk asked languidly.

That woke Angela. Pan snorted—nothing ruined a good sexual interlude like questions.

Questions were the province of Aphrodite, and Pan had no affection for the goddess who wanted to infect basic lust with love. Questions demanded answers; answers demanded trust and understanding, not passion. Sex didn't need anything but two healthy and horny bodies; love was the emotion that asked questions.

Sex was pure unthinking rut. Love was physical attraction blended with friendship. Aphrodite insisted that sex was far better when alloyed with love, but Pan wasn't so damn sure.

Love might make sex better, but love hurt more, too.

When the moment was over, sex just pulled on its pants and left. When *love* left, it had to pack its bag and have a scene. Love always left behind empty drawers in the soul.

Besides, you had to *work* at it.

The old god sniffed and disappeared back into vapor. This wasn't going to be any fun to watch.

"I knew you'd eventually figure out the question," Angela said.

Dirk frowned; actually, he'd been fishing for compliments, and already he didn't like the feel of what was on the end of his line. Angela's face was too serious.

"What question? The important one you said I hadn't asked?"

"Yep. That one." Angela sighed. She pushed herself upright, went into an effortless half lotus. "You want this straight or sugarcoated?"

Dirk pulled himself away from the sight of her body. This didn't sound good. Didn't sound good at all. "You twist me into knots, you know?" he began, but she interrupted.

"You're going to think I'm crazy, Dirk. Nuts. Is that what you want to hear?"

"It was just a simple question. I didn't need a dissertation." (Love always had to talk, too. Pan could have told Dirk that if he hadn't already left.)

"You wanted me to say I followed you because I couldn't stand to be away from you. You wanted me to say, 'Dirk, I realized that I couldn't live without you. I love you too much to be without you.' " Angela's emerald gaze bored into him; he found he couldn't look away and he couldn't lie. He felt his cheeks blushing. "Isn't that right?"

"Angela—"

She smiled sadly. "Well, it's partly true. I *did* miss you."

Dirk began to feel hope. Then she shook her head and continued. "You didn't understand what you were seeing when you came by my apartment that last night in Cincinnati. You won't understand this either."

"This is New York," Dirk said. "Next to California, this is nut heaven. Sure I'll believe you. Why not? Hell, last night the *Post* had an article about a man-sized killer dinosaur stalking the streets, and another about some nut wanting to start a chain of drive-in funeral homes. Some occult ritual isn't going to faze me at all."

"It's true," Angela said softly.

"Huh?"

"The dinosaur. The beast. I've seen it."

That was patentedly ridiculous. Dirk started to laugh, then suddenly realized that Angela was absolutely serious. The laugh trailed off into a cough. "C'mon, Angela. . . ."

"It's true. You remember Theopelli? You remember the ceremony you interrupted? The bowl? It took two days, but I managed to make a portal. Through it, I saw an apartment in New York. I looked into a room with a mage and the beast, and beyond it was another portal with a man or woman standing beyond it. There was enormous power being expended by all of us. I couldn't hold it very long, but I knew the answers were here. So I would have come here anyway, Dirk. It was more important for me to come here for that than because you were here. That you *were* here only made the decision much easier. But if they'd been somewhere else, I would have gone there."

"So I'm kind of an . . . afterthought." Even coming from him, the word hurt.

"No," Angela answered flatly.

She kept staring at him. Dirk rubbed his arm nervously. *Schmuck. You had to ask, didn't you?* "You know, it feels really weird to be sitting here naked talking about this. Why don't we get dressed and go out for break—"

"Dirk." Her hand stroked his cheek. She forced him to look at her. "I'm sorry. But you asked."

"You read too many fantasy books when you were a kid back in Illinois or wherever."

"I'm not from Illinois. I'm not from anywhere you know."

"Right. You're actually Shirley MacLaine and in a previous life you were Cleopatra or maybe Nefertiti. Both."

"Dirk, stop it. I'm from . . . well, a world very much like this. I've been away so long that the memories don't even feel real to *me* anymore, but it's true. I'm just not sure how to explain it to you, and there's no way to tell you just how important all this is to me."

"My God, Angela, you say that like I'm supposed to think that's more rational. This is ridiculous. This is *National Enquirer* material."

"Believe it. I knew you then, Dirk. I was in love with you there, too—you or someone very much like you."

Dirk pushed off the bed and strode angrily around the room. "You got pictures to prove any of this? Postcards? Hell, show me your levitating license. . . ."

In the middle of the tirade, her words finally penetrated. He stopped. "In *love* with me? Too?"

Angela nodded. "Yeah," she breathed. "In love with you."

He knew what he was supposed to say. He opened his mouth. "I—" he began.

"Don't," she said. "Don't say it just to be saying it. You're not sure; I can tell. I know this is fast. Sometimes that's the way it happens."

"I don't believe any of this," he said.

"I didn't ask you to. All you have to believe is the last part. Dirk, when I sent you away, it hurt me terribly. That's what told me how important you were to me."

"It hurt me, too."

Angela smiled, but there was weariness and sadness in her face. "Come here," she said. She stood up as he approached and molded herself against him. The kiss was first soft and tentative, a brush of lips. She drew back and looked at him. "You're frightened," she whispered, "and a little angry."

Dirk shrugged. Angela kissed him once more, and he felt all the irritation beginning to drain away. She tilted her head back; Dirk took the invitation and leaned down. This time the contact was longer, her lips soft and moist and full, parting with a hush of hot breath.

They pulled away simultaneously for an instant and then she clung to him with tightening arms, head against his chest. The catch in her breath almost seemed like a sob. "Angela?" He sighed and stroked her hair.

But when she looked up at him, she had somehow put away the emotions. She smiled, and if Dirk detected a certain masklike quality to her face, he chose not to notice.

Her hands were doing fascinating things at his groin. A part of him whispered that she was doing it deliberately to distract him, to stop him from talking about her past anymore, but it was a very small voice and easily drowned out.

"Let me show you how I got my levitation license— just so you know," she said. She slid down his body to her knees and smiled at him impishly. "Afterward, we can talk."

He didn't even notice when, afterward, they didn't.

The Reverend Abel C. Henderson's rooms didn't smell of sex. They held the fragrance of expensive cologne and cigars, of the remnants of last night's beef Wellington, of paste wax newly buffed on the hardwood floors.

The New York arm of the Church of Christ the Marvel had made excellent preparations for its founder's arrival in the city. The spacious apartments above the main chapel had been cleaned and polished, all the anemities had been laid out—the cigars, the meal, even a cut-glass snifter of Glenfiddich, for it was known that the supreme reverend had a fondness for an occasional glass of scotch.

It was heaven on Earth. Perfection.

Except in the room where Henderson kept Harold. That room smelled, well, of Harold-essence. Henderson's pet prophet was lolling naked on a couch covered with a white Persian rug. He was utterly wet, having just stepped out of a shower. Despite the shower, the rug was hopelessly soiled.

"Don't you *clean* yourself in there?" Henderson asked. "All you did was streak the dirt."

"I pretended I was standing in the rain. Only an idiot stands out in the rain, Abel. Turkeys drown in it. So I turned the shower off. It's not every man that can control the weather like that. It makes me feel omnipotent."

Henderson shook his head and puffed energetically on his cigar, wreathing himself in the perfume of Havana tobacco in self-defense and staring proprietorially out at the expanse of skyscrapers—the Church of Christ the Marvel owned a fair chunk of choice Manhattan real estate and a goodly number of influential politicians.

"We'll have seventy thousand people and more in Shea Wednesday night, Harold," he said. "Seventy thousand people paying to hear the word of the Lord.

That's omnipotence, or pretty close. I thought I'd start using your whore-and-sorcerer symbolism in the sermon I'll preach there; I'm still afraid it won't play in the south, but here . . ."

"Seventy thousand. Seventy thousand pious fools." Harold belched loudly. He turned on the couch, leaving a smear of moist dirt on the fabric that made Henderson wince. "There's a million wallets in the Naked City, but God knows where a naked person puts one. And Abel C. Henderson knows best how to pluck the green from those wallets. Praise the Holy Pickpocket."

"That green keeps *you* pretty damn comfortable," Henderson pointed out.

"I'm not comfortable," Harold said petulantly. He scratched his armpit. "I'm wet. I think there's bugs in here—I itched all last night. Besides, while you're making a few bucks, you're letting the important stuff go. She's still out there, Abel. The whore. She's out there and you haven't got her. They want to wreck us, Abel. They want to run us off the golden road to the Lord. You need to be heaven's police chief."

"Then convince me," Henderson said. He pulled over a chair and sat backward on it, leaning in toward Harold. The stubby cigar smoldered between his thick fingers, a ribbon of aromatic smoke coiling around Harold's head. "Tell me about how—now, how'd you put it?—that book of theirs 'holds all the power you'd ever dream of.' "

Harold made a face and coughed openmouthed. "Smoking's bad for you, Abel. You treat your lungs like a toilet, and they're hard to flush."

"I *know* that, Harold," Henderson said impatiently. "Quit trying to change the subject."

"It's the same subject, Abel. *Everything's* the same subject. You can't get away from it, even when your mouth smells like a week-old ashtray and your lungs are as black as the inside of a chimney. Abel, smoking was fine when it was part of a ritual, when it was a ceremony and a gift. Then it might have made some sense to take a bunch of dead plants, wad them up, and set them on fire so you could suck the smoke. But you're not doing it for the ritual, Abel. You're not doing it because it's part of the ceremony of life. To you it's casual—a habit and addiction. You slap the face of the old gods."

Henderson rubbed his forehead. There were times, he told himself, when having a pet prophet was a drag on the nerves. "What the hell are you talking about?"

Harold grinned at him with his ruined mouth. He scratched his pubic hair. "Can I convince you to stop smoking, Abel?"

"Hell no."

Harold nodded. He sighed, rose from the couch, and came over to where the preacher was sitting. He stood in front of Abel. Henderson, watching his face, didn't see it coming. Suddenly his right hand was warm and wet to the elbow, and Henderson could smell the sour tang of urine.

"*Jesus!*" he howled, dropping the cigar and leaping to his feet. "You *pissed* on me, Harold! Look at this suit—I'll have to change my clothes. . . ."

"You stopped smoking," Harold pointed out. He finished urinating on the floor, shook his penis to get rid of the last few drops, and smiled.

"Of course I did, you ass. What'd you think I'd do?"

"You admitted that you know smoking is bad for your health, but you wouldn't stop smoking until something nasty happened. I've also told you that it's important to find the woman, Abel."

"You haven't said why." Henderson gazed ruefully at his soiled sleeve and edged away from the spreading puddle on the floor.

"I don't *know* why, Abel. I'm a goddam *prophet*, not God." He was making a vintage Harold face, screaming now with spittle flying wildly, his long, unkempt hair flying as he gesticulated madly. "I get these fucking dreams and I interpret them as best I can but I don't *know!* Not exactly. I see change and destruction, Abel; fire and brimstone and all that Revelation stuff. I see the sorcerer, the whore, and I know they're out there waiting. I know that there's a book, a red book which can tell you how to read the future, and even how to change it. I know that you can gain power from it if you can read it. They're looking for that book, too. The last few nights there's been a hermaphodite, too."

Henderson was beginning to wonder if all this effort was worth it. Maybe Harold had finally gone completely round the bend. Maybe this prophecy was just as bananas as it sounded. He tsked softly. "What a shame. I used to have a hermaphodite once."

Harold wheeled about in midtirade, and his face beneath the stringy hand was almost comically sly. "Don't make fun of this, Abel. Think of what you could do if you knew how to predict the future. Think of knowing how to change the face of the world. Possess that book, Abel, and you will have *everything*. Think of the power if you knew exactly what was going to happen, if you knew exactly *how* to mold the future to your own shape."

Harold panted, sniffed, and wiped his nose with the back of his hand, leaving a moist trail across his right cheek. "But they're going to try to stop you. I know they're the portents of change, the vessels, and I know that *she*—the whore, Abel—is supposed to be with me. She's *mine!* And you, Abel C. Henderson, you are to be the world's new savior."

Harold was breathing hard, pacing the room. His bare feet stepped directly into the puddle on the floor. Heedless, Harold did a hard about-face and pointed at Henderson. "Are you going to wait until the whole fucking *universe* pisses on you before you find her and the book?"

Henderson looked from the twisted passion of his prophet to the soggy cigar on the floor by his feet. The ashes still trailed wisps of smoke.

Henderson sighed.

"Okay, Harold. Your point is taken. It's just a little hard to find someone when you don't know what they look like or where they are. If you could tell me their

The Abraxas Marvel Circus

names or what they look like, there wouldn't be any problem. A word to the mayor . . ." Henderson's eyes narrowed; he sniffed. He rubbed his chin thoughtfully. "Unless, of course, I can manage to make them bring themselves to me . . ." he mused.

A slow grin spread over Harold's filthy face. "You see, Abel. I knew you'd think of something. What is it?"

"Nothing much. Nothing very complicated at all," Henderson replied. "But I'll bet it works."

16: A Tossed Gauntlet on the Side

"Yes, sir, I do know that most people don't consider dying very funny. . . . No sir, I had nothing to do with instigating the story. The reporter just called. . . . Yes, I can appreciate the way people like me make everyone look at the business, but I don't see where drive-through funeral parlors . . . Sir, the use of Styrofoam coffins wasn't a *serious* suggestion. . . . Yes, I've noticed that business has fallen off. . . . I know a lot of my peers consider me a jackass, but you have to admit that I'm a handsome and articulate jackass—"

Ecclesiastes winced as the phone was slammed back on the receiver on the other end. "Dr. Jacobs, of the Guild," he said to Joan, who was examining the flowers in the front hall of the Remains to Be Seen. "He didn't seem to like the article in the *Sun* the other day."

Joan nodded, not really listening. She touched the silken petals of a rose, marveling at the texture. Herbie had skin like that—the Blind Cavefish boy. She heard Ecclesiastes pick up a copy of the paper from the lampstand by the telephone and rustle through the pages. "I can't say that it seems any worse than the other trash in here," he said. "But—"

Herbie's skin had been porcelain white and satin smooth, and his eyes had been startlingly pink. He had the trailer next to hers for over five years, and she could hear him scream in pain whenever sunlight snuck past the drawn blinds. Even bright spotlights blinded his sensitive vision. He'd stayed with Henderson until he was sixteen. One moonless night he'd simply run away. . . .

The rustling had stopped. Joan looked over at Ecclesiastes, who was dressed, despite the lack of any business in either of the two parlors of the establishment, in his customary outdated formal outfit, including white kid gloves. He was staring at the paper with a curious expression somewhere between bemusement and irritation on his half-Oriental face.

"What's you readin'?" Joan asked. "Them papers I give you for flowers? You figure them out?"

Her words seemed to shock Ecclesiastes out of his reverie. "No," he said distractedly. "Theopelli's mathematical shorthand isn't going to be decipherable. Not by me, anyway. As far as I can tell, they're notes toward a finished treatise which looks interesting. . . ." He smiled halfheartedly at Joan. "I was looking at an advertisement in the paper."

"Momma said you can't believe nothing you read, and it wasn't worth my time to learn how, so she didn't never teach me. Henderson said that people only believe half what you tell 'em anyway, so the bigger the lie, the more you get away with. Henderson claimed Herbie was raised by a fam'ly lost in Mammoth Caves for generations until they all had white skin and the sun burned 'em and they couldn't see nothing. That's what his ads say. Abel said no one'd believe the whole tale, but they'd still come to see just how much might be true. They did, too."

Ecclesiastes' lips were pursed tight. All his usual lightness seemed to have fled. His white-gloved hands crumpled the edges of the newspaper. "Henderson. Abel C. Henderson."

Joan grimaced. "The goddamn bastard," she agreed. "Lef' me to die."

"I don't believe half of this advertisement, either. Of if I do, I'm in deep psychological trouble," Ecclesiastes said. He looked so distressed that Joan came over to him. She patted his head the way she might a dog, shifting her wad of tobacco from one cheek to the other and pushing the ragged baseball cap back on her balding head.

"S'okay," she crooned. "S'okay." Her perception

jumped slightly. Ecclesiastes' shape melted into that of Herbie, sitting in a broken-down wooden chair, crying because a night under the lights in the freak tent had hurt his eyes. "Close them little pink eyes, baby. S'okay."

"Joan."

"S'okay."

"Joan!" The bark dragged her reluctantly back to the here and now. "Look at this." Ecclesiastes jabbed at the paper.

Meaningless black marks jumped under his prodding forefinger. "Uh-huh," she said. "Nice. 'S my favorite one to wrap flowers."

Ecclesiastes almost seemed angry. "Listen to me. 'The Hidden Sorcerer. The Beast that dwells with him. The Whore of Magic. The Hermaphodite. The Book in which the Future can be written. The Moment of Decision. The Most Reverend Abel C. Henderson, founder of the Church of Christ the Marvel, will speak on these mystical topics at his rally in Shea Stadium tonight.' "

Ecclesiastes set the paper down. His dark gaze fixed on Joan. "So what the hell's going on, Joan? You can't hit a person in the face with this much coincidence and not expect him to see it. You tell me Henderson used to run the carnie you were in. You give me Theopelli's notes—and the few hints he published about his late work said he called them the Destiny Theorems, and that's what I think they are. Then there's what I thought I saw in the lab the other night: the guy in the black robe; the alchemy set he had going in the apartment and the candles; that talking *thing* in the back; the naked woman. It was just my imagination, I thought. . . ."

Joan had begun trembling from the first mention of Henderson's name. The reality clutch in her head whined and slipped gears once more; Ecclesiastes and the foyer were suddenly liquid, insubstantial, overlaid with scenes from her past. She shivered, waiting for things to settle once more and to see where in her life she'd landed.

She began to cry, a girlish cry. They were in her and Betsa's trailer, the man and her. Alone. Outside, she could hear Henderson talking to Betsa. ". . . just leave me be, damn it! I can do what I want with her. She's mine; I paid for her."

"She's only twelve, Abel. She's too young." Betsa's protest was faint.

"She's old enough and it's about time she started earning her keep. Any way she can."

The voices faded as they walked away. Joan sniffed and stared at the man shyly. He sat in Betsa's chair, just staring at her. "You my daddy? Abel, he said you were. He said I had to be good to you and do everything you say 'cause you were."

"I'm not your daddy," the man said, but the answer seemed somehow wrong, jarring. The room seemed to shiver and nearly dissolve once again before settling.

"Betsa said you weren't my daddy, not really. She said it might hurt. You gonna hurt me?" Joan wiped at her nose and snuffled again.

"I'm not going to hurt you. No."

The trailer lurched with the words. Joan blinked and found herself back with Ecclesiastes. He gazed at her sadly.

"I want to see him," Joan said.

"Henderson?"

Joan nodded.

"Then we'll go," Ecclesiastes told her. "Tonight."

Joan wiped the last of the tears from her eyes. Her mouth was uncomfortably full of tobacco juice. She spat. "Thanks," she said. "I 'preciate it, betcha."

Ecclesiastes looked at the brown mess on the ceramic tiles with dismay.

"Well, at least you missed the rug."

"Alice!" Mundo roared.

"You bellowed, O Master Caleb?" the MindBeast answered from the kitchen.

She lumbered into the living room of Mundo's apartment cradling a thigh in her short arms. The thigh still had bits of blue stone-washed denim attached. Alice gave Mundo a needle-toothed smile and glanced down at the array of cards on the coffee table before the sofa. "I don't suppose this means that Alfred's finally found them? He seemed to find a lot of incentive in the fact you said I could eat him if he didn't have some results quickly." Alice frowned and shook her head. "That wasn't very fair, Caleb. After all, you haven't managed to do any better, and he's not exactly my type. Too stringy."

"I've been challenged," Mundo said, scowling darkly. "So has the Princess and the Adept who holds the papers. There's another player in this game: the High Priest. Take a look at this." He handed Alice a folded newspaper.

Alice peeled back a bit of denim wrapper and took a bite of the thigh. She chewed reflectively as she read.

"You should have expected it, Caleb," she said at last. "There had to be people from this world involved, too. All the old books hinted at it—someone from each of the Primes is involved in the Crux, every time. We're from one, the Princess is almost certainly from another. There had to be someone here, as well."

"I thought that would be the Adept, the ugly hermaphoditic thing."

Alice picked a string of muscle from between her teeth with a claw, stared at it, and popped it back in her mouth. "I have the feeling she's a rogue force, something the Crux has placed between us and itself."

Mundo sighed. In the dimly lit room, he was like a lost fragment of night. His dwarfish form leaned forward and scattered the cards with a grunt of disgust. "The cards say the same fucking thing," he said. "They show an active resistance, a new challenge, a gathering of forces. I need a beer."

"You've been here too long, Caleb," the Mind-Beast told him. "Caleb of Auremundo would have loved the challenge. He'd have laughed and started looking through some favorite spells. He'd have loaded up his staff with silver spells and headed out, cursing the whole time. You *do* still curse, don't you?"

"Fuck you. And I *have* been in the forsaken world too long. I hate it. I was ready for the challenge five years ago when I was sent. The Guild botched it, I tell you. I *told* Zee Cannelzu her crystals were out of calibration."

He flung himself back on the ragged cushions of the sofa. "Too fucking long," he muttered. "If they still *had* magic here, they'd sell it prepackaged, freeze-dried, and microwavable. It'd come in convenience packs with the surgeon general's warning label: 'Independent tests have shown that use of spells contributes to heart disease.' Disposable and biodegradable."

"So what are you going to do?" Alice persisted. "Besides the beer, I mean?"

"We're going to answer the challenge."

"A dwarf and a talking reptile might be a tad conspicuous."

Mundo glared at the MindBeast. Alice shrugged and took another bite of thigh.

"Just an observation," she muttered. "You don't have to take offense."

"Here's the paper. There's another article on the 'Dinosaur Murder' I know you'll enjoy. Though the reporter claims that it's really a big Irish setter gone mad. Seems it has fur, according to eyewitnesses to the last incident."

Dirk tossed the *Post* on the bed. It bounced once; the spreading waves toppled the deck of cards next to Angela. She'd spread out the black silk in which she wrapped her tarot, and several of the cards were laid out in a pattern across it.

Angela, engrossed, hardly looked up.

Seeing the cards again made Dirk feel edgy, even through the silly warm glow that seemed to come every time he looked at her lately. He remembered the unfinished conversation of the day before. "Listen, love," he said. "It's time we were heading for the club."

"You go on," Angela answered without taking her gaze from the cards. Then, as if realizing how cold she sounded, she glanced up and smiled absently. "I still need to get ready, Dirk. You go ahead. I'll be there before the first set; Stan said he'd save me a seat at his table."

"Right. You want to sit here and play cards some more."

He wasn't sure how that made him feel. He reached over the bed for one of the cards in the pattern: on the laminated surface, a dark-haired man in a strange cloak stood behind a table loaded with odd devices. The card seemed to intrigue him more the closer he looked at it. He closed his fingers to pluck it up . . .

. . . Angela slapped his hand away.

"Ow!" he yelped, frowning. "What the hell was that for?"

"No one else handles the tarot unless I'm reading for them. It dissipates the energy. I'd lose contact with the cards."

Dirk looked at his hand. The back was turning red.

"I'm sorry," Angela said. Her face had gone so ruddy as his hand. "God, I'm sorry, Dirk. I guess I shouldn't have done that."

There are moments when relationships totter. You climb up the steep slope of sex, across the moraine of trust, and up the cliffs of truth. At least once during that time, a ledge will crumble under your fingers and you'll hang there flailing over open space like Wile E. Coyote. Your next move will decide whether or not you wave bye-bye to the viewers and fall away into the deep perspective of the valley below until there's a little puff of dust at the bottom.

Poof.

"Kiss it and make it better," Dirk said.

The Roadrunner of Romance held out an Acme Inflatable Ledge; Wile E.'s flailing hand caught and held.

Angela sighed. She took his hand and bent her head over it. Her soft lips brushed his skin. "That better, love?"

"Much."

Dirk stooped down. Angela cupped her hand around his head and kissed him.

"Thanks," she said. "Thanks for understanding. That means a lot to me."

He nodded and touched her cheek. "See you later," he said. "I'll be waiting for you."

17: At the Old Ball Game

The holy radiance of the outfield lights shimmered in the brown smog. Out where Darryl Strawberry usually prowled, a stage had been set and there a thousand-voiced all-boys chorus filled the air with hymns instead of boos—the Mets were mired in a lengthy losing streak and had just dropped a doubleheader in Cincinnati. The infield was covered with rows of folding chairs seating those who had paid the higher admission to be on the grass closest to the stage. Their presence did little to abate Ecclesiastes' desire to vault the wall and run the bases.

His missionary mother, despite her American background, had had little interest in baseball, but his father had been an avid fan. Ecclesiastes had cut his first teeth to the sound of the Tokyo Giants' broadcasts, and Sadaharu Oh had been his father Yoroku's idol.

"Oh has mastery of *ki*, Ecclesiastes. He studied aikido so he could learn to use all his energy," Yoroku would say, sitting cross-legged on the tatami mats as the announcer's voice bounced over his father's small eighteen-mat dojo just off the main portion of their house. "Baseball is better religion than Christianity. Strike three; you go to hell."

"I *heard* that," his mother said from inside.

Yoroku chuckled and closed his eyes to listen to the next path.

"There's no way to figure a Holiness Batting Average. That's the trouble."

"The roustabouts used ta play baseball after they set up the tents," Joan said.

Ecclesiastes started, not realizing he'd spoken aloud.

The Abraxas Marvel Circus 147

"Sometimes I'd play with them," Joan continued, "but I was never no good at it."

She shifted the wad of tobacco in her right cheek to the left and spat in the aisle. There were audible sounds of disgust from the faithful around them. "At least you got the spitting down," Ecclesiastes noted. "You're all-star material with that. It's a start."

"Blasphemers," someone muttered from behind.

They were sitting along the third-base side, sixteen rows up from the field. They would have been great seats for a game—prime foul-ball territory, nice and close. The smell of stale popcorn and watery beer still remained in the park and the concrete under their feet was sticky. The chorus ended the hymn with a flourish of brass horns and prepubescent sopranos. The crowd applauded loudly, the pattering of hands sprinkled with "amens" and "hallelujahs."

"Speaking of ball games, the de Medici popes used to have the boys with the best voices fixed so they wouldn't lose their high range," Ecclesiastes noted. "Nipped them in the bud before the creative juices started flowing. It was considered a great honor for the family but probably wasn't a great deal of fun for the castrati in question."

Joan didn't answer, but the woman in the seat to Ecclesiastes' right gave him a glare, glancing up and down at the formal clothing and giving a disapproving sniff.

"You don't care for the tenor of my remarks, eh?" he told the woman with a grin, but any retort she might have made was drowned in the roar as the crowd rose to its feet. Henderson strode into view on the distant stage, the spotlights pinning him in a glare that his spotless white suit reflected back to the audience.

Henderson smiled beatifically to reveal teeth that would have graced any toothpaste advertisement, a Bible clutched in one upraised hand. He took a wireless microphone from an attendant.

"Bless you," his deep and vibrant voice boomed through the PA system, shivering the bleachers. "God bless you all."

The crowd roared their return blessing.

Alongside him, Ecclesiastes felt Joan rise to her sneaker-clad feet. Even through the crowd noise, he could hear the strange, ugly sound she was making deep in her throat, like an animal in pain. He turned; the expression on the stubbly, old man's face made his eyes widen. It was absolutely demonic. It was the flat, dangerous glare he'd sometimes seen on his father's face when he was engrossed in sword practice.

"Uh-oh," Ecclesiastes said. "I knew this was a mistake. I knew it."

"I have a message tonight," Henderson was saying. His voice was a thick, golden syrup. The tinny version Ecclesiastes had heard coming over his television speakers had been a poor sham. The man was good; there was a pull in his voice, a compelling sound of empathy and understanding. "The gift of the Lord came to me in dreams and revealed the Truth to my eyes. The Lord has told me that the signs are there for all of us to see. The forces of Satan have gathered. You see them, if you know where to look. You see them everywhere."

Henderson took a breath that shuddered in the speakers, and then he rolled in again, striding up and down the flank of the stage, his voice gathering speed and volume as he gesticulated with the Bible.

"You see them everywhere, I tell you. They're in the brazen flaunting of filthy sex on your television set every night. They're in the garbage filling your movie screen, in the obscenities that fill your books. They're in the 'New Age' nonsense, in a simpleton's belief in the power of crystals or cards or incantations. They're in the breakdown between the genders. The *Whore*, she is there. The *Sorcerer*, and *Hermaphodite*"—he screamed the words—"they are the signs of the final struggle."

He was impressive, Ecclesiastes had to admit. The man's voice was like an ice cube melting down the back of your shirt, and his cadence made you jump whether you believed the words or not. As Henderson stalked back to the clear acrylic lectern in the center of the stage, the crowd applauded him.

And as they quieted, waiting for him to continue, a loud, shrill voice cut through the night air.

"Henderson! You goddamn bastard! I'm not dead! You didn't kill me, you son of a bitch!"

Joan.

"Oh shit," muttered Ecclesiastes. Already, security was heading their way: blue-suited men with grim faces, walkie-talkies clipped to their belts, and suspiciously unholy bulges under their arms.

Henderson seemed to have heard Joan. He was peering through the lights in their direction even as he launched back into the sermon. "The time of decision is here. The Lord's hand is writing the book of the future. The time has come for each of us to say 'I am *yours*, Lord. I will do as you will. I will help.'"

"*'I will empty my pockets!' Tha's what you want the shills to say!*" Joan hollered back.

"Okay, old man. Let's go." The first security man's hand closed around Joan's arm under the torn windbreaker. Ecclesiastes, cursing inwardly, moved to intervene.

"Don't even think about it, buddy." The voice came from behind him. "Why don't you take your grandpa here and let decent people listen to The Man?"

The voice of Henderson thundered on. ". . . with your help and your prayers and, yes, your donations, we can win the Lord's battle. . . ."

"*Fuck you, Henderson!*" Joan bellowed.

"That's it," the security man holding Joan grunted. He pulled Joan away roughly. Ecclesiastes sighed. It was going to get ugly. He felt a hand on his own shoulder and wished he'd been a better student for his father. He gauged the room between the seats: *A quick turn, lock the elbow, toss the guy into the next row. . . .*

Joan grimaced, her face all scrunched up like she was about to explode in rage.

And the lights went out.

It was as if God had flipped the switch for Shea.

There was no noise—just that sudden, impressive blackness and an echoing silence from the speakers. The security men forgot about Joan and Ecclesiastes in the greater crisis. They listened intently to their earpieces and scattered. A slow panic was rippling through the stands. People were beginning to stand and look around, shouting. There were screams from those in the rest rooms. A few were already beginning to stumble toward the exits.

Ecclesiastes gaped.

In the faint light from the rest of the city, he could see Joan grinning, as if pleased with herself. "C'mon, 'Clese," she said calmly. "I told the bastard off, didn' I? He always hated it when the generator'd go in the middle of a show."

Sudden suspicion made Ecclesiastes hesitate, even as people began cursing and shoving, trying to get past the dam that was Joan and himself. If it hadn't been for that moment in the basement of the funeral home, the thought would never even have occurred to him.

"*You* did that business with the lights?"

"Sorta. Mostly it was that other guy. The dwarf, y'know. C'mon."

People surged after them as they finally began to move. From the stage, Henderson's mouth was moving, but you couldn't hear him at all over the crowd. The ushers were shouting for calm; security was trying to get people to stay in their seats. "Just a few minutes . . . Please . . ."

They pushed past and followed a small sidestream in the flood toward the field level "A" tunnel. As they entered the tunnel, the lights came back on with an audible electric snap. Henderson's voice could be heard once more, urging everyone to be calm and return to their seats.

Joan and Ecclesiastes found themselves alone in the tunnel. Ecclesiastes found that he had very little desire to return to their seats. "I think it's time for us to go," he said.

* * *

The taxi driver told her about the power outage as she got in the cab outside the hotel.

"Police radio said it was a real damn riot a few minutes ago. Alla power was out for a city block. Prob'ly some circuit let loose. You ask me, that Henderson should have ta pay for it, too. Preachers got money, every last one of 'em."

As she got out of the cab at Shea, she could hear singing from the field. The parking lots were still jammed; it didn't look as if too many people had left despite the problems. She went up to the gate guard.

"Reverend Henderson wants to see me," she said. "Use the phone and call him. Tell him I've come about the book. Tell Henderson"—she blushed slightly despite herself—"that the Whore is here to talk to him."

The security guard stared at her, but he'd obviously had instructions. He spoke into the field phone for a few minutes, still staring, gave her curt directions, and then waved her past the barricades.

No one else bothered her at all.

She had no idea how long this would take or what to expect. Part of her said that coming here alone was foolish. *You should have waited. You're not ready yet.*

But Henderson is here now. He must have the book. He must. The ad was too explicit to be otherwise.

Dirk was going to be pissed, that much was certain. Whatever happened, she'd be late at the club. She regretted that most of all; the last thing she wanted was to hurt Dirk again.

Certain things are more important, she reminded herself. *Remember why you were sent here.*

She knocked on the door and it swung open obediently. "Come in, please," a voice said.

She stepped inside. "I'm not going to mince words," she said as she entered. "If you have Theopelli's book, we've something to talk about. Otherwise, we're both wasting our time."

She turned around to face Henderson.

But it wasn't Henderson that shut the door. She'd seen the reverend's face in magazines. This was a filthy young man dressed only in a dirty loincloth, the front of which bulged conspicuously in her direction. He scratched at the matted hair of his chest and smiled.

It was about as ugly a smile as she'd ever seen.

"Hi," he said. "I've been waiting for you. I'm the Prophet Harold. I've had dreams about you. And now that we're introduced, wanna fuck?"

He came forward with his arms open as if he were about to embrace her. Angela sighed. She let him come within a pace of her, then held out her hand.

Something crackled and snapped like a blue-white lightning bolt. Harold yelled as he was flung three feet backward and up against a wall. He slumped to the floor rubbing his chest, where a burn mark in the shape of a handprint reddened the skin.

"Did you think I'd walk in here unprepared? Do you think I'm that stupid?" Angela said, shaking her head.

"You're gorgeous when you're angry," Harold said. "Your eyes flare like phophorus, your mouth twists and pouts. It makes me horny as hell. Let's dance the tango of love. Let's make the beast with two backs. Let's screw—though that's a bad metaphor. The motion's much more like a piston, don't you think? In, out, in, out." Angela doubted that he ever stopped babbling.

Harold started to get up.

"Move, and next time you're going to have to get your piston rebuilt."

Harold seemed to consider that. "I bet you fake your orgasms, anyway," he said sulkily. He grimaced and sat down again heavily.

"That's better. Now, do you have Theopelli's book?"

"The road map of the future? The atlas of paths? The coloring book of worlds?"

"Yeah. That one."

Harold shrugged. "No," he said. "Who's Theopelli, anyway?"

"Tell Henderson I'm sorry I missed him."

Angela strode toward the door. There *was* something here. Henderson—or at least this little weirdo—

knew more than she'd thought, but that skeptical part of her had been right. This wasn't the time. Already the little power she'd managed to hoard before coming here was fading. She needed to think this over, to plan, to do the proper rites. Then she'd come back.

The door opened for her. Four burly men in suits with gold crosses on their lapels pushed inside.

They reached for her.

Angela took out one too few of them.

Ecclesiastes steered Joan by the arm. Now that order was restored, the chorus was singing again. In a minute, Henderson would start in once more, and Ecclesiastes wanted Joan out of the stadium before that happened.

"What," Ecclesiastes said finally as they walked down the long tunnel to the exit, "happened back there?"

But it wasn't Joan who answered.

"She stole power from me."

Ecclesiastes was getting tired of voices from behind. He turned, very slowly, to see a dwarf dressed in a black robe standing at the upper end of the tunnel. He seemed vaguely familiar; Ecclesiastes was sure he should know him. With him was a thin man who seemed rather edgy and nervous. The dwarf frowned evilly at Ecclesiastes, then his somber gaze came to rest on Joan.

"I find that I'm very curious as to how she did it. She's left me very tired, and I thought I was protected against such thefts. But then I'm forgetting the polite introductions, aren't I? I'm Caleb Mundo. Unless I'm very mistaken, I'm also the Sorcerer our friend out there has mentioned. And this is the Hermaphodite, no? We have things to discuss. Alfred?"

The nervous man moved forward with Mundo's curt gesticulation, pulling a gun from his belt. It was obvious from the way he licked his lips and held the weapon that he was unused to it.

Ecclesiastes waited; the mistake came earlier than

he'd hoped. Alfred poked at Ecclesiastes with the snout of the weapon.

But Ecclesiastes wasn't there anymore. In the same instant, he had turned, his right hand dropping like a stone on Alfred's wrist. He grabbed, turned back with a quick hip motion, and with the movement twisted the joint. Alfred screamed and crumpled.

"Run!" Ecclesiastes shouted as he pulled the gun away from Alfred's fingers. He wasn't kind; he heard the forefinger snap under the trigger guard. "Run, Joan!" Joan was pounding away like a lumbering bear. Ecclesiastes raised the gun to keep the dwarf back.

Mundo scowled. He raised his hand, palm out toward Ecclesiastes.

Sparks exploded inside Ecclesiastes' head. He moaned, shuddering, and the sparks became a fountain of lava, bright and thundering and hot. Vaguely, he heard the gun clatter on concrete, then his knees buckled underneath him.

He slumped to the wall. The last thing he saw was the dwarf's face hovering over him.

18: Kansas City Without the Crazy Little Woman

Angela hadn't shown up by Jay's sound check. She still wasn't there when Dirk and Kyle went backstage to list the songs for the first set. Her chair at Stan's table was all too visibly empty when Savage romped onto stage to begin the first set.

Dirk didn't know whether to be worried or concerned. He settled for simply pissed.

"A romance is boring without a little mystery, Dirk," Jay said through Dirk's stage monitor as Dirk strapped on his bass. "You'd stop paying attention to her if she was always there."

Dirk glared up to the balcony where the soundman sat, and flipped him a quick finger.

Dirk's irritation actually seemed to work well with the group. Savage sizzled. Dirk had a manic, sour energy that drove the band and spilled out into the crowd. The club was once again packed, dancing and shouting and applauding after each number. Several of the local groupies had picked up the words to the songs; they sang along to their favorites. Stan seemed pleased; he gave them a thumbs-up sign after the first set. Dirk nodded and went backstage to change his sweat-soaked shirt and towel his hair.

Angela's chair was still frustratingly empty.

"Call her," Jay suggested when he came backstage. "That would seem the logical thing if you're worried."

"Thank you, Mr. Spock," Dirk grumbled.

"I could try to dig up Mikhail." Jay shrugged, deadpan. Stan's pyrotechnics expert hadn't returned to the club since the first night when he'd torched Dirk. "Maybe a little sacrificial hair burning—"

"Jay . . ."

"Hey, it worked before." He held up his hands to Dirk's stare. "Okay, I'm going back to the board now."

A waiter passed a note to Dirk from the owner of the club at the beginning of the second set. Dirk scanned it quickly.

> There's an old guy selling flowers in the club. Sometimes he sings "Kansas City" with the bands. It's okay if you want to let him. The crowd usually likes it. Your choice.

Dirk glanced up. There was an old man standing at the edge of the dance floor looking at him expectantly: a day's growth of beard, rumpled old clothes under a windbreaker, a Mets baseball cap pulled low over his balding head, a crumpled cardboard box full of carnations in his hands.

Dirk shrugged and passed the note back to Kyle. Why not? Angela wasn't here; he didn't particularly feel like playing, and it might be fun. What the hell. Dirk waved to the guy.

"Hey, we have a special guest for you tonight," Dirk proclaimed mockingly into his microphone as the old fart put the battered flower box on the edge of the stage and heaved himself heavily up. As the crowd whistled and applauded, Dirk leaned over to him. "What's your name?"

The guy mumbled something that sounded like "John." He had breath that could wilt steel. Dirk handed him the mike apprehensively, noticing that the man had oddly dainty hands once you looked past the dirt and the cracked fingernails.

"John," Dirk said to the audience. "John the Flower Man."

He turned to Kyle and Lars, waved to Jay up at the soundboard. " 'Kansas City' in G, okay? Just follow him best we can. Alf, you ready? One, two, and . . ."

They swung into the intro to the old blues tune, upbeat. Dirk expected this John character to fluff it like most amateur singers. He'd miss the first measure, start in a half-beat late and in a totally different key from them. He'd flounder around, forget half the words, and they'd end up in a musical train wreck with a good laugh at the fool's expense. Dirk rolled his eyes at Alf, who winked back. The intro riff descended to the start. . . .

John was right there. On the beat, on key, and with a surprisingly strong voice only a little muffled by what Dirk belatedly realized was a wad of chewing tobacco in his mouth. No wonder his breath smelled like a wet cigar. John swayed like a punching bag as he sang, his eyes closed.

"Shit, the guy's not half-bad," Lars stage-whispered to Dirk, strumming lightly on his Stratocaster. "But I'm glad he's on *your* mike." Lars laughed and moved across the stage.

They let him go alone the first verse, then Dirk and Kyle added impromptu background vocals the second. At the end of the second verse, John whirled around, snapping his fingers and shouting "Take it!" to Lars. The crowd screamed with him, cheering and laughing; Lars obliged them with a verse of screaming guitar licks. The band charged into the third and last verse, and John led them perfectly into a drum-flailing climax. John waved Alf on with a raised hand, let loose a surprising James Brown screech, and brought the hand down to silence and then thunderous, laughing applause.

Even Dirk grinned. It was camp, but it was good.

The old guy applauded with the audience, smiling shyly, then picked up the box of carnations.

"Now buy my flowers," he said, his voice gravelly now, though Dirk caught a hint of some of the odd delicacy of his hands in the soft voice. "Three dollars, cheap."

John hopped down from the stage. People gathered around the pudgy old man—the flowers were quickly gone, all but one bunch. That newspaper-wrapped bouquet John extended to Dirk.

"Here. Free to you," he said.

"You don't have to do that, John. Go ahead and sell 'em to your fans."

"Name's Joan, not John." The stubbled wrinkles folded into a frown. The back of his—well, maybe *her*—hand smeared tan juice across the tree-stump landscape of a cheek. Dirk could almost see the femininity in the eyes, the mouth. Maybe it *was* Joan, after all. Whichever, the face was suddenly very serious as it looked at Dirk. "You need flowers, betcha."

"Why's that?"

" 'Cause," Joan said. "They make you 'member me when you find your girlfriend's gone."

Lars overheard the last part; he guffawed. "Yeah, Joan's just the woman for you, Dirk. Keep her in chaw and she's yours forever. Bet she's a great kisser." He cackled.

Dirk scowled. "Shut the fuck up," he said. "Keep the flowers," he told Joan curtly, and started to turn away.

Joan shook her head. "Nope. You need 'em," she insisted. "When she ain't there, you come to me. 'Portant."

"Yeah. Right."

Lars, Kyle, and Alf all hooted in the background. Dirk wished passionately that Joan would shut up. He started to introduce the next song, but Joan reached up and grabbed his sleeve. Her face had a somber, almost scolding expression. "Very 'portant. Henderson's got her, prob'ly. You love her, right? You remember this, right?"

Her face was so intense that Dirk could only nod.

As if satisfied by that, she let go and her face crumpled back into an expression like a vacant lot. "You should see Betsa," she told Dirk. "She eat live chickens at ten o'clock. Good show. Feathers everywhere." She winked at him lecherously as the band howled. Joan walked away, whistling and still carrying the empty cardboard box.

For the rest of the night, the foam sheath over his microphone smelled like the bottom of a spittoon.

As his key clicked into the lock of the hotel-room door, Dirk felt a sudden premonition of something wrong.

He hesitated. The rest of the guys were already in their own rooms. If he went to get them, they'd only laugh. Dirk sighed. If there *was* an intruder, the bundle of carnations in his hand would be a useless weapon unless the guy had some horrible allergic reaction and went into an asthma attack. *Take that, you bastard, and I hope you wheeze to death.*

Dirk turned the key.

He wasn't certain whether he wanted Angela to be there or not. He wasn't at all sure how he felt about her. It was all too complex, and the hours at the club hadn't helped to sort out the feelings. There were shades of everything from love to anger to fear.

Besides, the feeling of *wrongness* wouldn't go away.

Beyond the wedge of light from the hallway, the room was black, the curtains drawn. It was deathly quiet . . . no, Dirk corrected himself. Not "deathly" quiet. Just *very* quiet. Dirk thrust the carnations into the room like a sword, waved it about. Nobody shot at it.

"Hello?" he called into the darkness.

The darkness didn't answer. "Turn on the light, idiot," he whispered to himself. "You'd think you were in a bad teenage slasher movie."

He flicked the switch to the right of the door and prepared to jump.

There wasn't a mutilated body on the bed. There wasn't a maniac wielding a butcher knife. There wasn't much of anything. Dirk pushed the door open gingerly and stepped inside. He kept the door open with a foot.

A black lace bra was lying across the top of the bureau, but it had been there when he'd left. The door to the bathroom was open and the mirror on the door let him see the whole room; he couldn't see anyone in there at all. The newspaper he'd bought was spread open on the bed.

"Angela?"

No answer. Dirk let the door close. "Shit," he said. He tossed the bouquet on the bed.

Feeling like a bad imitation of Philip Marlowe, he made a quick survey of the room. Angela's clothes were still in the drawers, an assortment of blue jeans, T-shirt tops, and loose cotton blouses and skirts. The cloth backpack she used for a suitcase was still behind the bathroom door. The room was neat and undisturbed. The pottery bowl and her tarot cards were both still where they'd last been placed. He couldn't imagine Angela leaving permanently without those two items.

Not a chance. She intended to come back here.

"No sign of foul play, Lieutenant," he muttered. "Not a clue anywhere." No lipstick-scrawled plea on the mirror, no note propped up against a perfume bottle. The desk clerk, when he called, had no messages from her.

The sick sense of unease snuggled into his stomach like a vulture.

It was as if she'd been reading the paper, got up from the bed, walked out, and vanished. *Poof.* Without even Mikhail's puff of smoke.

Dirk looked around the room once more, then, curiously, glanced again at the paper. The bunch of carnations lay there shedding dry petals, but something nagged at him. He looked more closely.

"That's odd," he said, and unwrapped the stems from their newspaper vase. He unfolded it, shaking his head. Joan's words came to him unbidden. They echoed mockingly.

You need flowers, betcha. They make you 'member me when you find your girlfriend's gone. Henderson's got her, prob'ly.

The page Angela had last read and the page Joan had used to wrap the carnations were the same. A half-page ad dominated the spread. It was outlined with an intricate geometric border, the boldface words spread out in plenty of white space.

The words leaped out like raking claws.

> The Hidden Sorcerer.
> The Beast that dwells with him.
> The Whore of Magic.
> The Hermaphodite.
> The Book in which the Future can be written.
> The Moment of Decision.
>
> The Most Reverend Abel C. Henderson, founder of the Church of Christ the Marvel, will speak on these mystical topics at his rally in Shea Stadium. 9:00 P.M. tonight.

The vulture inside clutched entrails and pulled. It began to feed.

"This can't be," Dirk told himself. "She's just out. She was late getting to the club. She'll be back any minute and I'll feel like an ass for thinking what I'm thinking."

But it was four in the morning, too, and he'd stayed at the club extra long just in case she finally showed up. For lack of a better idea, he called the desk again. "This is Dirk Masterson in Room 3818. I know she didn't leave a message, but did anyone at the desk happen to notice what time the woman I'm sharing the room with left?" He described Angela; he knew they'd know her—he'd seen them watching. Angela always had that effect.

"Just a moment, sir," the desk clerk said with an aggravated and put-upon tone. He came back a few minutes later. "The bellman said that he remembers her leaving about nine, sir."

The vulture cackled. It swallowed. "Thank you," Dirk said tonelessly, and hung up. He sat on the bed, staring.

When she ain't there, you come to me. Important.

"No," he said again. "It's just too damn weird."

He could just see himself stalking the streets of New

York, asking everyone if they'd seen an old man named Joan selling flowers.

On the other hand, he could toss the paper in the waste can and go to sleep. Maybe she'd be back in the morning.

Maybe.

Dirk sighed. He picked up the phone and called the desk. "This is 3818 again," he said. "I'd like to leave a message for my roommate. Tell her that if this had something to do with the damn cards, I'm going to burn them and break the bowl when I get back."

He put the key to the room in his pocket and left.

part three

"Nothing will ever happen elsewhere that does not also affect you."

19: The Fool, Reversed

His mother was wearing a priest's Roman collar and nothing else.

This was just a little strange, not only because she was usually an overly modest person, but also since it seemed to be snowing inside the little house near Osaka. She'd also been dead for nearly fifteen years.

"The Book of Ecclesiastes concerns itself with the purpose of our life here on Earth," she was telling him, heedless of the cold drifts piling up on her shoulders. "It admits to the existence of a divine plan. That's why I named you after the book."

"Right, mama-san," he answered. " 'A time to kill, a time to heal; a time to weep, a time to laugh.' I've listened to the Byrds, too. Don't you think you should put on a kimono?"

She leaned down and patted him on the cheek. Under the priest's collar, her body was that of a ripe young woman. Snowflakes swirled around her; the shoulder drifts avalanched over her breasts. They were very nice breasts, with perky little erect nipples, the skin puckered up around the twin summits. The sight made Ecclesiastes distinctly uncomfortable. Mothers weren't supposed to be objects of sexual attraction except to Freudians.

"Ecclesiastes," she was saying, "please don't be impertinent. You talk as if you don't like your name."

Her breasts swayed in front of his mouth. He wanted to reach out with a tongue and draw them softly in.

He decided to close his eyes instead. "Mama-san, don't you realize that names are important? Do you realize what school was like for me? Ecclesiastes Mitsumishi—I was the butt of jokes from both the American kids *and* from the Japanese. 'Hey, how's your brother Deuteronomy? I hear Exodus ran away from home.' You think it's a coincidence that I act a little odd?"

His mother was still patting his cheek: right, left, right, left. His cheek was beginning to sting. He opened his eyes again. The snowflakes swirled in spiral patterns around her.

"Albert Einstein, mama-san," he persisted. "You think he'd have come up with the Theory of Relativity if his name was Revelation Yamaha? No, he'd've invented a combination CD player and food processor. Would John Wayne still have had that macho image if his name had stayed Marion? Jeez, mama-san, a person's name and personality are cause and effect."

The patting stopped at that. Thunder growled around the peak of Fujiyama, which seemed to have moved very close to their house. The snowcapped volcano looked like a breast, too.

"You don't talk to your mother that way," his father said. He was wearing a *dogi* top as if he'd been practicing aikido, but his legs were in stone-washed blue jeans. Plastic Groucho glasses hung from his nose; his feet were in oversized clown shoes. "You owe her respect for giving you your very life."

He slapped Ecclesiastes hard across the face with a rubber chicken. Ecclesiastes' head rocked from the blow.

Which was very unlike Yoroku Mitsumishi. His father was a contemplative man who had never in Ecclesiastes' experience hit anything with a rubber chicken—or anything at all. On the mat, he had the ferocity of a wolf; off it, he was a lamb. Ecclesiastes wanted to rub his cheek but somehow he couldn't move his hands. The snow had turned to harsh, whispering sand driven by a hurricane wind. The abrasive stuff scoured the flesh from his father's face, leaving behind a grinning skull. The Groucho glasses, somehow, managed to stay on.

The ludicrous image bothered Ecclesiastes enough that he opened his eyes.

"That's enough, Caleb. He's coming around."

The reality—as it sometimes is—was worse than the dream. Ecclesiastes was looking at one of the darkest and dingiest rooms he'd even seen. It looked like a hotel room where you'd find pornographic books under the mattress and used condoms under the bed. The carpet was threadbare and appeared to have been cured for months in old Coca-Cola. The walls clung grimly to forty-year-old wallpaper faded to the color of old newspapers. All around the room there were candles, most of which had left small, shiny mountains of wax on the furniture. The furniture was Early Salvation Army.

Worse, he remembered it. This was the place he'd seen through a phantom hole in his lab wall.

Suddenly Ecclesiastes wasn't so sure this was reality after all. He seemed to have dropped back into Joan's fantasy again. Okay, he told himself, you've ascended from dream Japan to roach heaven, and you're tied to a rickety chair in the very middle of it. That was understandable; dreams did things like that.

He wasn't alone with the bugs, either. The dwarf Caleb Mundo stood with his arms akimbo in front of him. Alfred was huddled on the sagging couch, cradling a splinted hand in his lap. "I'll wake him up good. The bastard broke my damn finger."

The sight sparked a minor epiphany. Caleb Mundo and Alfred: they'd been in Joan's hallucination, too, before they'd shown up at the ballpark. Ecclesiastes tried to convince himself again that he was still unconscious and dreaming, but then he remembered Mundo raising his hand and gesturing. The pain he'd felt then had been very, very realistic.

Hallucinations that hurt deserved a certain respect, at least for the time being. He wasn't going to acknowledge they were *real* quite yet, but he'd give them his attention for a little bit.

So this was Henderson's Sorcerer. And the Beast that dwells with him . . . ?

"Quit whining, Alfred. At least you're still material," said a voice from across the room. There was an apparition there, like a pygmy Tyrannosaurus covered with a golden red fur pelt—a dinosaur through which Ecclesiastes could dimly see the outlines of the furniture behind. "This isn't fun at all, Caleb. You nearly lost my corporeal existence entirely."

"Give it a rest, Alice," Mundo growled. "How was I supposed to know she could do that?"

"She came close to sucking you dry, and then you let her get away," the dinosaur's ghost continued. "I thought you were better than that. My hands can't quite hold on to anything, and I'm getting hungry. How long is it going to be before you can stabilize me again? It hurts just to project enough to talk."

"So shut up."

"Caleb—"

The dwarf grimaced. "I don't know. A day or so. I'm tired. I had just about enough left to take out our friend here."

"In a day or two, I could get famished and very irritable."

"A little fast never hurt anyone. Think of it as purification."

"Easy for you to say," Alice said, sulking. "You're an omnivore."

"Nobody cares at all about me," Alfred moaned from the couch.

"I set the finger for you. If it still hurts, take some aspirin." Mundo turned to Ecclesiastes. Up close, his face looked worse than Ecclesiastes recalled: pocked, greasy, and folded.

"What are *you* to her?" Mundo asked, his face very close to Ecclesiastes'. There was a mole at the tip of Mundo's nose with a short brown hair planted in it like a flea's flagpole. It waggled at Ecclesiastes; an accusing finger.

For a chimera, a trick of the mind, he had awfully fine details, right down to oily pores. This was not looking good.

"I've seen you before," Ecclesiastes said. His throat

was very dry. That also wasn't a good sign. He never remembered having a sour throat in a nightmare before. This was altogether too realistic. "That night, you were the ones beyond the wall."

"Yes." Mundo's voice was a dry hiss. "Again, who are you, and what are you to the Adept?"

Ecclesiastes struggled against the ropes tying him. Whichever one of them had done it had earned his Boy Scout knot-tying merit badge. His circulation was effectively cut off; he could barely feel his fingers. His hands felt like two lead ingots glued to the ends of his arms. About all he could do was knock himself and the chair to the floor, but he didn't particularly see what that would accomplish other than giving himself a headache.

Mundo watched Ecclesiastes' brief struggle with amusement. "You'll pardon the bonds," the dwarf said, "but I'm really too exhausted to hold you with my mind. I've had to resort to crude physical methods. Now, the same thing applies to my questions. If I were stronger, I'd simply take them from you. Since your friend has used up my current store of power, I'll have to resort to painful crudity if you insist on persuasion. For instance, I'm certain Alfred would love to pay back the debt of his broken finger with, ahh, a certain amount of interest."

Mundo smiled, looking at Alfred and then back at Ecclesiastes.

"Yes, you see," he continued, almost genially. "He's even eager to do it. Now then, I seem to recall that I asked your name."

Ecclesiastes, looking at Alfred and Mundo, tried to decide what his father would have done in the same situation (granted, of course, that any of this was at all real . . .). Yoroku might not have been a violent man, but he had a lot of the old samurai mind-set in him. He seemed to accept pain stoically and took the Japanese concept of honor seriously. His father would have spit at Caleb Mundo and defied the dwarf to make him talk.

On the other hand, it hardly seemed worthwhile to defy what was probably a nightmare.

"My name's Ecclesiastes Mitsumishi," he said affably. "I own the Remains to Be Seen, the funeral home. I supply Joan with flowers."

Somewhere, ancestral spirits moaned in disappointment.

"I think you're leaving quite a bit out," Mundo purred.

"Hell, no one's got a name like that, Caleb, and no one in his right mind would name a fucking funeral parlor Remains to Be Seen, either. He's lying to you," Alfred added from the couch.

"Perhaps, perhaps not, Alfred. Look at him—no one in his right mind would dress that way, either. Mr. Mitsumishi?" Mundo leered at him.

"It's the truth. I'll swear it on a stack of my mother's Bibles—and she'd be pissed at you, Alfred. From what she said, she spent nine long months thinking very hard about my name. However, she'd have agreed with you about the 'right mind' part. You could look it up in the phone book, but I doubt you've left one lying around in the illusion."

"One gets the impression that you're not taking us entirely seriously," Mundo said. "That's the trouble with your world. Anything out of the ordinary, you deny. Mind you, I do it, too. Sometimes I go to sleep and think I'll wake up back in *my* reality, in the world *I* left. Even Alfred sometimes amuses himself with the notion that he's fallen into a prolonged dream and will someday wake up back in Theopelli's house."

Ecclesiastes felt himself start involuntarily with the name. Mundo, watching him carefully, laughed. "I thought so. So you *do* know more than you've told us. You wouldn't have taken Joan to see this Henderson if you were just giving her the flowers she sells, and you wouldn't have protected her from me. You even known where Theopelli's last papers are, don't you?"

"No. I don't know what you're talking about."

I have one piece of advice for you, his father always

said. *Never, ever, get in a poker game. You bluff about as well as granite floats.*

"I'll be damned." Alfred had a phone book open on his lap. His splinted, bandaged finger tapped a page. "There *is* a listing, Caleb."

Mundo smiled. His gums were bright red and receding. "Well," he said. "Then I think we'll just go have a look there. Alfred, you'll come with me. Alice, please watch our guest."

"You can have him for lunch as far as I'm concerned," Alfred said.

Mundo reached into Ecclesiastes' coat pocket. The dwarf pulled out the ring of keys. He jangled them in front of Ecclesiastes.

With the touch, the last shred of disbelief Ecclesiastes had faded. The hand was all too substantial, and the smell of old sweat lingered on Mundo's black robes.

"Hurry back," Ecclesiastes said, suddenly very nervous. "We wouldn't want Alice to get too hungry."

"Run!" Ecclesiastes had shouted in the tunnelway at Shea Stadium. Joan had seen the Sorcerer there, looking as black-clad and evil as he had when he'd been doing card tricks in the Marvel Circus. Of course, then he'd been Majesto, Sorcerer Extraordinaire and Mystifier of Kings, and he'd also been much taller, unbearded, and fair-haired. Somehow Majesto had condensed and turned dark. But then, Joan had certainly seen stranger things. If Majesto had turned into a dwarf, fine.

Dwarf or not, he *was* Henderson's Sorcerer; she knew that without being told.

"Run, Joan!" The shout came again, and Joan peered at Gil the Living Skeleton, standing outside Majesto's trailer and wrestling with one of the roustabouts. She could hear Henderson's echoing voice.

Henderson was coming for her again. She ran.

Joan had already been confused by the night. Henderson and she had never truly parted company, not when Joan moved through each day with the living, talking phantoms of her past. Joan had no concept of time at all. Past and present—they were always there, jumbled and shredded in the Cuisinart of her mind.

But there *was* "new." There were people and situations she had never encountered before and she was aware of them. She'd seen Abel Henderson on the outfield stage in the harsh spotlights. She'd heard the people around her screaming for him and in her mind she knew this was a "new" Henderson. This was a Henderson outside her experience. This was a Henderson who lived in a reality beyond the moment when he'd dumped her along a deserted Alabama backroad.

Seeing the new Henderson had summoned each of his myriad ghosts. In one unending, tortured second of time, they wreaked on Joan every humiliation and indignity she'd ever experienced at his hands. The sheer weight of her anger and pain made her howl.

In that instant, in her head, she felt something split wide.

Somewhere in the maelstrom of rage, she'd seen Something Else. She had no name for it. This was also "new," hovering beyond the rift in her mind. It was like a throbbing, pulsing ball of lightning, palpable and dangerous. She reached out with her anger and touched it, and she felt the thing draining energy from all around her, like a baby suckling on the breast of the city's power lines. The globe of energy burned and crackled, and Joan whimpered. She wanted to throw the fiery sphere at Henderson but it was slippery and hard to hold. She grunted and cast it away from her as quickly as she could, arcing and spitting sparks.

It spun like a wild comet past Henderson and careened into the centerfield lightpole. Circuit breakers there reacted far too late to the surge.

She turned her attention back to the elusive "now" and found it dark and nearly as noisily confused as her own brain. She followed Ecclesiastes, who kept wanting to turn into Gil or Betsa, and when Majesto had confronted them, Gil (or was it Ecclesiastes?) had told her to run. . . .

Joan wasn't quite certain what had happened after that. Chronology was a tentative thing with her. It was hard to keep a sense of urgency when the present kept trickling through the fingers of her mind.

Routine asserted itself. At some point she'd realized that it was late at night, and at night Joan was used to taking a box of flowers and making the rounds of the clubs, singing if a band would let her, because when she sang she sold more flowers.

That was about all the cause and effect she could manage to retain.

She *had* sung, too. Some new band. It seemed more had happened then. The mind rift yawned wide and black.

Somethin' else. Somethin' 'portant. She touched her head with a grimy hand. *That hole's new, sure. All sorta things leakin' out, betcha.*

She glanced at the ground and found herself standing ankle-deep in red Georgia mud. It had rained the night before, and the wagons were bogged down. The roustabouts were milling around, trying to get the wagons unstuck.

Joan grimaced and rubbed her head under the Mets cap, wondering if she should help even while the mud coalesced into a cracked sidewalk once more. But her head hurt too much.

The mind rift had been only a tiny fracture when she'd seen the dwarf and the naked woman in 'Clese's basement, she was sure. But tonight had ripped it open entirely. It throbbed inside like a migraine.

Betsa rubs my head when I got headaches. I'll find her.

Joan looked around. She was still holding her carnation box and seemed to be standing outside Roosevelt Park. Betsa wouldn't be here. She looked west. The buildings of Manhattan were all wrong. Unusual skyscrapers were poking up from the rotten gums of New York like new teeth, rising even as she watched. A latticework dome raced overhead from west to east, capping the island and blocking the view of the murky sky. Roosevelt Park disappeared under a glass-and-steel octagonal building.

This was "new," too. This was nothing she'd seen before.

Hand in metallic hand, two robots walked obliviously by her, staring into each other's burnished, glowing eyes. Joan gaped, openmouthed, tobacco juice running down her chin.

Then, with a disconcerting stomach lurch like the first drop in the carnie roller coaster, everything settled back into familiarity. The buildings were the ones she was used to seeing. The dome had turned back into a greenish night sky. Joan wiped her chin and swallowed bitter saliva. She moved the wad of tobacco to the other cheek.

"John! Uh, Joan! Shit. Hey you!"

Joan turned, squinting myopically. "Betsa? I got this damn headache. . . ."

"Listen, I'm glad I found you. I have to ask you about what you said."

"I said I got a headache, Betsa. You rub my head, okay?" Joan took off the baseball cap and pointed to the dandruff-laden and scaly scalp below. "Here."

Betsa seemed downright reluctant to do as bidden, which wasn't like Betsa at all. But at last Joan felt fingers kneading her scalp and she sighed. "That's good. Thanks."

"You're welcome, I guess. Hey, about what you said at the club . . ."

"About my headache? Feels better, a little, sure."

"No, not about the headache, damn it." Betsa's voice was full of exasperation, and Joan peered at her. Betsa was frowning. Sometimes the raw meat Henderson gave Betsa was bad and she had stomach cramps. When that happened, Betsa was a little testy.

"You get maggots again?" she asked. "Tonight, I tol' Henderson he could get fucked, Betsa. Right out loud. How 'bout that?"

Betsa seemed confused. She stopped rubbing Joan's head, and Joan put her cap back on. Betsa shook her head. "You said that my girlfriend would be gone.

You said when I found that she was, it was important that I come to you. How'd you know?"

"You got a *girl*friend, Betsa? I didn't know you was no lezzy...."

"Oh, *hell!*" Betsa stamped her foot. The sun was coming up around the carnie. Joan could hear the roustabouts beginning to get things ready in the cook tent. They must've got the wagons free. "This is hopeless," Betsa said. "Look, just forget it."

Joan squinted. Betsa's face ran like a wax figurine in an oven and became someone else: a man with longish, brown hair and eyes that couldn't decide between blue and green, maybe about thirty or so. Memory dredged up a scene. "You were in the band," she said, pointing at the man who'd been Betsa. "I sang. 'Kansas City,' 'member?"

"Yeah. That's right. You gave me flowers."

Flowers. The mind rift throbbed, and Joan groaned in response. The hole was leaking again; there was just too much flowing out of it, visions like a hundred TV sets going at once on different channels and she couldn't hold it all, just try to catch pieces of it as it flew past. Joan gaped, bewildered, trying to cope with it all and make any sense of what she was seeing. It had never been like this before; this was "new," like too much today.

She tried to relay all the sights as they shot past her like bright meteors. "Henderson's got her ... she need you, but you can't do it alone ... you go with the Sorcerer and that weird thing he has, maybe ... Henderson, he's got the sheriff ... there's someone else with your girlfriend ... the dead guy, you gotta talk to him ... there's a book ... and a bowl...."

The mental TV sets sparked and went dark. The rift was just an aching black void again. Joan shrugged. "I sold all the flowers," she said. "Don't got no more. Sorry."

"I don't need flowers. What about Angela? You said there was someone else with her."

Joan shrugged. "I jus' told you what I saw. It's gone now. It hurts, too."

"The damn bowl. I'll bet you saw cards, too."

Joan surveyed the quickly fading images in her head. Already they were nearly lost. "Dunno," she said cautiously, scratching her chin. "Maybe. Pretty uns. Better'n the ones Betsa and me used. Betsa knew which were aces 'cause they got crinkled corners. We'd play poker, sometimes. Gil, he used ta get mad when we played 'cause Betsa cheated—"

"Right, right," the man said quickly. He frowned. "I should have figured it was the cards," he muttered, looking back at the city.

"People think you weird if you talk to yourself," Joan told him. "Bad habit, sure." She switched the tobacco to the other cheek again and spat on the sidewalk. She wiped her lips delicately with the cuff of her windbreaker.

"Right. And you're Miss Manners." He kicked at a concrete bench support. "This is stupid. There's no reason in the world I should be bothering with this. It's almost morning and I should be in bed."

"You love her, huh?" Joan asked unexpectedly.

The man looked startled by the question. He frowned and pushed his long hair back from his forehead. "Yeah. I mean, I think so. . . . It's all happened so fast."

Joan shrugged. Betsa used to read her stories late at night when the wagons were moving slowly toward the next town—fairy tales, mostly. In each of them, there was an implacable interior logic and a distinct moral obligation. The sound of Betsa's untutored voice and the creaking of the wheels over rough southern roads came back to her now.

It seemed to her to be very simple. "You love her, and she's in trouble. You gotta go rescue her. I'll help."

The man gave a bitter laugh. "You'll have to excuse me, but the only white charger I ever owned had a stick for a body. Besides, I have a gig to play, and how do I know that she didn't just walk out?"

Despite the sarcasm, his words resonated with the sound of Betsa's voice. The mind rift was throbbing again, like a live thing. Joan held her head in her hands. Scenes drifted by her again, and she plucked one from the flurry and examined it. "If she'da just left you, she'da taken the cards, the bowl, betcha."

"What?"

Joan had grabbed him by the sleeve, tugging at him desperately. "They still in your room, huh? We gotta get 'em. She'll need 'em when we find her."

"Wait a minute. . . ." The man pulled away from her, frowning. "I haven't said I was going to do anything yet."

Then he shook his head and shrugged.

"If Lars sees us, I'll never live it down."

20: Far Ago and Long Away

"I wouldn't eat you, really," Alice the MindBeast said to Ecclesiastes. Insubstantial or not, her breath still smelled like the garbage dump behind a slaughterhouse. Then a contemplative and very human frown flicked over her reptilian face.

"Unless you were already dead, of course," she added. "No sense in letting good food go to waste. People always seem to think I'm vicious, and I'm not. Really, I'm quite friendly. Alfred was just trying to scare you because he's scared himself."

Alfred did a very good job, Ecclesiastes was tempted to say. *I can understand his feelings.*

"That's very comforting," Ecclesiastes said in what he hoped was a pleasant tone of voice. The claws on Alice's handlike paws and the doubled rows of pointed incisors in her mouth didn't exactly inspire images of Disney-cute animals. "One shouldn't judge by appearances, I always say."

Alice nodded. "Absolutely. Couldn't have said it better myself." She peered sidewise at Ecclesiastes: his Victorian formal wear, the top hat, the dapper white gloves. "On the other hand, if you're trying to run a business, *you* might try dressing to the expectations of your clients. You'd probably make more money. That seems to be important here."

There is very little in life more strange than being lectured by the ghost of a furry lizard who sounds exactly like your father. "My clients are generally dead," Ecclesiastes said flippantly. "The way I dress doesn't matter to them."

Alice continued to stare. Her round, vertically slit

eyes didn't blink, which Ecclesiastes found distinctly disconcerting after a few moments. "All right," he conceded at last. He gave her a lopsided grin and tried to shrug—the ropes around him made the gesture impossible. "My clients are usually the relatives, and yes, they *do* care what I look like. Death shouldn't be so damned serious, that's all. I'm just trying to inject a bit of life back into death. It's fine to grieve, but you have to go on. By making the family and friends focus on me—even if they get hostile, which happens occasionally . . ." She stared at him. "Okay, *often*— I can begin the process of catharsis for the survivors."

"Intellectual double talk. Infantile rationalization," Alice scoffed. She waggled a finger in front of his face. "You're making excuses for your own problems. I suspect it's your own fear of death you're denying."

Memory: a flotilla of glowing rafts swaying gently through the night on the soft downstream current to the sea. Bearing away his mother's soul. His father watching calmly while a young Ecclesiastes raged. "Why aren't you crying? She's gone away forever." Yoroku shook his head slowly. "No one goes away, Ecclesiastes. They only go to a different place. What is the good of crying about that? There is nothing we can do about death. It simply is."

The words hadn't convinced him then; they were salt water in the raw open wound in his life.

He cast the memory away and scowled. "I'm not in the habit of discussing pop psychology with figments of my imagination. If you want to do something useful, you might untie me; I haven't been able to feel my hands for the last ten minutes."

"You're just angry because I hit too close to the mark," Alice retorted. "And I'm a figment of *Caleb's* imagination, not yours. *And* I can't untie you—even if I had the inclination, and I don't—because your friend has made me immaterial."

With a sniff, she returned to the other side of the room, where she busied herself puttering around a scarred kitchen table laden with vials and jars. Her puttering was pointedly useless: her clawed fingers kept slipping through the jars.

Mundo and Roundbottom came back after several minutes of awkward silence had passed. The dwarf was, if possible, in a fouler mood than before. He tossed the sheaf of notebook paper down on the coffee table and glared at Ecclesiastes.

"You lied to me," he said.

The sight of Theopelli's work dispelled the last shreds of the notion that this was simply a prolonged and very vivid nightmare. Ecclesiastes tried to smile disarmingly and failed. "Sorry," he said.

Mundo pounded the papers with a fist. "Look at them!" he shouted. "This is not science. These aren't incantations or alchemical formulae or anything at *all* useful. They're just mathematics. Garbage. Page upon page upon page." Droplets of saliva sprayed with each consonant.

"I could have told you that," Ecclesiastes said. "I didn't understand them myself. Now if you'll just untie me, I'll be going."

"You forget which world you're in Caleb," Alice said from behind the table. "The incantations of this world are written that way."

"It's *still* sloppy work," he insisted, then turned back to Ecclesiastes. Mundo tapped the pages. "Does the Adept understand this?"

"Joan? Hardly. She was going to use them to wrap flowers."

"Don't mock the Adept. She can do things I'd not thought possible."

Ecclesiastes remembered the hole in the wall of his lab and the last evening at Shea all too well. He hadn't even the slightest notion of mocking Joan at all. Her mind might be like a vase dropped on the floor and glued back together by a blind man, but she certainly had *something* he hadn't quite figured out yet.

Mundo was pawing through the notes, with Alfred peering over his shoulder. "That's them," Alfred said. "Yep. Them's the notes I was tellin' you about and you're going to pay me for."

"I wouldn't get your hopes up about that." Then Mundo peered quizzically back at Alfred. "How about you, Roundbottom? Do *you* know how to read any of this? Did Theopelli talk to you about his theorem, confide in you?"

Alfred shook his long head. "That old fart? Not a chance. He wouldn't even talk to the people that called him or wrote. How'd he use to say it? 'You could add the IQs of every last tenured professor and still not be able to join Mensa.' "

"It's useless, then." Mundo sighed. "We need Theopelli himself."

Alfred laughed. The sound was like a crow cackling in a tin can. "Right. The bastard's dead eight years now."

"That's not the problem," Mundo growled back. "Any decent sorcerer can remedy that little obstacle. If we were talking a half century or so, then we might have something significant. The problem is that the customs here are primitive and barbaric. I don't know what they might have done to the body."

Mundo's words found a resonance somewhere deep in Ecclesiastes' mind. Death not a problem? Death had been Ecclesiastes' obsession for years, and this dwarf dismissed it as a casual obstacle. Ecclesiastes felt such a rush of mingled emotions that he forgot about Joan, forgot about the fact that Mundo had kidnapped and threatened him. He began to speak, almost hurriedly.

"Actually, local regulations and individual preferences vary a bit. You don't *have* to embalm, but not everyone knows that. In modern embalming the blood is drained from a vein and replaced by Formalin injected into the carotid or some other main artery. That's simple enough. Cavity fluid is removed with a trocar and replaced with an alcohol-based preservative to keep the body from shriveling and the skin from turning brown as it'd do otherwise—"

Ecclesiastes stopped. Mundo was staring at him thoughtfully. "Well, I'm a mortician, after all," Ecclesiastes said. "And a fan of Theopelli's. So have some compassion and untie me before rigor mortis sets in."

"Ooh, flowers!" Joan exclaimed on entering the room. Dirk closed the door hastily behind her as she lurched to the bed and the carnations she'd given Dirk several hours before. They were visibly wilted.

"They need water," she said to him accusingly.

"Then they perk up, betcha." She held out the bunch to Dirk; the blooms sagged over her clenched fist.

"Yeah. Fine. Go ahead."

Dirk sat on the bed as Joan went into the bathroom humming. "You gotta make a decision," he said to himself. "You gotta figure out what to do."

Finding Joan hadn't made his situation any clearer for him. If anything, he was more confused now than he had been after finding Angela gone. He couldn't believe he'd actually brought this stinking street character back to his hotel room. He felt trapped, snared like a rabbit in some invisible mental netting.

Ever since you met Angela. Ever since she walked into that club. She fucking put a spell on me. Why me? All I wanted was to play some music, and if that didn't work, just settle down and teach history at some quiet university somewhere. I didn't ask for this weirdness. I didn't ask for it at all.

He looked at the *Post* on the bed, still opened to the Reverend Henderson's ad. He swiped his arm brutally across the coverlet, sweeping the paper to the floor with a sound like swift fire. Joan came out of the bathroom, leaving the water running. She'd taken off the windbreaker and rolled up her sleeves; her flannel shirt was half unbuttoned. Between the gaps of the buttons, Dirk thought he saw sagging feminine breasts.

"Here," she said, "I put 'em in water. Look good, huh?"

The old man—or woman, or whatever—had somehow found Angela's bowl, *the* bowl. She'd cut off the blooms (actually it looked as if she'd simply torn the heads from the stems); they floated in the pool of water. Joan balanced the bowl on the fingertips of one filthy hand.

"Pretty," she said.

Dirk lurched from the bed and snatched the bowl from her. "Jeez, be careful. If that thing's really as old as Angela said it is—"

That was all he got out. Dirk had a breath in which to think *I should have known*—before reality did a half gainer into the pool of floating carnations.

He had the same sense of being in another person's body that he'd had the last time he'd held the damn thing. He cradled the bowl, but his hands weren't the hands he was used to seeing. They were old, knobby-veined ones with arthritic joints. Dirk was staring down into the glazed depths of the bowl, and the flowers there were not carnations but tiny blossoms with delicate yellow petals and red veins. The water was fragrant with spices and puddled with droplets of pungent oil that held shimmering spectral colors. He pursed his lips and exhaled; the petals skated and swirled to the sides of the bowl. He bowed his old head over the bowl. (The hair falling in front of his eyes was stringy and bone white.)

There, in the rainbow depths, something moved.

Images formed, melted, coalesced again, then firmed and brightened. He was staring at a scene as if he were floating several feet above the landscape. Angela was there, along with a wild-looking young man accompanied by a portly, well-dressed older gentleman. There was a house behind them, a rambling and huge edifice set among palm trees.

A sense of urgency and panic filled him. He felt very afraid, and looking at Angela made him want to reach out and comfort her. Her face was troubled, and she hugged herself as if terrified.

"Angela," Dirk breathed, and the word rippled the water's surface. The scene wavered, the unknown mansion dissolved, and he was back in the hotel room once more.

He was looking directly into Joan's old, folded eyes,

and there was a sad understanding in them. "You see? 'Portant," she whispered.

"It was somewhere in the south, Florida maybe. . . ." Dirk shakily put the bowl down on the dresser. He didn't want to touch it ever again.

Someone knocked at the door. With the sound, some of the sense of urgency faded into irritation.

Angela, Dirk thought immediately. *She's back, and all this nonsense was for nothing*. He wrenched the door open with a melding of relief, concern, and anger.

Lars was standing there. "Hey, Dirk, we're heading out for break—"

Lar's eyebrows raised. He snorted. "She-it," he said.

"Hi," said Joan. "He's too tired, betcha."

Laughing, Lars looked from Joan to Dirk. "Oh, I'll just bet he is, too," he said. Lars slapped Dirk on the shoulder, struggling to keep his face straight. "Kept you up all night, did he? No problem, man. No problem at all. We'll see you later, huh?"

His amusement exploded in a braying guffaw. Chortling breathlessly, Lars headed down the corridor to the elevators.

Dirk stared after him, feeling the heat radiate from his cheeks.

Somehow, it made the eventual decision that much easier.

21: Fate's Accomplice

The subtropical sun could have used shades, so bright were its aching reflections from the wave tips of the Gulf. It gazed proudly over the baking white sands of the beach and applauded the heat ghosts dancing between the palm trees. This was a wonderful day for skinny-dipping or contracting a melanoma of the skin, depending on your outlook or the state of the ozone layer.

Angela, who burned easily, stayed in the grudging shade of a large beach umbrella. Those parts of her that stuck outside her terrycloth beach robe were liberally smeared with number-thirty sunblock. Harold, whose leathery and remarkably hairy skin seemed impervious to ultraviolet bombardment and whose feet didn't seem to notice the fact that hamburgers could have been grilled on the sand, frolicked buck-naked in the sunlight. His lack of clothing lent emphasis to the erection that lurched upward every time he glanced at Angela.

"Don't point that thing at me. It might go off," Angela told him. She knotted the robe tighter about her body.

As if grateful for her attention, his cock nodded its red-capped crown and bobbed stiffly upward a fraction of an inch. Angela had to admit that it was a moderately impressive sight, if one could ignore the body to which the equipment was attached.

Unfortunately, that was rather difficult.

"A man can't help these things, Angela," Harold said. "Testosterone flows like lava; the blood sloshes into erectile tissue; the testicles throb with rush-hour sperm jamming the sexual freeway. We were destined for each other. You'd have to expect that you'd make me hot."

It was the same line he'd given her since New York. At least so far all he'd done was expose himself. Angela had expected him to try to rape her the night before, had in fact resigned herself to the inevitability of the attempt. Henderson kept his pet prophet well protected, and the guards who watched Harold also were stone-facedly unconcerned with her. "She stays with Harold," was all Henderson had said during the quick flight south in his private jet. "I don't want her to leave the compound."

On the other hand, she didn't think they'd give him any help, and Harold she could handle—or *not* handle, as the case may be.

She half slept huddled in the corner of his room, listening to Harold's endless manic prattling, enduring his grossness and waiting. It had been one very long night.

Talking seemed to work best with Harold. In conversation, he seemed to pay less attention to her body.

"Tell me again how you think we're 'destined' to be together, Harold." He'd mentioned that several times during the night.

Harold grinned at her. He squatted in front of her blanket and plunged his hand into the sand, pulling up a fistful of white crystalline grains that trickled through his grimy fingers.

"I get visions," he said. "God reached in and stirred my brains with a cruel ladle. Head cheese. Brain pudding. Primordial soup. Everything's crossconnected now. *Zap!* I hear colors. *Zoom!* I smell the velvet. *Zing!* I taste the dark sound of a cello. And He also gave me the Sight. I dream the world. I saw your nakedness, heard your moans of passion, smelled your sweat, touched the soft folds between your legs, tasted your arousal. I saw us coupled together on the sand, your legs and arms wrapped around me as I plunged in and out, in and out, in and out, in and out. Faster, faster, faster!"

His eyes had closed, his cock had come back to full attention. His hand stroked the underside gently. Angela crossed her legs and hurried to interrupt him.

"I have a lover, you know," she said. The excuse had worked, if erratically, in the nightclubs back in Cincinnati. If he'd stay away, she wouldn't have to do anything else. She really didn't want to hurt him. "We're nearly married," she added.

"We're *all* married. The river to the sea, the ocean to the sky, the earth to the sun. Yet a relationship can't stop a comet from crashing into us and making a general muck of things. Relationships fall before destiny."

"I agree that destiny is very important, Harold." It was obvious that this wasn't going to be easy. On the other hand, he hadn't so much as touched her yet. "But there's no such thing as a single destiny. I know. I'm not even from this world."

"Your lover is an alien?" He shook his bedraggled head at her. "I may be a little odd, but I'm not *crazy.*"

"Yes . . . no . . ." Angela sighed in exasperation. "You don't understand. I really don't expect you to. I met him in Cincinnati."

"That explains it. Look, I know you. I know you're a heathen, an apostate. You're the Whore. I saw you and a man without clothes, and you screwed him in the middle of some pagan ritual. New Age stuff. Crystals, channeling, and sex. Looked like fun."

His smile was as radiant as the sun. Angela was beginning to wonder if you could get sunburn on a penis. The concept seemed rather painful.

"Harold, you're misinterpreting what you saw."

"Nope. You were fucking, and you were sitting on him. His cock bent to the left. I'll bet it was seven and a half inches long, and he had lots of muscles, a big strawberry birthmark on his left cheek—the bottom one—and no brains whatsoever. He was having trouble keeping it up because you kept playing with this bowl instead of him."

Inexplicably, she found herself blushing. That was Edgar—whatever Harold was, he was embarrassingly accurate. She remembered the birthmark and the rest.

"You still don't understand. Sex sometimes helps to power a ritual, yes, but that doesn't make me a whore."

"The Sorcerer doesn't do it that way."

"Who?"

"Your friend. The dwarf dressed in black. He's got a familiar, some weird creature, but they don't screw."

Angela remembered the ritual, and the little man in dark robes. "Him," she said. "The Mage. He's not from this world, either. And he's not my friend. He's working against me, as far as I know."

"Aliens again?" Harold asked. He sounded disgusted. His toes dug into the burning sand. The tide was beginning to come in; a curl of water lapped around his ankles. Like a nudist's sundial, the shadow of his erection pointed to Angela. Half-past a navel in the afternoon.

"Not aliens," Angela told him. "Other destinies."

The use of his favorite buzzword brought Harold's attention back again. "Destiny. I saw a book; the book in which the future is written."

"The other part of Henderson's ad. I remember it."

"I told Abel," Harold said proudly. A length of seaweed had wrapped around his foot. He reached down and put it in his mouth, chewing a moment before spitting it out. "I told him you'd come. You know the book. I know you do. Abel wants it—same as you, same as the Sorcerer. With the book, you know how to make things happen. Gives you lots of power, doesn't it?"

He grinned again, and this time there was nothing amusing in Harold's smile at all. It was cold and dead, fixed on his face like a death's-head.

"Having the book won't do Henderson any good," she insisted. "He won't be able to understand it."

Harold just grinned. "Not on his own. But the Fat Man knows, and he'll tell him."

"The Fat Man?"

"The guy who wrote the book."

"He's dead."

"Lazarus rose from the dead. People still see Elvis.

There are precedents. Nothing's permanent." He looked down; he'd gone flaccid. "Not even me," he said sadly. "But that can be fixed."

He reached down to fondle himself, and Angela pulled the beach robe tight once more.

"*Ouch,*" Harold grunted. He let go abruptly and examined himself in dismay.

"Should've used the sunblock," Angela said.

22: Remains to Be Seen

The grounds of Summer Grove were incredibly lush, the grass as thick and soft as a baby's diapered bottom and the unreal emerald green of a postcard from Ireland. Among the rolling hillocks were pools of sky blue water in which pristine white swans preened. The place was gorgeous and fantastically expensive.

None of the permanent residences seemed to have grave concerns about either of these two attributes. Or, if they did, they kept their mouths shut.

Being dead, that was relatively easy.

Ecclesiastes had thought that the ten-acre-or-more grounds of Summer Grove Cemetery—Cincinnati's most exclusive final resting place—were impressive by daylight. By night, he wasn't so certain. The ornate mausoleums with their intricate cornices and elegant statuary were shrouded in darkness. The shade under the oak, maple, and sycamore groves was dense and impenetrable; at 4:00 A.M. the sound of traffic on Summer Grove Avenue had ceased and the cemetery was, well, dead quiet.

Ecclesiastes had dealt with corpses for years.

He'd played normal student games with the donated bodies at Morticians College. Most of the teachers said, as long as they wouldn't be quoted, that such things tended to give the students a necessary distance from what could be a disturbing occupation. Ecclesiastes himself had been the perpetrator of what later classes told him was a legendary prank.

He'd made the tape from the soundtrack of his roommate's porno tapes. Sour old Professor Ames, who had the general pasty and sunken look of a corpse

190

himself, had heard the theatrical and loud moans and panting from well down the hall; he'd come barreling down the corridor with an eager, grim smile on his face, going white with rage when he realized that the sound was coming from behind his closed office door. Professor Ames had flung the door open with a triumphant shout, thinking he'd caught two students in flagrante delicto (and in a rather imaginative position at that) on top of his desk.

The uproar when he'd discovered the truth had been gratifying. Professor Ames had never been quite the same afterward.

In his own work, Ecclesiastes had seen corpses sit up suddenly in the middle of the night with involuntary muscle contractions; he'd heard them grumble and moan with gas. He'd stitched them and pressed their cold flesh and arranged their stiffening limbs. The visible residue of death—after a while—didn't bother him at all. He'd seen all the faces death had to offer.

So there was little reason for him to feel like he was living a Vincent Price movie now as he, Mundo, Alfred, and the ghostly Alice slunk through the Summer Grove grounds toward Theopelli's crypt.

But he did. He very much did.

On the other hand, he found himself enormously curious. He might have come along on the expedition even if Mundo hadn't threatened to have Ecclesiastes' kneecaps broken by his drug-dealer friends, his funeral home burned to the ground, and a curse of impotency laid on him for the rest of his life, should he refuse.

Ecclesiastes was either stuck in a nightmare, was having the worst case of acid flashback yet on record, or had been kidnapped by refugees from a lunatic asylum. All these options had their drawbacks when it came to explaining just what was going on, but whatever it was seemed likely to be, well, *interesting*. If nothing else, the *National Enquirer* might be persuaded to consider an article afterward. Since it didn't seem feasible to escape just yet, Ecclesiastes had decided to cooperate for the time being.

When the police came, he could always claim to have been an innocent hostage.

They waited in the shadow of a sycamore tree until the security guard passed on his rounds, then ran to the crypt they'd surveyed that afternoon. It was one of the expensive affairs, like a one-room Greek Acropolis. The massive door was, at the request of Theopelli's will, unlocked, but the hinges made an impressive groan as Alfred pushed them back. No one had visited Theopelli in the eight years he'd been dead. No one liked him well enough. They were greeted with a damp, musty, *old* smell.

"I don't like this," Alfred whispered, as if Theopelli could overhear. Overall, Ecclesiastes had to agree with the sentiment.

"Shut up and get inside." They filed inside, and Mundo pushed the door shut once again. Mundo flicked on a shielded flashlight. Its tiny beam picked out the sarcophagus set on a concrete slab in the middle of the room. He played the beam over the walls; it looked like the set of *Cleopatra,* a temple complete with altar; candelabras everywhere and unlit torches set in the walls; tall ceramic jars sealed with wax around the walls. There were no windows in the place at all.

"Alfred, get the candles and torches lit," Mundo said. The dwarf plopped a duffel bag down on the floor. He began pulling out a selection of odd items.

"You know this won't work," Ecclesiastes told him hopefully. "You can't bring people back to life."

Mundo ignored Ecclesiastes and continued setting up. "Oh, it's not *easy,*" Alice answered for Mundo. "Caleb's done it, oh, one and a half times since he summoned me from the ether."

Ecclesiastes decided to ignore the ether and summoning references. "One and a *half* times?"

"He did bring King Evan back after twenty years when Evan's daughter died and there weren't any more heirs for the throne, but the flesh restoration didn't take. No one could stand to be in the same room with the king, and the fly problem in the summer—"

Ecclesiastes gulped and nodded.

"The problem is going to be whether Caleb has the power," Alice continued cheerfully. "He's still recovering from the drain your friend the Adept put on him. That's why he hasn't bothered to make me entirely corporeal again—he's conserving strength. And it also depends on the will of the dead person. If they don't *want* to come back, it's usually impossible to force them."

"I wouldn't think many people would voluntarily remain dead," Ecclesiastes said. "It seems people are usually trying to avoid that state."

"Oh, you'd be surprised. Think of how you hate to wake up and get out of your warm bed on a cold winter's day. My information's all secondhand, mind you, but I'm told being dead's actually not as bad as it's been made out to be."

Mundo was prying the stone lid of the sarcophagus off with a crowbar. "Give me a hand here," he said. Ecclesiastes went over. The lid was carved and filigreed. He ran his fingertips over the words there. "What is this?"

The words were written in a triangle, sets of them around the edge of the lid like a frieze:

```
ABRAHAS ABRAHAS ABRAHAS ABRAHAS ABRAHAS ABRAHAS ABRAHAS ABRAHAS
 ABRAHA  ABRAHA  ABRAHA  ABRAHA  ABRAHA  ABRAHA  ABRAHA  ABRAHA
  ABRAH   ABRAH   ABRAH   ABRAH   ABRAH   ABRAH   ABRAH   ABRAH
   ABRA    ABRA    ABRA    ABRA    ABRA    ABRA    ABRA    ABRA
    ABR     ABR     ABR     ABR     ABR     ABR     ABR     ABR
     AB      AB      AB      AB      AB      AB      AB      AB
      A       A       A       A       A       A       A       A
     AB      AB      AB      AB      AB      AB      AB      AB
    ABR     ABR     ABR     ABR     ABR     ABR     ABR     ABR
   ABRA    ABRA    ABRA    ABRA    ABRA    ABRA    ABRA    ABRA
  ABRAH   ABRAH   ABRAH   ABRAH   ABRAH   ABRAH   ABRAH   ABRAH
 ABRAHA  ABRAHA  ABRAHA  ABRAHA  ABRAHA  ABRAHA  ABRAHA  ABRAHA
ABRAHAS ABRAHAS ABRAHAS ABRAHAS ABRAHAS ABRAHAS ABRAHAS ABRAHAS
```

"'Abraxas.' An ancient charm. A spell," Mundo replied. "It invokes the gods to aid with health and restoration. Your childish 'abracadabra' is a powerless bastardization of the word. I'm surprised Theopelli knew it," he said grudgingly.

"He seems to have known a lot more than you thought, Caleb," Alice said. She was examining the room, peering at the jars. "He has power runes on the vases, too."

Mundo grunted and levered up with the crowbar. The lid moved, scraping loudly. Ecclesiastes and Alfred helped him slide the lid to one side and lower it to the floor. Mundo peered into the sarcophagus.

He nodded. "It's as you said, Mitsumishi. Good."

On their arrival in Cincinnati, Mundo had insisted that Ecclesiastes check with the mortician who had dealt with Theopelli's body. His colleague, a man named Schueller (who unfortunately also remembered Ecclesiastes' short-lived business in Cincinnati, the Stiff's Upper Lip), had been more than willing to complain about the arrangements demanded in the will.

"Theopelli was a real nut case, but then most everyone knew that before he died. *You* might have liked him, Mitsumishi. Your kind of customer. He left specific instructions that no organs were to be donated, and he sure as hell made sure no one would want them anyway. The embalming was the barest minimum. He wanted the brains, the intestines, and the other internal organs removed, washed in wine, and placed in jars which were to go in the crypt with him—the jars were full of some herbs he'd ordered. I had to put the heart back into the body cavity, then fill the rest with more herbs and oils—perfumed stuff that smelled like a cheap whore on a drinking binge. The incisions were to be stitched back up again and—this is the weirdest bit, and it was a damn good thing he got legal permission for everything before he died because otherwise I would have refused—we pickled the body in saltpeter in my back room for three months. Then we had to wash it again and wrap it like a mummy. At least he paid well, or his estate did. I tell you, I've never done anything like that before, and I'll never do it again."

Mundo, dangling over the sides of the sarcophagus with his feet off the ground, was examining the corpse, peeling long linen strips from the body. "This is good. The lack of blood is a bit of a problem, but . . ." He hopped back down and pointed at Alfred. "You—go open the jars. Mitsumishi, come here. I need your help."

"Mundo, I don't usually have much to do with bodies after they're interred."

"I notice Alice is nearly material again. She's probably getting hungry, and if she won't kill you herself, *I* don't have any problems with the concept. And there's still your sex life."

Ecclesiastes looked at Alice, who smiled toothily back to him. He moved to the sarcophagus and peered inside.

Theopelli had never been pleasant to look upon. Death had only enhanced that particular trait. The wrappings had left a gummy residue on his face, the various treatments had turned his skin the color and texture of shoe leather. His nose hadn't been fixed after its fatal encounter with the desktop, and the right eyelid looked suspiciously convex. Without the normal padding, his cheeks had sunken in, giving him an anorexic look at odds with his obese body. Mundo was stripping away the remainder of the linen, revealing the body beneath. Schueller had made a long incision from breastbone to groin; the stitching of the cut had been perfunctory at best.

And Theopelli smelled not like rotten meat but like a sweet, decaying apple.

"Cut him open," Mundo said to Ecclesiastes. The dwarf stabbed a surgeon's scalpel into Theopelli's chest in front of Ecclesiastes.

"I don't think—"

"Nobody would ever look for your well-gnawed bones in here, would they, Mitsumishi?"

"I'm doing it. I'm doing it." Ecclesiastes took a deep breath, wiggled the scalpel out of Theopelli's chest, and ran the blade down the length of the body. The sweet smell intensified. Below the incision he could see a black, wet mass like sphagnum moss dipped in used motor oil. He cut down further and the skin parted more, revealing the gray muscles of the heart nestled in the abdomen.

There was an audible *pop* behind him as Alfred breached the seal of one of the jars. Ecclesiastes glanced behind just in time to see Alfred get violently sick. As Alfred heaved on his knees, Alice sidled over to the jar and peered inside.

"Intestines," she said to Mundo after a quick glance. "My favorite."

"When he's finished losing his dinner, make sure the rest of the jars are opened. Mitsumishi, we need to dig this stuff out."

Ecclesiastes made a face. "Rubber gloves?" he asked hopefully. Mundo had already plunged his bare hands into the soft, squilching mess.

"It's powder of myrrh, aromatic resin and perfumes, and various herbs. There's nothing to hurt you." He pulled out a double handful and tossed it to the floor. "Do it."

Ecclesiastes sighed, pushed his sleeves up, and helped Mundo eviscerate the corpse. Alfred had recovered and, breathing heavily, was opening the remainder of the jars. After most of the packing was out, Mundo straightened up. "All right. Bring the jars over here."

"What are you going to do?" Ecclesiastes asked. He had a horrible suspicion that he already knew.

He did. "We're going to put the organs back in, of course. You can't revive an empty shell. Now, hold the skin open." With Alfred's help, Mundo tipped the first of the jars over the sarcophagus. Gray-blue, slimy intestinal coils slithered over Ecclesiastes' hands and into Theopelli. Ecclesiastes had to fight not to add his own dinner to Alfred's. The other jars followed: liver, stomach, kidneys, lungs. Mundo shoved them into the husk of Theopelli with no regard to their natural order. Then he gestured at Ecclesiastes. "Fine. Sew him up again."

"Just like that? I don't know where you come from, Mundo, but things usually need to be attached to each other to have any chance at all of working—not that I think you have a prayer anyway. You know: the hipbone's connected to the thighbone, that kind of thing. You just threw the stuff in there like it was a tossed salad."

"Yum," Alice commented. Mundo glared at her.

"Where *I* come from," Mundo replied darkly, "the old ways were never lost. There are other connections than those of merely physical. Your society has forgotten them, or certainly your type of butchery of the dead would not be allowed, but they are still there. The body is simply the *khat*, what I am interested in is the *ka*."

"Those are old Egyptian terms. History of Embalming—we studied them."

"They are the *correct* terms. You would know them, too, if things had happened differently in your world."

"I still don't see—"

"Then be quiet and watch, and you will. Now, stitch him up so I can proceed."

Ecclesiastes did as bidden, shaking his head the entire time. Theopelli's skin was like parchment; though he tried to be careful, it kept tearing. Mundo merely grunted when he pointed it out. "The act and intent are all that matters. Appearance is of no importance."

Ecclesiastes finished with a long sigh of relief as he backed away from the sarcophagus. Mundo had set up an array of candles around the sarcophagus and sketched a pentagram on the floor of the crypt with chalk. He connected the Macintosh computer to a battery pack: its screen was flickering with strange symbols and words, among which Ecclesiastes recognized the occasional "abraxas."

Finally, the sorcerer pulled a vial of powder from the duffel bag and spread it over the corpse. A blue smoke filled the stone cavity and spilled over the edges like dry-ice fog, filling the interior of the temple with a smell like roses. Alice was chanting near the door, her stubby Tyrannosaurus arms held out to either side of her massive chest. Ecclesiastes looked at Alfred, who shrugged back. They both stayed near the door.

There was a sudden definite smell of ozone. Small pale yellow lightnings sparked and sizzled in the sapphire fog within the sarcophagus. Mundo was walking slowly around the coffin, speaking in a loud, low voice in some language that Ecclesiastes didn't know. At each corner of the pentangle, he paused to throw more powder into the interior of the sarcophagus, and each time it flared like burning magnesium. The interior of the crypt was very hot, very bright, and extremely smoky. Whether the ritual worked or not, Ecclesiastes had to admit the special effects were nice.

Mundo had completed his circuit of the pentagram. "Alice?" he said.

"I'm done, Caleb. The computer's run the program, too."

"Then let's see what happens." Mundo slipped an ornate knife from underneath his robe, bared his arm, and plunged the blade deep into his forearm, making a long cut that immediately began flowing blood. He moved to the sarcophagus, raining red droplets over the corpse. "Life for life," he said.

Ecclesiastes could have sworn that the blood sizzled as it disappeared into that bright, throbbing cloud that filled the interior.

The glowing atmosphere of the sarcophagus pulsed, throbbed, and erupted with light. An enormous thunderclap boomed in the same instant, and the sound pressure slammed against Ecclesiastes' chest and tossed him against the wall of the crypt. He lay there stunned for an instant. Worse, he'd gone blind. He could see nothing at all. The others were shouting in the darkness as well, cursing. Ecclesiastes fumbled around him; his fingers closed over a cold cylinder and explored it: Mundo's flashlight. Ecclesiastes thumbed the switch.

A beam of blessed yellow sliced through the murk. Ecclesiastes let out a breath he hadn't known he'd been holding; evidently the explosion had blown out all the candles and torches.

"That was impressive, Caleb," Alice's voice said. "Did it work?"

"I don't know. Mitsumishi, shine the light over there." Mundo's voice sounded weary and hoarse. Ecclesiastes flicked the beam over to the sarcophagus. He gasped.

There was movement in the center of the room: a hand gripped the stone slab from inside. A head followed as the corpse sat up. Pale eyes opened and blinked into the flashlight's glare.

"It's about time you people got here," Theopelli said.

23: Dirk Hits the Beach

The little runabout bobbed in the gentle swells of the Gulf of Mexico outside Tampa Bay. It smelled the way the inside of an old tuna tin smells after sitting out in the sun for a week. Essence of dead fish. The bottom of ancient pilings.

Dirk felt like a character trapped in the old paperback mysteries he often read on the road. He tried to imagine that a committee of handpicked fictional advisers were with him in the tiny fishing boat.

The sun was rising, as swollen and red as a drunk's eyeball after a night's binge. The water had the oily sheen of blacktop under an old car. Philip Marlowe unscrewed the top of a hip flask, took a slug of rye, and gave the empty flask a casual half toss over the side. He eyed the widening ripples, a bull's-eye for a passing gull. "There'll be a woman in it," he said with a dry, sandy rasp. "There always is."

Shut up, Marlowe. Just give me some advice here.

He looked up. His flat eyes had all the expression of tarnished pennies. "Oke. I do whatever anyone pays me a buck to do," he drawled. "Unless it's murder. Then I gotta ask two-fifty. Last tough I tangled with had a jaw you could crack diamonds on."

You're a smartass, aren't you. Always one for the flip answers. That's all you got to say?

"I'm just a shamus, a private dick. If I had brains, I'd be a cop on the mob beat holding my hand out for the take. That's where the real money is."

Bye, Marlowe.

Splash.

Travis McGee nudged Meyer. "We should've brought

the *Busted Flush* instead of this tub. Now listen, Masterson, you know how I work, don't you? I won't take every job that comes along, and I don't work at all unless I need the money and the job interests me. I get half the value of whatever it is I'm supposed to recover."

Fine, McGee, but what the hell can you do with half an Angela? You're too busy doing clever philosophizing with Meyer. Go back to your houseboat, both of you.

Splash.

Splash.

"Dames. They're nothin' but trouble. You see a bimbo with good gams and you get all silly. Ya gotta slap 'em around every once in a while."

Bogey, you'd never survive today with that unliberated crap. Play that song again, Sam, and take the falcon with you.

Splash.

At least the boat couldn't hold Nero Wolfe without taking in water over the gunwales. Besides, he'd never have come out of his greenhouse. As for the cinematic heroes—they tended to use more firepower and pyrotechnics. Dirk figured he'd just shoot his foot off with an Uzi.

Which left no one in the boat but Joan.

"Yo-ho-ho," she chirped.

". . . and a bottle of rum," Dirk added. He stared at the Florida shoreline through a pair of cheap binoculars. The sun was burning off a slight haze; he could see Henderson's mansion glinting like a polished tooth on the shore. From what Dirk could see through his lenses, Henderson was no doubt quite an addition to the rich neighborhood.

A fair amount of the Church of Christ the Marvel had been funneled into creating a lavish home for its founder. There wasn't a blemish anywhere on the extensive plush lawns where sprinklers tossed sparkling mists into the air. Ornate topiaries lined the curved, crushed-shell drive. A helicopter sat on its pad on the roof; in the extensive flower gardens, a squadron of gardeners were bent over, industriously weeding. Along the beach, a suspicious-looking pair of blue suits with mirrored shades were walking and staring out into the Gulf.

"It's fun playing pirates with you, Petey," Joan said. She'd been in some fugue state since they'd pushed off from the slip in Clearwater. She kept calling him Petey. She kept mangling the phrases, too. "There was a crow's nest in the mainsail, but I got rid of it."

"Thanks," he said.

"Arrr," she growled. "Ye'll walk a blank, me hearty. You stepped on the cat with nine tails."

Dirk had about four hours in which to rescue Angela, no idea how to go about it, and his partner was a tobacco-chewing, fat, and possibly female Errol Flynn who kept flubbing her lines. Great.

He'd played detective all day yesterday, first finding the crew at Kennedy Airport who had serviced Henderson's Lear jet. It had taken the sight of a couple twenties peeking from his fingertips, but they'd told him that yes, there *had* been a woman with Henderson and the other weird guy, some chick in a wheelchair who was asleep or sick. Their description matched Angela well enough.

Dirk contemplated going to the police, but only for a few moments. That didn't seem smart. The Church of Christ the Marvel was simply too large, too well respected, and too influential. He might as well try to serve an indictment on the pope. The Church of Christ the Marvel subsidized an army of lobbyists, contributed heavily to favored politicians, and generally paved any avenue to influence with dollars. He could hear the conversation with the desk sergeant.

I think my girlfriend's been kidnapped by the Reverend Henderson. She's not in her room, the paper's open to his ad, and the crazy hermaphodite I'm with thinks so, too.

Yeah, sure, buddy. No problem. Come along into this nice little padded cell and we'll check it out, betcha.

The Abraxas Marvel Circus

Monday was an off night for the band. At least that worked in his favor. Dirk had flown down to Tampa that evening with Joan, but he needed to be back later this afternoon to play. He'd optimistically booked tickets for three on the 4:00 P.M. flight from the airport.

Now that he was here, it was a lot easier playing hero in his head than actually doing it. It wasn't as if he could walk up to the front door and ask for Angela back. *You're jeopardizing your musical career and spending one hell of a lot of money on a lunatic and— just incidentally, illegal—rescue mission for a woman you've spent a total of maybe three weeks with. Does that make sense?*

No, shouted his intellect, but was quickly drowned out by his libido, the aching hole he'd felt leaving Angela in Cincinnati and again last night when he'd found her gone, and the entire right side of his brain.

Love's an art. And like any art, it doesn't make sense, it shouted.

As if in affirmation of that, Dirk saw movement through the binoculars. A door opened in the rear of the mansion. Two more of the mirror-shaded blue suits stepped out first, followed by Angela and someone dressed like a scrawny and wild-haired Tarzan. The group headed down toward the beach near a stand of plams and scrub brush.

"Angela," he said out loud. His heart was suddenly hammering at the cage of his ribs. His pulse pounded like a bass drum in his skull.

Suddenly it didn't seem so crazy after all. Suddenly it seemed, well, *destined.* There was only a few hundred yards of surf, two guards, and a scrawny apeman between Angela and himself.

Those were acceptable odds for a hero.

Dirk turned the boat south along the beach, putting the brush between himself and the people around Angela. At the same time, he made a show of casting a fishing line out. He turned off the inboard Evenrude and let the boat drift in the northeast current.

"Joan?"

She was standing in the bow, one foot up on the gunwale like a pudgy George Washington crossing the Delaware. "Captain," he tried again, and finally she turned.

"Yes, Mr. Christian?" She gave him a wrong-handed salute. Shaking his head, Dirk returned it. "I 'spected the nekked savages to be out in their boats by now," Joan said. "Blow me down. Batter the hatchets."

"I'll go see what's keeping them, Captain," he ventured. "It's very important that when I call, you come for me." Joan only glared at him theatrically, sticking out her lower lip.

"Sir," Dirk added.

"That's better. You'll 'member some r'spect or I'll slap you with irons."

"Yes sir." Dirk fumbled in the locker under the seat. He stuffed an oilcloth-wrapped parcel in the back pocket of his jeans. The only thing on the boat that even vaguely resembled a weapon was a twelve-inch Maglight, but the heft of it was nice and solid. He stuffed that into his belt.

"She's idling now. Just push this lever all the way down and steer it closer to shore when I call, okay?"

"I know how to handle my ship, master," she said haughtily. "I'm wearing Davy Jones locket."

"Right. I forgot."

Dirk checked the shore one more time. From their position, he could see the back door of house but not Angela and her guards. One of the burly mirror-shade guys was just going in the door, which meant that if he was lucky, there was currently only one left with Angela and Tarzan. He slipped off his shoes, stripped off his shirt, and slid over the side of the boat into the bathwater-warm Gulf.

"Watch out for sharks," Joan said.

That pleasant thought made him swim a little faster.

Dirk felt confident. This was going to work. He'd get Angela and they'd hightail it back to New York. He'd play; Angela would finally tell him what all this was about, and they'd press charges against Henderson. With the attendant publicity, which Stan Federman would be sure to take every advantage of, Savage would be in demand everywhere. The second album would hit the *Billboard* charts, they'd rerelease the first. He and Angela would stay together. They'd put the damn bowl and tarot deck on their mantelpiece.

A perfect ending.

Dirk didn't even feel worried anymore as his feet touched sand and he waded ashore. He flipped the Maglight once in his hand. It was heavy and reassuring.

He moved into the brush. He hadn't gone more than a few yards when he heard voices.

". . . embarrassing place to be sunburned, certainly." Angela's voice.

"It's worst when I have to pee," a male replied. "It burns like Abel's hellfire. Like the clap—which, if you ask me, is a bizarre nickname for a sexually transmitted disease. I had it once and didn't have the slightest desire to applaud."

Dirk decided he didn't like the sound of this conversation at all. He hadn't come a minute too soon. He slid through the thick tropical foliage.

The blue-suited guard was busy scanning the bay and had made the minor mistake of putting his back to the palms beneath which Dirk crouched. Tarzan didn't look like much trouble—he obviously wasn't hiding anything under the skimpy loincloth he wore, and his muscle tone was nonexistent. Angela was wearing a one-piece suit under an open robe, sitting on a wooden lounger, and hugging her knees to her chest. She seemed tired.

Destiny. No problem.

Dirk burst from cover swinging the Maglight. It thumped against the guard's skull with a satisfying dull *thunk;* the man crumpled bonelessly to the sand.

"Dirk!" Angela cried.

She started to get up from the lounger, but Tarzan grabbed her arm.

"I think you'd better look behind you," Tarzan said, and Dirk laughed.

"C'mon, man. I've read that garbage in every half-baked detective story ever written. That's the oldest ruse in the world," he said. "I look, and you take the chance to jump me. I'm not that stupid."

"Dirk—" Angela began, but Dirk waved a hand.

"It's okay, Angela." He snarled at the scrawny man holding her. "Just back away from her, asshole, or you get the same routine I gave Mirror Shades." Dirk hefted the flash menacingly.

Tarzan let go. "C'mon, Angela," Dirk said. "We've got a boat waiting."

And about the same time, Dirk heard the crunch of sand under heavy shoes. Behind him. "Oh, shit," he muttered, and then something about the size and general weight of Rhode Island slammed into the back of his head.

His last thought was that sand really didn't taste very good at all.

The world came back with mixed results, which was pretty much as he'd left it. It returned in the shape of a woman's face (which was pleasant) and a pounding headache (which wasn't).

"Angela," he breathed, and spat a few clinging crystals of sand from his lips. He was in a room somewhere. He could smell salt air and hear the waves.

That wasn't a good sign. He tried to sit up but the headache convinced him to stay down.

"Nice rescue, Dirk," Angela commented. Then she smiled and the headache didn't matter quite as much. "But I'm awfully glad you tried, anyway," she said, and leaned down to kiss him.

24: Abracadaver

"I've always prided myself on being a good judge of human character, and I was certain no one could be more unpleasant than Caleb," Alice the MindBeast whispered to Ecclesiastes. She glanced at Theopelli. "But I guess everyone's entitled to a mistake now and then."

They were seated in a second-floor study at Three Norns. Ecclesiastes' clothing was already a mess, but he was afraid to sit down for fear of ruining the suit entirely. If there were a museum for dust, a number of exhibits could have been stocked here. Theopelli's home was filthy, run-down, and foul.

The house matched its owner perfectly.

Their band of graverobbers had driven from Summer Grove Cemetery to the Holiday Inn room they'd rented. Theopelli had refused the bath Mundo offered (that Mundo had, in fact, insisted on) though he had condescended to wash off the worst of the clinging oils and sundry anointings from his arms, face and several chins. Then they'd made their way west on I-74 to Three Norns, arriving just before dawn.

Theopelli's resurrection hadn't improved him a great deal. His right eye was swollen almost entirely shut, and what peered from behind the slit was wholly red, though Mundo claimed that the revival process would heal even that grievous injury. Theopelli's nose looked to be permanently squashed upward and to one side, lending Theopelli's features a certain porcine quality. That seemed to suit him quite well.

And he stank. The car ride had been barely tolerable even with all the windows open. Ecclesiastes had no idea what the rental agency was going to say when they dropped off the car at the airport. Mundo maintained, defensively, that the stench was a temporary by-product of "backward and ridiculous burial practices" and not a result of his lack of skill. Theopelli didn't seem to notice or care about the body odor. Alfred claimed it was no different from when Theopelli had last been alive and living at Three Norns.

Mostly, they all tried to stay downwind.

"God, it feels good to be able to fart again," Theopelli said.

"He's back to normal," Alfred observed glumly. "Damn it anyway."

Theopelli ripped open one of several packs of Hostess Twinkies he'd insisted they stop to buy. He stuffed the first cake whole into this mouth.

"Best damn snack in the world," he mumbled around the Twinkie wad. "Brain food." He broke open the second Twinkie and plunged his forefinger into the center, gouging out the filling. "Now, where the hell are the rest of you?"

Mundo had been watching glumly. "Not even so much as a 'thank you,' " the dwarf had grumbled as they'd left the cemetery. "He even has the nerve to complain about how stiff he is. Hell, he hasn't moved a muscle in eight years. What'd he expect?"

"What 'others'?" Mundo asked now.

Theopelli licked Twinkie fluff from a forefinger as plump as a cheap cigar and crammed the rest of the snack after it. His thick brows lowered and knotted. He didn't bother to wipe off the finger before he waved it at Mundo. "Don't you *dare* tell me you fucked that up, too," he thundered.

"Look, you conceited, arrogant son of a bitch," Mundo shouted back, "I've spent three of the most miserable years of my life trying to figure out the signs. I've put up with drug pushers and salesmen; I've dodged your police and the IRS; I've lived in a hovel that the damn roaches complain about. I've given up my entire career to come here. I've conjured a MindBeast, found your goddamn papers, *and* brought you back to life—a fact I'm now beginning to seriously regret. Don't you give me any crap about fucking up."

They glared at each other like tomcats over a tabby in heat. Theopelli rustled cellophane menacingly. "You're from the Amenhotep IV split, aren't you? You didn't think you'd be the only branch involved, did you? You didn't think you'd be enough by yourself? I set this up so that the Gnostic and the local focus would be here, too. This is important, you little black turd. Now, where *are* they?"

"The Princess and the Adept? Are they the ones you're talking about? Well, I don't know *where* they are, Theopelli. I don't really care. I thought *she* was working against me, and the Adept slipped away."

"So you're telling me I'm surrounded by incompetent assholes. Great." Theopelli let the wrapper drop to the floor. ("Just like old times, all right," Alfred whispered to Ecclesiastes.)

Mundo was practically frothing at the mouth. Alfred looked too cowed at seeing his former employer alive once more to dare speak up, and Alice was simply staring at Theopelli as she might a potential meal.

Whatever insanity Ecclesiastes had stumbled into, it didn't look friendly. He cleared his throat.

"Excuse me," he said in what he hoped was a conversational tone, "but would anyone mind telling me what's going on?"

Theopelli squinted as if noticing him for the first time. "Awfully goddamn tall for a chink, aren't you? Who the hell are you?"

Ecclesiastes blinked at the insult and decided to ignore it. Eight years of being dead gave a man a right to be a little snippy, he told himself. "I'm a friend of Joan—the Adept. I had your notebooks." Ecclesiastes smiled tentatively. "I even used to follow your papers in the journals once, back in college. They were always interesting."

Theopelli grunted. "I doubt you understood them. No one else could, either. What month is it?"

"May."

Theopelli farted again, grunting. "Hell, it's *all*

fucked up. You people were supposed to have me out by October last year. No wonder . . ." His voice trailed off. "Who won the last presidential election?"

Ecclesiastes told him.

Theopelli grimaced. "It's worse than I thought." Ecclesiastes tended to agree, but didn't say anything. Theopelli was frowning at Mundo again. "We're going to have to recalculate everything, and I can't give you any guarantees. If your people had sent someone halfway competent—" he began.

Mundo kicked over a carved oaken chair, sending a cloud of dust into the air. "I have degrees from both the Thebes Arcanae and the Luxor Temple," the dwarf declared, thumping his barrel chest. "I studied with Ma'at himself for half a century."

"Perhaps you were a slow learner."

"I should have left you for the worms, you bloated toad."

"But you couldn't, could you? You didn't dare. Your world doesn't stand a chance without me."

"*What* are you two talking about?" Ecclesiastes interrupted.

"History," Alice told him.

"More precisely," Theopelli sniffed, "the making thereof. You see, all those nuts who go around claiming that the end is near—well, they're exactly right, in a way."

If A equals B, and B equals C, then A equals C. Logic.

If A causes B to occur, and B causes C to occur, then A causes C. Cause and effect.

A never moves by itself. Inertia.

And if old A *doesn't* get up and jostle B, then poor C never has a chance and ceases to exist at all.

Just the facts, ma'am.

As a boy, Theopelli had always been fascinated by little logical conundrums:

If a tree falls in a forest and there's no one to hear it, does it make a sound?

Is there an end to the universe, and if so, what's outside it?

What is there about love that causes an otherwise normal person to behave like a blithering idiot?

Fascinating stuff.

Early on, Theopelli also began to realize that history depended more on who was doing the writing of it than what might have actually happened. History, as it is said, is written by the winners. The losers always get the bad press. Long lists of kings and generals, battles and famous dates were all right, but they were the end results. Nothing else.

History was and is a whole line of very visible C's marching dramatically across the stage. Occasionally you might catch a glimpse of a furtive B; *never* did you see the A.

Never at all.

Things began to click in Theopelli's mind not long after that fateful day in Boston when Willis McAllister shredded his brains with a bullet in front of the young derelict Theopelli. After a time, he realized that some of those childhood conundrums weren't so ho-hum after all.

The sound of the falling tree is entirely secondary to the question Does the tree fall at all before there's someone there to observe it?

The problem is not whether the universe has an end, but whether there's an end to the number of universes.

The lovesick blithering idiots wonder what in the world's wrong with the *rest* of us.

Theopelli's delving into the mathematics of fate, into what Newton might have called the Great Clockwork of God, showed him some curious wiggles in the equations. Just as the existence of unknown moons in the solar system was first surmised by perturbations in the predicted orbits of the known worlds, so Theopelli noticed other realities floating about the perimeter of our own fate.

He realized that whether the tree fell or not depended on which forest you were looking in at the moment.

He saw the complicated superstructure of A's that held up the final C of history. The main trunk of this particular tree went straight for long periods, then suddenly reached a gnarl, where it would branch and intertwine. From that point, other smaller branches would shoot out, and the main trunk would continue onward until the next branching.

He could see partway down the other structures projecting out from the main trunk of reality, the "what if" worlds. He saw the connections between those alternate realities and this world and knew that things must occasionally cross between—which went a long way toward explaining several bizarre myths and sightings in what he'd previously considered the realm of blithering idiots and Californians.

Theopelli knew that he could also, by using his equations, project himself into the dim future. Theopelli knew that all the names and dates of recorded history were just the outer surface of the tree. Really, they weren't that important at all. Underneath, the A that made life twist and turn and branch and flower, was mind-set.

Belief.

Attitude.

He saw the crux toward which they were currently heading, and he didn't like the shape he saw leaving that point.

Theopelli was nothing if not arrogant. He decided that if he didn't like it, he would change it to suit him.

Ecclesiastes realized just how far he'd stumbled down the path to La-La Land by the fact that he didn't even question Theopelli's ability to do such a thing. He supposed that seeing a dead man return back to life was enough to shake even the most dogged skepticism. Not even the Great Kreskin, Doug Henning, and David Copperfield together could have done that.

Still . . .

"Just like that?" Ecclesiastes argued. "You don't like it so you're going to play God and change it? You have to have one gargantuan ego to consider your personal view of the universe to be the best one."

"Listen, because I'm obnoxious doesn't mean that I'm wrong," Theopelli shot back with a sidewise glance of his bloodshot eyes. He was childishly sullen. "Egoism is often packaged with brilliance. Two for one. A special offer."

"And just what is it you claim to have seen, Theopelli?" Mundo asked. He was pacing the study near Alice.

Theopelli turned to the dwarf. He snorted, his nostrils flapping. "You know well enough, or you wouldn't be here. So does the Gnostic." He swung ponderously back to Ecclesiastes. A forefinger the size of a small hot dog prowled the edges of a Twinkie pack on the table.

"Anytime any choice—*any* choice at all—is made, new shadow realities are born. Most of them are ephemeral, fleeting. They're gone in the same instant, at least from our point of view. But—rarely—humankind comes to a group decision, where a philosophical viewpoint is decided. *Then* the process is powerful enough to create an alternative world that lives, one that moves alongside our primary reality with its own people and its own societies. To the point of that branching, we share a common past, but our futures are radically different. With great difficulty, a person can cross even that boundary.

"In *our* reality, for instance," he continued, with the dry, flat delivery that university professors use in required courses, "the Pharaoh Amenhotep IV was a rebel. He renounced the old gods for a single deity he called Aton and changed his name to Akhenaten. His new religion didn't survive his death. The priests and sorcerers quickly reverted to polytheism. But the damage was already done. Akhenaten had put a dent in humankind's perception of the universe and changed everything thereafter.

"Now in our ugly short friend's world, those events never happened, at least not that way. Some hidden B's, set in motion by forever unknown A's, altered the course, so C—Akhenaten's rebellion—never occurred. Our sorcerer's world is *still* entirely polytheistic. Things we regard as magic and superstition are the norm there, if I'm not mistaken. What we call science never came into being at all."

"And it's a damn better world," Mundo scoffed. "At least you can breathe the air."

Theopelli only looked pleased.

"Spells? Incantations? Mundo went to university for *that* stuff?" Ecclesiastes ventured.

"The only thing that matters is belief," Theopelli answered. "Tell me, why do airplanes fly?"

Ecclesiastes blinked. "Huh?" It wasn't the kind of question one fielded every day. He tried to remember fuzzy articles from *Popular Science*. "Roughly, the propeller or jet gives you thrust, and when you have enough forward momentum, the airstream flowing over and under the wings causes it to lift. Something like that, anyway."

"*Wrong!*" Theopelli shouted triumphantly. He reached for another Twinkie. "Airplanes fly entirely and *only* because we believe they can."

Ecclesiastes started to laugh and thought better of it. "Forgive me," he began, mostly because his father had taught him that it was polite to apologize before calling someone a flat-out liar, "but I think that's just about the stupidest thing I've ever heard."

"That's because you have the mind-set of this reality," Theopelli answered around the Twinkie. Sugary crumbs sprayed on the "t" of "reality." "You believe in science. You believe in mechanics and physics and aerodynamics. You have faith in them, and your faith and the faith of the billions of others here make it work."

Ecclesiastes was shaking his head. "I'm sorry, but you're not making any sense."

"Prove it wrong," Theopelli declared.

"A remote-control plane—" Ecclesiastes began.

"—is still piloted by someone who believes such a thing can fly. And even if you had one person in this world who really, truly, didn't believe it, he would be so overshadowed by the utter faith of all the rest that it wouldn't matter."

"This is ridiculous. By what you're saying, it wouldn't matter if the wings fell off a plane. If the passengers didn't 'believe' it would fall, it wouldn't."

"Ahh, but everyone 'knows' that you need the wings to fly. No one could convincingly believe otherwise. So if they fell off, the plane would go down. Inevitable."

Ecclesiastes continued to shake his head, and Theopelli opened the last pack of Twinkies. "You believe in science, Mitsumishi, Mundo here believes in spells," Theopelli continued. "His world is still peopled by mythological creatures such as his familiar, and for them, they're real. Science works for you, spells work for him. Magic, mathematics: it's all the same, ultimately."

"Spells sure as hell saved your ass from the maggots," Mundo growled.

Ecclesiastes decided that none of this was worth arguing about. He wasn't going to quite *believe* any of this sophistry yet, but then Theopelli had been convincingly dead just a few hours ago. Maybe he had to make allowances for that.

"All right. Granting your argument for the moment," he said, "you still haven't said why Mundo and the woman are here. They have their reality; we have ours. Why should they care?"

"Existence," Alice answered, sounding as mournful as a mythical furry lizard could sound. "To use Theopelli's mediocre tree analogy, a branch cut from the trunk dies."

"I'm lost again," Ecclesiastes sighed.

"How many *kamis* are there still left in Japan, the old demigods? How many leprechauns are still in Ireland? How many dragons in China, feathered flying serpents in Central America, stone trolls in Finland? The main trunk has narrowed, each time. And by doing that, we're choking ourselves." Theopelli unwrapped the final Twinkie and looked at it sadly. "The tree is rooted in chaos.

"Once there were thousands of branches," he said, "but we've closed them off, one by one. There are only a few left, and the avenues between them and us close each day. *We* don't notice when they die, not really, but everyone there does. They know. They experience it. And, like a tree, the branches also sustain us. I think we're in danger of killing ourselves, too. The world is becoming too familiar. We all see the same sights, we all believe the same truths. We're becoming too much the same."

Theopelli paused dramatically. "We need to reintroduce chaos into the world."

For a moment, a new vision of Theopelli stood before Ecclesiastes. As the dawn began to flood through the dusty old rooms, he thought he saw through the gruff exterior of Theopelli to the soul beneath, and he was awed by what was there.

"You really care, don't you?" Ecclesiastes said. "For all your bluster and self-centeredness, Theopelli, you care. You can't bear to think of all the lives that would end, of the generations that would never see life. You don't want to see all those people die. You believe in magic and happy endings."

In Ecclesiastes' mind, the angelic Theopelli nodded sadly. A silver tear like a liquid diamond rolled down the fat cheek.

But the real Theopelli brayed like a donkey. The vision dissolved in front of Ecclesiastes, and the sunlight seemed only mocking. The fat man stuffed the Twinkie in his mouth.

"Shit, no," he said. "I don't give a fuck about that at all. In the world that would come to being without my interference, the theorems behind my work won't be valid. If I don't change *that*, then the old fuddy-duddy bastards who said I was wrong will never have to eat their words. I want to see the looks on their faces when they see what utter shits they are."

He snorted, amused at the horrified look on Ecclesiastes' face. "What's the matter, slant eyes? Don't you like the idea of saving the world for the wrong reasons?"

25: Weighing the Anchorite

Joan turned the boat around. She followed her first mate's movement on the shore toward the group of pirates burying treasure on the beach. She saw the pirates club Petey to the sand, and she leaned far out over the gunwale of her three-masted schooner, dangling with one hand from the rigging with her wooden leg braced against a belaying pin.

"A vast hair, ye curvy frogs!" she screamed. "Ye leave me mate, or I'll have your keel hauled, betcha!"

That got their attention.

They looked up and pointed to her with their ferocious curved sabers. Two of them grabbed Petey and a native woman and ran back up the trail toward the fortifications. The remaining pirate ran down the beach and around a curve in the shore.

"Cowards!" Joan screamed at them. She drew her own saber in challenge, waving the bright polished blade wildly. "Cowards! Are ye afraid my steel won't taste good? We've got broad sides on our ship, sure."

Behind her, she could hear her crew muttering, daggers clenched in their teeth, each and every one of them wearing a red silk bandanna and eyepatch. They swarmed in the rigging, growling like madmen. The wind was picking up; she could hear it howling through the torn sails. Salt spray splashed over the bow, the deck dipped and swayed.

The dreaded North Easter.

"Lash the boss's son to the wheel," she cried. "Cut the jig loose! Don't poop on the deck! They'll be comin' after us. Ho, is Jolly Roger aloft?"

Roger leaned down from the top of the mainmast. "Here, Captain!"

"What do ye see, matey?"

"Vessel approaching off the starbird bow!"

Joan looked left, shading her eyes with one long-fingered hand to better peer through the salt mist. She couldn't let them take her, not with the cargo she carried on this voyage. The queen's prized magical bowl was still aboard, and the queen needed the bowl.

Captain Joan would sooner die than surrender.

"Aye, I see 'im, Roger. They'll be trying to get our quarters in the wind, but we're not going to let them, betcha. Bring us around, bring us around!"

Joan took the wheel herself, spinning it madly. The ship's hull creaked and groaned, heeling over the side and the crew screamed, grabbing wildly for ropes as everything on the decks shifted. But she was a good ship and Captain Joan had never been bested in ship-to-ship combat.

Mother had loved old sea movies. She'd made Joan watch whenever one was on television. Joan had learned quickly that one of the worst things she could do to Mother was to interrupt when a pirate movie was playing. In self-defense, she'd learned to love them herself.

"I seen 'em all," she screamed to the wind and the crew and the sea. "A hun'red times, prob'ly. Captain Joan always wins. Arrrr!"

The ship was aimed directly at her enemy now—she could see that it flew the hated flag of Spain, and she spat. Cannons boomed from the frigate, white puffs of smoke belched out, and cannonballs ripped holes in Joan's sails. Behind Joan, the rear mast snapped like a twig and men screamed, but she only laughed.

"Delay that, second mate!" she cried. "We ram them! Prepare two boards!"

Closer, closer: the bow wave was tremendous now, and she could see the frightened faces of the crew on the frigate. She had them. The ship's figurehead was aimed directly at their middle and they were too close for the cannons. The frigate's crew screamed, waving at her, but Captain Joan bore on relentlessly, holding the wheel steady.

Still shouting, the frigate's crew abandoned ship, leaping overboard. "Ye see!" Joan shrieked. "Ye see, you cowards!"

She spun the wheel at the last moment. The ship turned like a balky, angry sea dragon, the sides of the two ships scraping loudly. Then she was away again, the frigate's crew cursing her from the water as she passed.

"Captain!" Jolly Roger called from above. "Another ship, ho! A Spanish gallon!"

Captain Joan scowled. Yes—she was a gallon all right, four-masted and with sails like a bank of clouds on the horizon. Captain Joan admired the ship even as she hated her. The second mate came up behind her as Joan paused to gauge her enemy.

"Ye canna outrun her," the second mate said with a distinct Scottish brogue. "I'm already givin' ye everything she'sa got, Captain. She canna give no more."

"I'm aware of that, mister," she snapped. "Then we'll fight. Our sixteen men will play dead man's chess with her. We'll grapple the irons while they're hot. Turn us about!"

Once more, the ship canted into the wind. The crew primed the cannons on the foredeck, loading them with grapeshot to tear the sails and rake the decks of the enemy ship. The two vessels maneuvered in an intricate dance, playing the winds and each trying to cross the other's bow to unleash a deadly broadside. It was Captain Joan who won that battle of wits. Her craft was smaller and slower, but more nimble in the tricky crosscurrents. She slid across the front of the enemy.

"Fire!" she cried, and her cannons bucked and roared. Captain Joan leaned over the wheel and laughed, mocking the enemy crew, who bristled with steel on the deck. Their mouths were open in amazement as their ship came dangerously close to Joan's stern.

Joan sought to find their captain. She wanted to see

who commanded her, wanted to know her enemy. She saw him on the foredeck, his hands white-knuckled on the wooden rail.

She knew him. She knew him well.

Henderson. Fucking goddamn Abel C. Henderson.

Seeing that face made reality shift around her. The smell of black powder and the boom of cannons became diesel fumes and the puttering of inboard motors. The spoked wooden wheel in her hands became a plastic half wheel; her three-master dissolved into a sixteen-foot, battered Criscraft. Henderson stood on the foredeck of a long, sleek launch passing just behind Joan and turning back toward her.

Her boat bobbed in the heavy swell of the launch. The motor had gone dead. "Henderson!" she shouted. "I didn't die!"

"Joan? My God . . . *Joan?*" she heard him say. His florid face went pale. "Get her. I don't care what you do, but *get* her!" he shouted to the crew.

Grappling hooks gouged huge splinters in the wooden sides of the Criscraft. Screaming in anger, Joan ran to pull them out, but Henderson was alongside now. His hirelings swung over the rails onto Joan's boat.

"Leave me alone!" Joan shouted, but it was too late. Three of them grabbed her and lifted her kicking and screaming from her feet. They swung her up onto the deck of Henderson's boat.

Henderson was still pale. His smile looked like a wound in his face.

"Welcome aboard, Joan," he said. "It's been a long, long time."

Ecclesiastes possessed a vivid imagination. The ingenious and rather liberal erotic images he conjured up during lonely nights are best left private.

Among other type of fantasies he cultivated, one was a rather romantic image of the working scientist. He could see the stalwart Ph.D. posed in front of a blackboard, the front of his (or *her,* Ecclesiastes' raised consciousness prodded) lab smock powdered with the confectioner's sugar of chalk dust, the slate a landscape of incomprehensible squiggles.

Like most fantasies, masturbatory or otherwise, the reality certainly fell short of the eventual truth, Ecclesiastes thought. He looked at Theopelli in disdain.

Theopelli worked not hunched over old tomes piled on a desk in front of a blackboard, but slouched in a Laz-E-Boy recliner, the keyboard perched on his ample lap, the cord trailing over to Mundo's Macintosh computer on the coffee table. Plastic keys rattled like cheap castanets under his pudgy fingers. Mathematical symbols marched across the blue-white screen.

At least part of the fantasy was right. They *were* incomprehensible squiggles.

No, fantasies were best left untouched by reality, Ecclesiastes decided. The actual experience would never be as good.

"You know, he has fantasies, too, and they don't involve light bondage and leather," Alice said to Ecclesiastes.

Ecclesiastes reddened slightly. Alice looked at him with her long mouth slightly open. Her breath smelled like undercooked hamburger. "You read minds, too?"

Alice nodded. "Yep," she said. "A little. It depends on the intensity of the thoughts. You know, I really doubt that breasts like that are possible except in zero gravity."

Ecclesiastes decided to change the subject. "So what's he thinking?" he said, nodding toward Theopelli. The gross man wasn't wearing the fantasy lab coat but a soiled bathrobe found in one of his closets the night before. An eight-year wait hadn't improved its appearance. Its front was littered with potato-chip crumbs. Theopelli's hand prowled the bottom of the bag. He looked dejectedly at the salty remains he dredged out. Cross-legged in front of Theopelli, Mundo was dealing tarot cards. Alfred was downstairs, fixing supper.

"Theopelli? Aside from thinking that we should've bought a bigger bag of chips and that everything's Caleb's fault, he's trying to figure out what we need to do next."

"Great. Is what he said about these other worlds really true?"

"You should see Caleb's world. It's a mess. Half the population's dead and dying already—wars, pestilence, famine. A lot like New York and L.A., only everywhere. I imagine the same's true with the Gnostic woman's world."

"And what's going to happen here?"

Alice looked smug, grinning with all her teeth showing. "Boredom."

"Boredom?" Ecclesiastes echoed flatly.

Alice prodded him on the shoulder; she'd returned to full materiality overnight. "Why do airplanes fly?"

"You want my answer or Theopelli's?"

"The only reason any magic exists in your world at all is because there's a few people—a very few—who haven't accepted all the answers. You know, it's only when people aren't satisfied with the current way of doing things and go looking for something better that you get any progress. When you believe all the answers, when there's only one Truth, everyone's satisfied. But when that's the case, magic dies and progress dies. You get boredom. It killed the dinosaurs, too." Alice shrugged, a gesture that looked more like a shiver. "So Theopelli thinks you need some uncertainty put back in the world. Chaos. The unknown."

Ecclesiastes found himself nodding in agreement. The world Alice depicted sounded like a world in which his funeral parlors would go bankrupt in an instant. It sounded like a place where Ecclesiastes would find nothing to laugh at, nothing to wonder at. Things were bad enough now.

"You see," Alice said. "You agree. You want the same thing Mundo wants, that Theopelli wants. That's why you stay, because even though you deny half of what you've seen, deep down you really *want* it to be true."

"But how do you do it?" Ecclesiastes asked. "How do you 'put chaos back'?"

"Mundo thinks it a matter of shaking people's belief, of making them confront something they've denied. How Theopelli would do it, I don't know."

Theopelli stirred in the recliner. The keyboard fell to the floor as he stood up. "We need more chips," he declared loudly. "And Twinkies. Lots of Twinkies. We're going to Florida."

"Florida?" That brought scenes of palm trees and bikinis to Ecclesiastes.

Alice snorted. "Your mind's a one-track gutter," she whispered.

"That's were the Marvelites' headquarters is," Henderson answered. "Nothing exemplifies blind faith like organized religions. They're a symptom of everything that's wrong. Henderson's already shown an interest in you people; Florida's where Reverend Henderson lives and where I surmise Adept and Gnostic have gone. There's still a chance we can make the change."

Theopelli looked at Alice and shook his head. "We just have to figure out how to bring the goddamn dinosaur along."

26: The Attack on Fort Marvel

As strategy, Theopelli and Mundo's scheme had all the brilliant panache of Custer's stand on the low ground of the Little Big Horn. It shimmered with the inspiration of the Light Brigade's charge into the world's largest shooting gallery for cannons. It ranked with Napoleon's desire to visit Moscow in midwinter.

Or, as his father might have said, Theopelli might have been one of Hirohito's generals, advising the god-emperor to invade the United States with bombs and planes instead of electronic goods.

If Theopelli and Mundo wanted to inject chaos into the world, they didn't have to do it with their own plan, especially when it included Ecclesiastes.

What they came up with was the most harebrained, backward scheme Ecclesiastes thought possible. The trouble was, no one else seemed particularly disturbed by it.

The headache was gone. That was good. Angela was there and alive and in love with him.

That was *very* good.

But . . . they were prisoners of the second largest organized church in the USA. He and Angela had watched Joan's gallant sea fight and capture from the window of their fourth-floor "cell," and as far as Dirk knew that meant their last realistic hope was gone.

That was bad.

Especially since all of that was now two days in the past. Joan, Dirk assumed, was locked up somewhere else in the complex. Henderson refused to answer any of the questions Dirk asked about her. He also refused to let them go. Dirk should have been back in New York that first night to play. The band didn't know where he'd gone; they'd probably had to cancel the club gig, Stan Fedderman had most likely dropped them from his stable of groups, and Dirk could forget the recording contract, Savage, and his musical career.

That, he supposed, was very bad.

At least Dirk thought it should be.

In between bouts of happy and almost oblivious lovemaking with Angela, he tried to convince himself that he was depressed. Sometimes he succeeded. It was a schizophrenic few days in any case. Like Dirk, Angela's moods were alternately black and desperately jovial. She seemed to be waiting.

The only consolation Dirk had was that Angela seemed genuinely impressed by his gallantry. She also seemed largely amused by it.

The bright Florida sun peeked through the wooden shutters with a quiet embarrassment. Their room, though as large, spacious, and palatial a suite as any prisoner could ask for, was nonetheless fifty feet or so above the ground and too isolated from the main section of the mansion for the central air to have much effect. The windows had been firmly nailed shut. As a consequence, except when Harold and Abel Henderson paid one of their frequent visits, Angela wore nothing but one of Henderson's undershirts and white cotton panties, and those only because bare skin stuck to the wooden chairs in the humidity and the cotton absorbed the sweat.

To Dirk, she looked ravishing. Angela was in one of her up moods. She brushed damp hair back from her forehead and smiled at him when he turned back after staring out at the placid Gulf.

"Dirk, really, your coming here after me was awfully sweet of you. I almost cried when I saw you tearing from under the palms, swinging your flashlight. It was very brave and quixotic, and certainly out of character."

He'd started to grin, but the last words made him

tilt his head. "Out of character?" That didn't sound promising. In fact, it sounded suspiciously patronizing.

"It was daring. It meant taking a risk and maybe looking foolish. It meant not being safe. That's not like you."

She said it with a smile. It still hurt. His ego began bleeding all over his pride.

"Just a minute, Angela," he protested. "I left a comfortable teaching job to become a musician with no guarantees that anything would ever come of it. I've spent three years living out of a suitcase and a hotel room. That's not taking a risk? That's playing it safe? I don't buy that."

She wasn't going to allow his righteous anger. She poked him in the stomach under the "I'm a Marvelite" T-shirt Henderson had provided him, and she snickered.

"C'mon, Dirk. First of all, you know you can always fall back on teaching if music doesn't work. Playing rock star is a fantasy, not a risk. You're young, you don't have a family or a wife or own a home. You didn't have to leave anything behind. You've been indulging yourself, and that's about as safe as you can get. Admit it."

She prodded him again.

"No," he said stubbornly. "I won't. And I suppose you think *you're* the one who's taken all the risks."

If he'd intended to hurt Angela in return, he succeeded. He could see that immediately. Angela's good moods were fragile; this one exploded like the Hindenberg.

During the last few days, she'd told him the long tale of her past. Dirk still wasn't sure how much of it he bought, but there was obviously more going on here than he'd first been willing to believe. If this other world of hers was a fantasy, she'd invented a remarkably detailed madness, and he'd found the history fascinating.

In her world (Angela told him), the rising Christian Church hadn't been able to solidify the Roman bishops' authority over the rest of the church. Confronted by the heresy of the Gnostics (most of whom claimed that Christ had never physically risen, who sometimes taught that there were several Gods, and who numbered among their holy scriptures the gospels of Mary Magdelene and Thomas) the bishops hadn't been able to consolidate their stand. Instead, the Gnostic sect continued to grow.

And like a toppling row of dominoes, that failure to codify and unify the new religion had rippled down through the rest of history. Christianity never solidified as a religious or a political entity. With the Gnostics' influence from Eastern mysticism and magic, East and West met and mingled far more quickly.

The empire of Rome encountered the Tsin Dynasty of China and helped them defeat the Hsiung-nu Huns to the north; open trade was established by the fourth century A.D. Oriental metaphysics merged with Western sciences into a new ideal. Christianity (much changed under Gnostic influence) was simply another of the dozen or so official state religions tolerated by Rome. The New World was discovered in the ninth century; settlements were established by 1000 A.D. The Roman Empire didn't fragment and fall, but became a disassociated Uber-empire, adjudicating and overseeing the separate local governments.

And, in recent times, it had all gone to hell. The Four Horsemen were riding roughshod over the land. Because of—if Dirk credited Angela's reasoning—*his* world.

"Yes, I'm taking a risk," she told him, and her mouth had turned down, and the jade eyes shimmered with threatened overflow. Angela hugged herself and withdrew from him. "I left *everything* behind me. Dirk, if *I've* made a bad decision, a hell of a lot more people than just me suffer. And I may have already made that decision, Dirk. I let myself get involved with you."

That stung.

"Don't look at me with those sad cow eyes," Angela told him. "I'm not trying to hurt you, and I don't regret it. I just wonder if I didn't let my feelings for you interfere with my reading of the situation. I didn't have to let Henderson capture me, but I did. I thought I could keep you out of it that way."

"Whoa." He waved a hand at her. "You're telling me you *let* yourself get caught? That's the first I heard about this."

"It's true. And I stayed by choice, too. I thought . . . I thought the others would be the ones to come after me, or I might find them here already. I . . . I didn't think you'd be the first one to show up."

"And now what?"

Angela shrugged. "I don't know," she admitted. "It seemed to make sense at the time. But I made a mistake. I didn't really think Henderson would make a move that night at Shea, so I didn't bring the cards or the bowl with me. It was stupid. Stupid. Without them . . ." She smiled sadly. "So I'm still waiting."

And Dirk remembered something.

"I have the cards," he said.

For a long, long moment, Angela didn't say anything at all. She stared at him, one eyebrow higher than the other. Her hands went to her hips and the sadness was gone, replaced by something else, something dangerous.

"*You,*" she said finally, each word separate and very distinct, "Have. Them."

"Umm . . ." Dirk licked his lips. He didn't like the look she was giving him. Not at all. "Yeah, well . . ."

"Here? Now?"

"Uh-huh. Had them in my back pocket, wrapped in oilcloth. Henderson's guards looked at 'em, gave 'em back."

"For the last *two days* you've had them."

Dirk shrugged.

"You wouldn't by any chance have also brought the bowl?"

He gave her a lopsided smile. "Well, yeah, it was in the boat, too. Joan—"

He didn't have time to say more. Angela leaped at

him. Her arms went around his neck and she hugged him. "You're an absolute asshole," she whispered, her face very close to his.

Then she kissed him. "But I love you."

This time her mouth opened as they kissed. Her tongue went spelunking. Her hands went from the back of his head down his spine and cupped his rear before migrating to the front of his jeans. Her mouth pulled away from his wetly.

"You're awfully crowded in there," she said. "I think you need some more room."

His zipper rasped. "There. That's better," she said. Holding him that way, she led him to the bed.

"We'll approach from the five points of an imaginary pentangle drawn around Henderson's mansion," Mundo said. "Each of us will carry a lit candle. As long as we stay together, the pentangle will protect us—you each have an FM receiver linked to me. We've already alerted the media, so they should be waiting. When Henderson comes out, that's when I'll make the move."

"Look, why don't we just call the papers and tell them all about you and Theopelli?" Ecclesiastes asked. He was sweating under the wilted collar of his formal shirt. Somewhere along the line he'd lost the silk bow tie, and it was simply too hot to wear the coat. He felt positively slovenly, and he didn't relish the thought of getting thrown in jail, whether he saved the world or not.

"No," Theopelli said emphatically. "You're an idiot, Mitsumishi. It won't work that way. I thought you Japs were good with logic. All we'd get out of that would be to become one-day wonders of the local press. No, we need a direct confrontation now. We need national coverage so that the Gnostic and the Adept can find us. Once we're all together, we'll have the power to do something public and dramatic. What we have to do is shake the foundations of belief. There's too much inertia to overcome the situation any other way since you people were too damn late."

"I won't do it," Ecclesiastes declared. "Look, I can agree with you people in principle but I wouldn't last a week in jail. Besides, the shame would kill my father."

"Impotence," Mundo proclaimed. "Broken knees. Funeral homes burned to the ground. I have friends in bad places. And Alice is getting very hungry."

Alice shrugged. "A little bit, yeah," she said. "It comes with being material."

Ecclesiastes looked at them: Theopelli, Mundo, Alice. Alfred was slumped in a chair of their motel room, no help at all.

"So—where's my candle?" he asked.

The image was grainy and slightly out of focus, but Harold could see well enough to be furious.

"Look at that, Abel!" he screamed. "They're fucking again. The beast with two backs. She's pulling him down on top of her, wrapping her legs around his back as he enters her, letting him lick her nipples. . . ."

Abel was staring at the video monitor, a slight sheen of sweat on his expansive forehead. "I can see all that, Harold. I'm not blind."

"You'll go blind if you do what you're thinking of doing, Abel. And you a man of God." Harold stared at the flickering images on the screen, moving together in the dance of love. "Aargh!" he throated out. "The woman's mine. She's mine. I don't know why you put the two of them together, Abel. You *knew* what they'd do."

Abel glanced at Harold and the erection that despite the sunburn, insisted on flaunting itself under his loincloth. "You couldn't do anything even if you wanted to," he pointed out. "And you know why I put them together—so they would talk."

"So they'd fuck. So you could tape it all and play it back at night, beating your meat in time to the grunts and moans. Trying to achieve a replayed mutual orgasm. Slow motion and freeze-frame." Harold panted dramatically, throwing his head back.

Henderson blushed. "Harold—"

"It's okay, Abel. I know you're not really a man of God. All you want is the power and the money that goes with your position. This is just another carnie for you, bigger and brighter and more lucrative. Fine." Harold thumped himself on his bare chest, his scraggly beard whipping back and forth as he shook his head. "But *I'm* godly, Abel. God gives me the visions. And this offends me."

"You're standing there with a hard-on, screaming about how she's yours and how you'd like to be screwing her yourself, and *you're* godly? Look at you, you won't even take your eyes off the monitor."

But Harold was ignoring him. Intent on the screen, with his thin mouth pressed into a tight line, he was— very carefully avoiding the tenderest sections of sunburn—masturbating.

Abel sighed. He was beginning to regret following Harold down this particular prophecy. The little illegalities were starting to pile up, and while the church's influence could bury quite a lot, there was always some danger in too much bad press, as his lesser cousins among the fundamentalists had discovered. Maybe he should have been content with what he had. Maybe this time Harold wasn't seeing the future but only his own madness. Abel didn't deceive himself that any of Harold's visions came from God. No, Harold was just erratically prescient. Gifted. An idiot savant of prognostication. But maybe this time Harold was simply insane.

Maybe.

On the other hand, some of what he'd heard from Angela and Dirk had been interesting. She was looking for the same book, and now he knew that a man named Carlos Theopelli had written it, and that it was mathematical in nature. He knew that she also believed there was a (unbelievable!) sorcerer involved, from yet another world, if he could credit that at all.

So far, Harold's visions and Angela's comments matched, wherever they were coming from.

And then there was the incredible coincidence that

Joan—poor Joan, of all the haunted and guilty ghosts of his past—should find him again.

Leaving Harold to his self-ministrations, Abel went to see her.

Ecclesiastes supposed that he shouldn't have been surprised when Theopelli and Mundo gave him the pentangle point defined by the Gulf of Mexico. About the only good thing he could say about it was that his clothes were ruined anyway. He slid out of the rental motorboat into waist-high swells, which made it difficult to hold on to the candle, much less keep the taper lit.

He didn't make it far toward the shore before he saw two security guards tearing down the beach toward him from opposite directions. The closest was a middle-aged, out-of-shape man with jowls like a broken-down hound. Dogface had his gun out as Ecclesiastes stumbled through the surf near the shore.

"Stop right there," he snarled in a classic southern-sheriff twang. "Hold your hands way up there, boy, and don't even think of movin'."

Dogface looked like he was used to being obeyed. Ecclesiastes lifted his hands high, still holding the candle. Hot wax dripped down his sleeve.

"Call the rev'rend," Dogface said to his companion, a much younger version of himself. "Tell 'im we got another loony on the beach."

The tiny speaker in Ecclesiastes' ear hissed and crackled. "Mitsumishi, goddamn it!" Mundo's voice. "Keep moving. The pentangle's falling apart."

Ecclesiastes took a step forward. That brought Dogface's gun barrel back up. "Boy, don't even think it," he said. "I told you to freeze, and I don't give a shit how hot it is—you make like a Frigidaire, son."

"Mitsumishi! I'll grind your nuts to powder with a sledgehammer. I'll pull your teeth out with rusty pliers. Move it, man. They can't stop you."

Ecclesiastes moaned. "Mitsumishi!" Mundo screamed in his ear.

Ecclesiastes took another step.

"Son, now, I'm not fooling. You so much as twitch and I'll take out your legs. You unnerstan'?"

"Mitsumishi!"

Dogface looked uncertain. Maybe he was bluffing, maybe he was too kindly to actually shoot. Ecclesiastes took the step. Dogface frowned, his eyes went hard, and he squeezed the trigger.

Ecclesiastes closed his eyes. He heard the shot and waited for the pain.

It never came. Ecclesiastes opened his eyes again. Dogface, with a puzzled expression, fired off another round, then the whole clip. Bullets sprayed seawater all around Ecclesiastes, but he remained, somehow, untouched.

Ecclesiastes grinned. He laughed. He lowered his hands. Cupping the flame of the candle and smiling broadly, he stepped onto dry land, his shoes squilching wetly. "A nice day for a miracle, isn't it, sir?" Ecclesiastes said to Dogface.

The security guard reached out for Ecclesiastes, then jerked his hand back. "Ouch!" A crackling burst like static electricity had leapt out from Ecclesiastes' arm; Dogface's cuff smoldered.

Ecclesiastes chuckled. "All right, Mundo," he said. "Maybe this is going to work, after all."

With Dogface and his friend trailing alongside him, he walked toward the house, whistling.

The hole in Joan's head had been growing larger and it hurt. The feeling she had was much like what she remembered when the Marvel Circus had worked the Alabama coast. Sometimes a storm would move in from the Gulf. All the afternoon before there would be an aching, tense stillness. Finally, the sky would darken to blue black on the horizon and there would come a flickering of distant lightning. Hours later, the actual storm would break in a flurry of hail and wind.

That was the way the rift felt. She could see the gales gathering.

Joan was adrift. She'd never had the world act so

unstable before. Everything was fluid and flowing; nothing stayed the same for more than a few minutes.

It was very disconcerting.

"Joan?"

The familiar and hated voice of Henderson spoke from the grate at the door of her trailer. Betsa had gone to another trailer for the night, indulging the sexual tastes of some country rube. Joan figured Henderson had found somebody for her.

"Go 'way," she said. "I got my period." That sometimes ended things—in fact, her menstruation was erratic and fitful.

"I'll have one of the servants bring you something," Henderson said.

That changed everything. Now she was in one of the movies she'd seen on television. "Not now, Jeeves," she said. "I'll be fine."

"Joan, just what are you doing here? Can you tell me? Did Dirk tell you anything about the bowl?"

Joan looked to where the bowl sat on the table. She'd filled it with flowers again. Flowers reminded her of New York, and for a moment she was back on the urban streets. "Flowers look pretty, huh? You buy 'em, three bucks, cheap."

"Joan, you're not making any sense. Come back to reality."

That sounded like something Majesto the Magician used to say when he was doing his show. "I know the patter, too," she told Majesto. " 'Behind the curtain of reality, there are worlds where other gods live.' I 'member."

"Sir?" The interruption came from the door. A concerned face appeared.

"What is it?" Henderson asked.

"Well, sir. That's just it. We're not really sure, but I think you ought to come upstairs immediately."

Naked and flushed from their lovemaking, Angela laid out the cards, staring intently at each of the brightly colored images as she dealt them into an intricate crossed pattern on the floor.

"I knew it," she breathed. "Dirk, they're somewhere close. I can see the Mage's influence in the layout, and the Dead Man . . . They're close."

Dirk had been staring out the window. For the last few seconds he'd been standing in silent shock. Angela's words released him.

"I know," Dirk said. "Umm, darling, there's a dinosaur at Henderson's front gate holding a candle."

Angela laughed. "The bowl, Dirk. I need it."

"Joan has it, if anyone . . ." he began, but Angela was already bounding off the bed.

"Call the guard," she said. "Get him to come in here."

"Neither one of us is dressed. . . ."

"Just do it, Dirk."

Her tone didn't leave him much chance for argument. Going to the door, he knocked. There was a bored and muffled "Yeah?" from outside.

"Can you come in here for a second? We've got a slight problem. . . ."

A key rattled in the lock. The knob turned. "What kinda problem—" the guard began. At the same moment Angela leaped forward. The guard had time for one startled (and appreciative) look before she touched him. There was an audible, sinister sizzling when her fingers touched his chest, and the guard slumped to the floor.

"Jesus," Dirk said. "Could you have done that all along?"

"I told you so, didn't I? Come on, we don't have time for that now."

She was already through the doorway. Dirk hesitated, wondering whether he should grab for clothing, then sighed.

Feeling slightly embarrassed and very exposed, he followed.

Dogface and friend followed Ecclesiastes every step of the way, though neither one made another attempt to restrain him. Dogface was consulting with a walkie-talkie to someone in the house and waving his arms around as he explained the situation.

For his own part, Ecclesiastes was feeling decidedly cocky about things by the time Mundo's voice crackled in his ear again. "Around the front, Mitsumishi. Henderson's come outside."

Ecclesiastes nodded to no one in particular and gave Dogface a big wave and toothy smile. "Follow me," he said. "We're going around front."

In the courtyard before the entrance, Henderson stood before a squadron of his blue-suited people. A minicam crew from a local TV station had arrived, along with a few reporters from the papers; they crowded around Henderson. The reverend looked bigger and softer than the television version Ecclesiastes had seen. He also looked a lot more confused and uncertain, though Ecclesiastes supposed that seeing the five of them camped out on the front lawn might disconcert anyone.

"Just *what* is going on?" Henderson thundered in his best evangelical voice.

Theopelli answered. "Come now. You don't know? Christ's sake, man, you're not very swift on the uptake. We have here most of what you were advertising for in New York. I'd like you to meet Caleb Mundo, the sorcerer, and Alice, the beast who dwells within him. We also have Ecclesiastes Mitsumishi, a slant-eyed undertaker, and the scrawny hillbilly is Alfred Roundbottom, my manservant. As for me, my name is Carlos Theopelli."

Theopelli smiled. He was still wearing his bathrobe, and it had come partially untied. Underneath, Ecclesiastes could see a dirty pair of Jockey shorts. "I'm the genius who wrote the book you've been searching for," Theopelli continued, and thumped himself proudly on the chest. "I was dead, and I have risen again. Now, that tends to rip one great big frigging hole in the exclusive Resurrection Club, doesn't it?"

Henderson looked at each of them, then eyed the minicam suspiciously. He almost smiled, in the way Ecclesiastes imagined that a piranha might. "I don't think we need to be making a scene out here, my friends. I'd suggest that we all come inside. We can talk in private. . . ."

"Not a chance, dickhead," Mundo grunted before Theopelli could answer. "We're just here for one thing. Theopelli tells me that if you have your way, my world gets squashed. So I'm going to make certain that doesn't happen. I'm going to shut you up. Permanently."

Mundo said it dramatically enough, but Ecclesiastes saw the uncertain look Alice sent his way. Mundo's statement brought the weapons out from under the armpits of the blue suits around Henderson, but all Mundo did was sniff derisively.

"Sophomore-level magic," he said. "Any decent graduate could do it. Just flex the local magnetic field . . ." Mundo snarled, gestured, and the guns flew from the blue suits' startled grips. They lay on the lawn like bright metal birds.

Mundo laughed his dark, sinister laugh. "You have the wrong idea entirely, Henderson," he said. "I'm a sorcerer, remember? I don't need guns or violence to deal with you. My realm is the arcane. Magik with a 'k.' What you'd probably call evil devil worship. But then, you're stupid. You have a dangerous tongue, though, a tongue that I'm going to cleave to the roof of your mouth. I'm going to make you *mute*, Henderson. I'm going to make your tongue sit in your mouth like a dead thing so you can't talk at all. Not ever again."

Abel Henderson was used to threats.

Anyone remotely famous became very familiar with them. There were enough cranks and crazies out there to send death threats to several editions of *Who's Who*. Loonies with guns Henderson took seriously enough that he made certain that the local sheriff was always pleased with him, and that his security staff was quick and efficient.

Loonies with "magical" threats he wasn't quite so worried about. Hell, Joan was weird enough for any three patients in the Florida State Mental Facility. Angela, Harold's "whore," had done some strange stuff, by all accounts, but she certainly hadn't shown him anything since.

Henderson had seen every carnie magician in the world. He remembered Joan's Majesto, too, and though the guy had been good, there were others better. Henderson had seen elephants disappear, watched a small city's worth of big-breasted stage assistants in skimpy outfits get cut in half and magically glued back together. He'd witnessed levitations, summonings, disappearances, distortions, manipulations, and transformations.

He was certain of one thing and one thing only.

Each and every one of the millions of stunts he'd seen performed had been a fake. A trick. The result of misdirection, stage props, sleight of hand, or a combination of all three.

This ugly little dwarf might have something to pull the guns from the hands of his people. Some heavy-duty electromagnets planted just under the ground might do it, and hadn't the groundskeepers been working out here just last week? Mindyou, this was a *good* stunt, but it was just that—a stunt. There was no way Mr. Short-and-Ugly was going to make Abel C. Henderson stop talking. Still . . .

It was always best to know the ground rules before you called a bluff. Especially when the press were watching.

"Let me get this straight, brother," Abel said. "Y'all are going to strike me dumb. From right over there. Without touching me or getting any closer at all."

"You got it, bozo."

Abel looked at them. This was the damned oddest bunch of loonies he'd ever seen, and they matched Harold's prophecies uncannily, down to the guy dressed up in a furry lizard suit. Maybe this was exactly what Harold had been talking about. Maybe this was the opportunity he'd been gabbling about for the last several months. The news coverage would guarantee airplay, maybe even something national. This was bizarre and visual. It was *made* for television.

A little publicity never hurt.

"Even if I believed you could do it," Henderson intoned, "the Lord protects me. My voice is His, my friends, and He does not take lightly those who mock Him." He was gathering speed and resonance now, half turned to the cameras. "Those who dabble with magic and the occult are placing themselves in jeopardy, for that is Satan's world. I tell you, your souls are in mortal danger."

"And your tongue is in deep shit. How's it taste, Reverend?" Mundo asked.

Henderson shook his head sadly, like a father to an errant, misguided son. "I place my trust in the Lord. You can do nothing to me. Nothing at all."

The dwarf cackled. He spat. He held out the guttering candle in his hand, closed his eyes, and began to sway back and forth. It wasn't a bad show. Henderson could have used the short little fart if he were still running the carnie racket. The dwarf was a natural.

Now the "sorcerer" was muttering gibberish like the faithful who sometimes spoke in tongues at Henderson's own meetings. The dwarf had some visual gimmick going as well—there was a greenish fog swirling around him, and ugly yellow sparks flared in the midst of it. High-class stuff, Henderson realized, real Industrial Light & Magic quality, like the electromagnets in the ground. *Expensive* stuff. Whoever was backing these people (the Catholics? maybe the Baptists?) had money to burn. Henderson began to wonder if maybe he hadn't made a slight misjudgment.

It was too late now.

The dwarf reached a shrieking crescendo. Henderson could hear a wind howling around the little man; even in broad daylight the sparks were blinding. The dwarf howled as if in pain and gestured toward Henderson.

Ecclesiastes saw the whirlwind strike Henderson full in the face. A flurry of bright fireflies careened past the burly preacher and disappeared. Henderson *felt* Mundo's spell. Ecclesiastes could see it. The reverend's eyes were dazed; Henderson staggered backward a step as if someone had just slugged him in the jaw.

"Got him!" Ecclesiastes whooped, slapping Alice on the back.

Or trying to. Ecclesiastes' hand went clear through her.

Henderson's mouth was open. For a long second, nothing at all came out of it. Henderson shook himself, straightening his yellow silk tie. The minicam crew moved in close.

"Praise the Lord!" Henderson said. "Hallelujah!"

His voice was utterly and completely normal.

27: Every Now and Then

"Just what's so important that we have to run around the place in our birthday suits?" Dirk huffed as he followed Angela down a flight of stairs and into the main wing of the house. Angela seemed to know where she was heading—Dirk trailed her naked, muscular back through a series of doors and into another stairwell.

"I've been wrong," Angela called back over her shoulder. "We've all been wrong."

"Huh?" Dirk was beginning to breathe heavily. Angela was definitely in better shape.

"Theopelli's book, Dirk. It's really just a guideline, like the tarot. What's going to make a difference for my world isn't equations or signs in the cards: it's the people those things represent."

"Like"—huff—"Joan?"

"I can *feel* her, Dirk. She's got a pull like nothing I've ever felt before. I thought that *I* was the focus, and I'll bet the Mage was thinking the same thing. I thought I was the one supposed to do something, but it wasn't me. Not at all. I think it's Joan. Joan's the key. We're just here to lend her the power."

They reached the bottom of the stairwell. Angela wrenched open the firedoor and went through. The heavy door shut before Dirk, panting, could get there. Taking a gasping breath, he pulled it open again. "Slow down, would you?" he called, stepping through into the corridor beyond. "The last time I saw Joan, she thought she was a pirate captain. You want *her* to make a decision on the kind of world we live in—"

He stopped, nearly running into Angela.

"Oh my God," he said.

* * *

"Shit!" Alfred howled. He dropped his candle; it went out immediately in the sandy grass. "It didn't work, it didn't work." He began to moan.

Ecclesiastes looked from Alfred, whose face had gone a pasty, terrified white, to Theopelli's frowning scowl, to Mundo. The dwarf was on his knees. He was sweating far more than could be attributed to just the black robes and Florida heat. He slumped as if exhausted.

"*She's* here, damn it," the sorcerer muttered. "She did it again. I could feel it. Sucked it all out of me, just drained it." He pounded his fists on the ground.

"Joan? She's *here?*"

Mundo sighed. He suddenly seemed very old and not nearly so dangerous. He nodded.

The cameraman for the news crew was openly joking with the female commentator. Henderson was chuckling himself. Alongside Ecclesiastes, Alice was little more than a faint outline, like a heat ghost wandering over blacktop.

"You would have been tasty," Alice's faint voice whispered to Ecclesiastes. The voice was almost too soft to hear. "Bye, 'Clese. I enjoyed it."

"Just a little diversion," the preacher told the press. "Some folks that need the Lord's help. It's all over now, folks, so let's all go home." Henderson turned to Theopelli, swaggering with victory. "Why don't you come in and talk? I'd like to know more about you and your book. The rest of your friends can leave. I don't think there's any reason for me to press charges. They all look pretty harmless."

Henderson chuckled.

Ecclesiastes decided that indecision made Theopelli's face look more like a bloated fungus than usual. The recluse's bloodshot right eye was puffy and black-rimmed. His already round shoulders slumped; his skin had a gray pallor that reminded Ecclesiastes of the first time he'd seen Theopelli in the cemetery.

"It's over," Theopelli said. "We were too late."

"No," Mundo wailed, still on his knees. His dark

gaze flared and his hand fisted on his lap. "You can't say that. You can't let that happen."

"I can. I did," Theopelli answered. "I told you that one person or one group of people can't change the world, not unless they're at the exact place at the exact moment. You weren't. I tried to fix it, but I told you it wasn't certain. You failed."

"You're saying that my world's dead now?" Mundo's fist opened.

"It's even worse than that. Now the world will never know my true genius," Theopelli replied. Ecclesiastes could see tears of disappointment in the man's eyes. "You might as well go," Theopelli said. "Chaos is dead. Belief won."

Alice had faded away altogether. Alfred had already taken Henderson's opening—his dwindling figure was moving at a fast half trot down the long driveway. The minicam was packed away, and the reporters were getting into their cars.

They pulled away.

The moment that was to have altered the very mindset of humankind wasn't *totally* a dud, Ecclesiastes decided. At least it didn't look like he'd be going to jail.

The door to the room was two-inch-thick laminated oak banded with iron. The tiny window cut into it was barred and grated; the lock was a drop-bolt masterpiece and the massive hinges were plated stainless steel. It was a monster, not quite jailhouse quality but obviously designed to discourage anyone from leaving the room it guarded.

At the moment, however, the door smoldered on the floor, the hinges snapped clean from the steel doorframe, the oak warped and blackened, the lock a melted, smoking puddle.

However, it wasn't the door that stopped Angela and Dirk in their tracks. It was what stood on top of it.

"Hey, Petey! You part of the peep show now, betcha."

Dirk blinked. It didn't help. Whatever was standing

on the door must be Joan. The voice was certainly hers, though there were shifting overtones in it like something heard through a ring modulator.

But it certainly didn't *look* like Joan.

Oh, it had the general lumpy outline of that street character, but the figure shimmered optically in and out of phase. It was impossible to pin down any of the details. Everything shifted, like movements seen out of the corner of the eye but gone when you turned to find them. It *hurt* to look at her. It was like trying on someone else's glasses, the prescription of which was totally wrong: Dirk kept squinting, but couldn't bring her into focus.

She was something glimpsed in the middle of a downpour of mirror shards. In a way, it was almost attractive.

"Don't let Henderson see your friend, Petey," Joan said. "He take her, sure. He like tits. He use ta say, 'Tits sell tickets.' "

"Joan, what's going on? Are you okay?"

"I think so. S'pretty, kinda. See all sorts'a stuff: mountains, trees, clouds, animals, people. All round me." Something that might have been a hand shot from the bundle of motion. "Whoo! See that'n? Like fireworks. Purty as flowers."

Then her voice became darker, disturbed. "Thing is, I keep seein' Henderson, too. Lots of the little bastards."

Angela was edging past Joan toward the room. *The bowl*, she mouthed to Dirk, and gestured past the doorway.

"Joan, did you bring the bowl with you?"

"Sure, Petey. In the room. Henderson thought it was a 'tique, so he kept it." Angela had gone into the room, out of sight. Joan, or the cloudy, sparkling thing she'd become, stepped down from the door and began moving toward the stairwell. "I put flowers in it. Gotta go, Petey. Gotta find that bastard."

"Sure. No problem."

Dirk let Joan pass him, pressing against the wall. He didn't want any of whatever she was to touch him.

When there was an opening, Dirk hurried into the room after Angela.

As it turned out, there was an extra person in Joan's old cell.

Harold was there, too, and he had the bowl.

It was awfully hard to see. The mind rift had exploded like a volcano and entire landscapes were racing out of it along with bits and pieces of Joan's own life.

It was very confusing, but Joan knew how to deal with confusion—you simply pretend it's normal and flow with it. All the sounds from outside were distorted, and there were inner sounds as well: voices were talking to her from all directions, shouting, pleading, insisting. Joan wasn't exactly sure what it was they were trying to tell her to do.

The rift made a din of its own, a grinding howl like a bad bearing on a car wheel. But there was power in the energy flowing from the mind fault. Joan sensed that she could use it as she had in Shea Stadium. She just had to find the right place.

Joan wasn't certain where that might be. Whichever way she looked, there was something new. Still, in front, like a roadway seen through the barest clear patch on a fogged windshield, there was Henderson. Her hatred of him pulled her toward him. The crackling energy she'd stolen guided her.

Joan plowed through the main door of the complex, which exploded into splinters as she approached. The security people who were racing toward her suddenly stopped at the sight, and Joan plowed through them like the Big Apple wind blowing trash along a gutter. That made her laugh. Joan moved out into hot sunlight; the rift glowed, sucking at that energy, too. She had never felt so vital, so potent. Her hand, when she put it in front of her face, was incandescent. Joan marveled at it.

More images raced past her, screeching. Joan was loose in time and space, unfettered. She saw parts of her life, all jumbled and out of order, interspersed with landscapes and faces she'd never seen before at all.

She found it nearly impossible to concentrate on her one obsession, but through the visual and aural brilliance she could see the group gathered on the lawn. Some were people she knew. There was 'Clese; there was the dwarf magician.

There was Henderson.

"You son of a bitch!" she bellowed. Joan raised her hand and gave Henderson the finger. She was as startled as the rest when an arc of blue-white resplendence seared from the upraised fingertip, crackling loudly. The bolt discharged on the ground two feet in front of Henderson. The flare hit like a grenade, splattering him with grass and sandy dirt. A ring of orange flame guttered around the perimeter of a foot-wide hole.

"Whee!" Joan giggled. She blew on her finger like a movie gunfighter with a smoking six-shooter. "Gotcha now, Henderson, betcha!" She aimed her finger at the preacher, who blanched and backed away from the apparition.

"Stop! You're wasting the power!" An obese and remarkably ugly man next to 'Clese and the dwarf was shouting at her. The other voices chimed in through the static-filled din. The ethereal voices shouting along with the ugly man.

No. You have to retain the power for other tasks. You must open the gateways.

A dark nodule floated in front of her, a sphere of utter satin black that even the dazzling sun couldn't illuminate. Deep inside it, as if Joan were gazing into a pool of impossible depth, there were faint glowings, tiny microbes of light.

Distantly, she heard the dwarf gasp. "Gods, Theopelli, she's got a gateway up somehow. *I* couldn't do that, much less open it. How—"

Direct the forces here. The voices were aiding her, but Joan frowned. She didn't trust voices in her head. Too many of those she heard had hurt her.

"Fuck you," she said.

Please? Now the voices had all become Betsa's voice, echoing, pleading. *Joan, I need you. You have to save me. Please do this for me.*

Joan sighed. "Okay, Betsa. For you. You hate Henderson, too."

Joan pointed her finger at the sphere. Lightnings hissed and flickered again, and a bitterly cold wind raged from the darkness flailing at her. Joan's baseball cap went flying from her balding, crewcut head. The flecks of light grew and brightened. But then, as if weary of their long climb from the darkness, they began to fade again, receding into the black depths of the sphere. "Betsa?" Joan called.

She felt tired. Very tired.

"She doesn't have enough," the dwarf was saying. "Damn it, she doesn't have enough."

"It wouldn't matter anyway," the ugly man said. "She doesn't know what to do with it."

"It's very pretty don't you think?" Harold said. "It'd be a true shame if I dropped it. Crack, crack, splinter, splinter. And all the king's horses and all the king's men couldn't put the bowl back together again, though I must say it's always puzzled me why the king would expect his horses to have any success at all. Most horses of my acquaintance have no manual dexterity at all."

Harold's manic eyes skittered above the scraggly, thin beard. To Dirk he still looked like a starving Tarzan, bare feet, loincloth, and dirt streaked on his sunken, hairy chest. Harold leered openly at the naked Angela, then scowled at Dirk.

"Do you know how old the bowl is, Harold?" Angela asked him. "Thousands of hands have held it, innumerable rituals have gone through it. If you drop that bowl, it can't be replaced."

"I know," Harold admitted, and in his wild eyes, there was a trace of awe. "I can feel everyone who ever used it. Even the glaze throbs and burns; just holding it makes me feel like I'm someone else. But I'll still drop the bowl," he added. "You're going to use it to leave. You're going to use it against Abel and me. That's not a nice thing to do to your future husband."

"You've called me the 'Whore of Magic,' Harold. You'd marry someone you call that?"

Harold nodded. His breath was fast and shallow. "Yes. Yes. I do. I, Harold, take this whore to be my lawful wedded wife. Love, honor, and respect, and all the rest. The visions said we'd be together. I saw you naked, you and me together."

"I'm naked now, Harold." Angela ran her hands down the flank of her body. Harold's gaze followed the gesture, snared. He was beginning to drool.

"Angela . . ." Dirk began.

Angela ignored Dirk. Her hands came up, cupped her breasts. "You know why the visions called me the Whore, Harold? Do you know what starts the ritual?" Angela asked.

Harold shook his head.

"Sex," Angela answered. "Screwing."

That elicited an immediate and noticeable reaction from Harold. Dirk stared at the rising centerpole making a tent of Harold's loincloth and then at Angela. "Wait a minute—" Dirk protested, but Angela didn't even look at him.

"If the bowl's destroyed, I won't have a need for you, Harold. Your visions were right. We *are* meant to be together. I need you. But I need the bowl, too. Please, put it down."

Harold started to obey, then stopped. His erection twitched under the coarse fabric at his waist. "You want to destroy Abel and my church."

"No," Angela said. "This isn't about you and Henderson at all. I just want other choices left in this world, that's all. I want my people to live. That's not wrong is it?"

Harold shrugged. He seemed caught between his visions and lust.

"I want you, Harold," Angela said. "I want you inside me."

Harold shivered.

Lust as it often has, won the battle. The brain screamed commands, but desire had cut the communication lines to the body and need swarmed over the bulwarks of reason. The Voice of the Phallus was all Harold heard. Hormones raced triumphant through his body, sounding the victory of testosterone.

Harold put the bowl down on the floor. He ripped off the loincloth, exposing his still-sunburnt but rampant manhood. "Yes," he said. He moved toward Angela.

Dirk hit him like a linebacker, shoulder down. The impact drove Harold into the wall. The breath went out of the prophet with a gasp; his head slammed against concrete blocks with a sound like someone rapping on a ripe watermelon. Harold's eyes rolled back in his head and he slumped to the floor.

"You didn't have to hit him so hard," Angela said ruefully. "But you picked up wonderfully on your cue."

Angela pressed up against Dirk. She hugged and kissed him fiercely. Dirk thought that she was simply being grateful until he felt her hands on his genitals. "Angela!" he said. "Not now—"

She continued her ministrations, her breath hot on his neck and ears. "I wasn't entirely lying to Harold, Dirk. Why do you think I needed Edgar that night in Cincinnati? A ritual's an engine—it doesn't work if you leave any of the parts out. Dirk, I need you to make love to me. Now. If you ever wanted a quickie, this is the time. Or should I wake up Harold?"

That decision didn't require any thought at all. "So . . . where do you want to do this?"

Angela laughed. "I thought you'd come to that conclusion," she said. "Right here will do."

Leaning back, she pulled him down on top of her on the floor.

The dark sphere was fading. Joan yawned, wanting just to close her eyes and go to sleep. The mind rift had started to close once more, the odd landscapes sliding back into the gap like melted Bosch paintings. The horrible roar around her was subsiding; her vision of Now was opening again.

The rift voices wailed. Joan felt a compelling sadness. "Sorry, Betsa. I tried. I'm jus' sleepy, that's all."

Joan thought she'd sit down here on the grass. She was even too tired to yell at Henderson.

But just as her knees started to buckle, Joan felt a recharging of her vitality. This infusion was different from the other energy, which had been dark and somber—this was scintillating, blazing. The mind rift cracked wide once more; the sphere, now interlaced with brilliant, metallic hues, bobbed before her once more. Joan's ears were filled with a new roaring.

Now, Joan. Do it again.

Joan pointed her finger into the well of the sphere. As before, fierce lightnings flared and poured into that depthless space. The coruscating forces seemed to strike bottom this time, bouncing from the inner walls of the sphere and redoubling. The globe blossomed like a flower made of fire and parti-colored smoke. The flecks of light inside exploded like soft fireworks. The force of the explosion threw Joan back, and the globe became a roaring hurricane that engulfed all of them.

Then, very suddenly, everything was silent.

"She opened the gateway. I don't know how, but she did."

Mundo stared in wonder. The Adept stood on Henderson's lawn, but the area around them was bounded by a hemisphere of glowing white. The glare was nearly blinding—Mundo's sensitive eyes were watering helplessly. The Adept herself was swathed in shimmering, swirling bands of pure, aching color; Mundo could barely see the figure behind it. She emanated a deep, resonant, throaty purr like a thrumming dynamo.

Mundo, Ecclesiastes, and Theopelli were to one side; Henderson was standing in slack-jawed shock before the Adept. The forces involved in opening the gateway had pulled in two other people. On the other side of the Adept, Mundo could see a naked couple. He recognized the woman—the Princess of Pentacles. She looked to be as exhausted as Mundo, leaning heavily on the man beside her. That told Mundo where the

Adept had found the power: she'd stolen it from the Princess, as she'd stolen it from him.

The interior of the globe was not itself featureless. There were luminescent openings at either end, lustrous portals leading out into landscapes that were not part of the Church of Christ the Marvel's estate. One of those landscapes was achingly familiar. Mundo had not thought he'd ever see it again. The sand, the sacred river wending its way northward.

"Luxor," the dwarf said. "Home."

The Adept must have heard him. The glistening being's face seemed to turn toward him. "Yours?" she said, her voice garbled behind the screaming wind sounds.

"Yes. My world."

"Then you belong there, betcha."

"I would like to go back, yes. For the short time it has."

The Adept raised her hand, but Theopelli interrupted. "Wait!" he said. "I want to go with him."

Mundo turned.

"You? You said my world would be dead."

Theopelli shrugged. "It might be. I don't know, not now. Nothing went as I intended. But even if nothing changes here, being dead wasn't so bad the first time around. Why not go? No one's going to credit my work. I think I'd like to see a world where science and technology never took hold."

"Hurry up," the Adept said. "I'm tired. Ready or not . . ." She waved her hand.

The winds swirled around them, phosphorescent and loud. Howling with them, Mundo and Theopelli were swept away.

Dirk saw Mundo and Theopelli carried through the gateway in a rippling cascade of glowing energy. The door to that world closed behind them.

Joan was weakening now, the hemisphere beginning to close in once more. Dirk knew, somehow, that the other gateway wouldn't last very long at all.

Dirk had an answer before he asked the question.

He could tell by the way Angela was staring at the green hills and white buildings beyond the lambent perimeter of the remaining opening. "Yours?"

Angela nodded. She was crying. "Roma," she said. "The same as I remember it."

"You want to go back there." It wasn't really a question.

"Yes. Yes, I do." The answer was too quick for Dirk's peace of mind. Angela sensed it. Her hand touched his cheek.

"I'm sorry, Dirk. I've been gone a long time; I want—I need—to see my world again. I want things to be familiar for a little while."

"Safe."

Angela smiled. "Yes, I suppose." She sniffed and brushed at the tears with the back of her hand. "Dirk, I do love you."

"I know. Me too."

Angela nodded.

Dirk knew that there was more he was supposed to say. He was balanced on a crux himself. Savage, the recording contract: they were all hanging fire back in New York. Even if he were too late to salvage anything from this band, there could be another. And teaching was always a possibility. He'd enjoyed that.

You've been indulging yourself, and that's about as safe as you can get.

Angela's words came back to Dirk, bitter and sour tasting.

"You goin' too, betcha," the glowing thing that was Joan said to Angela and Dirk. "I can send you both, sure."

He knew he had to make a decision. Quickly. He also knew that his decision would irrevocably change the rest of his life.

One way or the other.

He could feel himself holding back, hesitating. He felt like he'd been placed blindfolded and disoriented on the edge of a cliff. He had to take a step, and for all he knew it would send him falling down to destruction.

Or to use cruder analogy, Dirk's mental tires were spinning in the snowdrifts of cowardice.

"Dirk," Angela said, and when he looked at her, he saw that her eyes were wide and moist and very, very serious. "I do love you. Yes."

"But?" Dirk said cautiously.

Dirk thought it was a very bad sign that she didn't smile at that. "But," she said, "I have to be honest with you, too. Remember when we first made love? I told you then that you reminded me of an old lover. That was the truth. He's *there,* Dirk. Back there in my old world."

The portal opening was beginning to fade like an old photograph. Behind him, he could hear Joan grunting with effort. "Just what does that mean, Angela? What are you telling me? That you love this guy more? What?"

"I'm telling you that I don't know. I've been a long time away. Things change, people change. I know what I feel for you now. What I'll feel for *him,* or what he might still feel for me—I can't tell you." She gave him a wan smile and touched his cheek. "I can't say what will happen, Dirk, and I won't give you any promises I can't keep. Mine is a different world with different moralities. You asked me to go to New York with you; I didn't go. The reasons don't matter—I just told you no. I can understand if you say the same to me now."

"Shit or get off the pot," Joan interjected behind them. Rainbow spectrums chased themselves around her glimmering body. "Hurry."

"Angela, do you *want* me to go with you?" Dirk asked.

"Yes." Her answer was quick and definite. "Of course I do, you idiot."

The blindfold of indecision came off. Mental tire treads grabbed pavement with a squeal of certainty.

"Then let's go," he said.

Angela hugged him. They were still embracing when Joan made a sweeping movement with her hand. The last of her stolen energy swept them up and through the gateway.

The globe collapsed back into nothingness.

The mind rift sealed itself shut.

* * *

The world was as it should be.

That was a big disappointment.

Henderson was standing on the lawn as before. If he looked rather dazed at the moment, he was rapidly regaining color now that the episode was over. Ecclesiastes saw no sign of Mundo, Theopelli, the naked couple, or Alice. They'd vanished back into their own worlds. Joan was standing alongside him, but Joan was no longer the Psychedelic Wonder. She was the old Joan: the grizzled old man face, the dirty-bedraggled clothing, the lumpy body and womanish hands.

As normal as Joan could be.

The sun was beaming down on the Gulf. Gulls wheeled overhead and the tang of salt water flavored the breeze. It was just another Florida day.

"Nothing's changed," Ecclesiastes said, and vast chagrin filled his voice. He turned to Joan, who favored him with a wide smile.

"Hi, 'Clese," she said. "Purty fireworks, huh? Fourth of July, early."

"Nothing's changed," he told Joan again. "They're all gone, but Theopelli said they would have gone anyway. The old fart might have been able to change things just by being here and proving he was a former corpse, but he's gone, too. None of the newspeople saw any of it, so no one's going to believe us if we tell them. It's just our word against Henderson's and I already know how that would go. Theopelli said we had to put some chaos back in the world, had to add the unknown, and we didn't. Not really."

"The Lord protects His own," Henderson said. The reverend took a deep breath. Ecclesiastes knew that the man was looking at the familiar setting around him and already dismissing what had happened. His security people gathered around Henderson quickly, but they were putting their guns away.

"Nothing's changed, Joan. You opened the doors but they sealed right back up again. It didn't do any good. Maybe the situation's changed wherever they've gone, but it's all the same here." Ecclesiastes sighed.

"You won," he said to Henderson. "Wherever your path leads, you won."

Henderson gave them a wide smile and a wave of benediction. His confidence was coming back rapidly. "I told you, my son, the Lord takes care of us. Joan, it was nice seeing you again, but I don't believe we need to worry about each other any longer. You can tell them whatever you want. No one's going to believe a crazy old woman and an Oriental kook anyway. See that they get off the grounds safely, boys. I'm going to see about Harold."

Nodding to Ecclesiastes and gesturing to his security, Henderson turned his back on them and went back into the mansion.

"C'mon," Ecclesiastes said to Joan. "We might as well get going. Dogface looks impatient."

But Joan wasn't paying any attention to Ecclesiastes. She was staring at a distant corner of the grounds. "Look," she said. "Henderson'd love *that* for the circus, sure."

Ecclesiastes squinted, shading his eyes. He sucked his breath in with surprise.

Something—some*one*—was slipping through the brush and into hiding. Ecclesiastes had only a quick glimpse before the figure was gone behind a screen of brush and palms. He couldn't be certain with the brilliant sun and deep shadows, but for that moment, he would have sworn that the creature had the torso of a human male and the lower extremities of a goat.

Ecclesiastes's thin Oriental face creased into a smile. He began to chuckle.

"C'mon Joan," Ecclesiastes said. "We can leave here now, betcha."

Still laughing, Ecclesiastes put his arm around Joan. Together, they began walking away, the brush rustling behind them.

Stephen Leigh is the author of eight science fiction and fantasy novels and several short stories, and is a contributor to the Hugo-nominated WILD CARDS series. His interests, vocations, and avocations include music, art, computers, aikido, history, the physical sciences, and finding spare bits of free time. He would like to invent the thirty hour day. He is married to the delightful and lovely Denise Parsley Leigh; they have two and no more children, Megen and Devon. Mr. Leigh swears that THE ABRAXAS MARVEL CIRCUS is not entirely autobiographical. Really. Some of it never happened.